"FULL FATHOM FIVE, A DEAD MAN LIES..."

The diver saw a parrot fish and red snapper, but was intrigued by a little green fish, following it down into a wide cleft in the reef. It was on its way to join another, which was feeding on something under the pink coral. Curious, she swam closer.

What had drawn them? It appeared to be something shiny and round, like a brown marble on the fine, white sand. A marble? She reached down to retrieve it. But it was lodged in something under the sand.

Running out of breath—and patience—she brushed the sand away. The air in her lungs exploded into her face mask as she screamed. The marble was an eye, in the face of a man...

W9-BQV-593

more . . .

A MATTER OF ROSES

"Well-developed characters, an authentic Massachusetts location...and a complex plot make this a gripping read."
—*Publishers Weekly*

"Chock-full of action and character subplots, this debut mystery (and series) is totally captivating."
—*Library Journal*

"A terrific little thriller...a sweet-smelling, suspenseful rose—but watch out for thorns!"
—*Cape Cod Journal*

"Recommended to readers who don't like sugarcoating but who enjoy spiritual truths included in their mysteries."
—*CBA Marketplace*

A Matter of Time

Also by David Manuel

A Matter of Diamonds
A Matter of Roses

A Matter of Time

DAVID MANUEL

WARNER BOOKS

An AOL Time Warner Company

Faith Abbey is in spirit quite close to the Community of Jesus, the
ecumenical religious community of which the author has been a
member for 29 years.

This book is a work of fiction. Except as noted above, names,
characters, places, and incidents either are products of the author's
imagination or are used fictitiously. Any resemblance to actual events,
locales or persons, living or dead, is entirely coincidental.

If you purchase this book without a cover you should be aware that
this book may have been stolen property and reported as "unsold and
destroyed" to the publisher. In such case neither the author nor the
publisher has received any payment for this "stripped book."

WARNER BOOKS EDITION

Copyright © 2002 by David Manuel
All rights reserved. No part of this book may be reproduced in any
form or by any electronic or mechanical means, including information storage and retrieval systems, without permission in writing from
the publisher, except by a reviewer who may quote brief passages in
a review.

Cover design by Diane Luger
Cover art by Stanley Martucci

This Warner Books edition is published by arrangement with Paraclete Press.

Warner Books, Inc.
1271 Avenue of the Americas
New York, NY 10020

Visit our Web site at www.twbookmark.com

 An AOL Time Warner Company

Printed in the United States of America

First Warner Books Printing: May 2003

10 9 8 7 6 5 4 3 2 1

To
my dear friends
John and Barry French,
boon companions
on the pilgrim's way

acknowledgments

The hardest part of writing fiction occurs before the actual writing begins. When everything is still up in the air, when the pieces have not fallen into place, and the characters have yet to reveal their past, a writer needs uninterrupted time and unrestricted space. Eventually he must narrow his focus, as a chess master reduces his world to 64 squares. But in the beginning, he needs to ramble, mentally and physically.

Few locales are as ideal as the beach house of Charlie and Katy Towers of Jacksonville, Florida. Atlantic Beach is the best drifting/musing beach I know of. I take this opportunity to acknowledge the kindness and generosity of Charlie and Katy, who make their house available to me each February.

I would also like to acknowledge the invaluable input of my two editors — Time-Warner's Sara Ann Freed, whose wise and perceptive suggestions improved this book immeasurably, and Paraclete Press's Lillian Miao, whose encouragement at a moment of deep discouragement was crucial. I should also mention my brother, Bill, and his wife, Christy, whose eagle eyes at the galley-proofing stage have saved me much embarrassment.

Finally, I would like to express my gratitude to John and Barry French of Scottsdale, Arizona, who have opened their home and their hearts to me for early work on each of these mysteries.

A Matter
of Time

1 | the dream

A wall of green seawater crashed against the front windshield of the boat's cabin. From the windshield's corners, white hairline fractures streaked like lightning across the Plexiglas. One more wave like that one would stove it in and send them straight to the bottom.

And Brother Bartholomew, peering out into the eerie, gray-green half-light of the storm, could see it coming. Building, directly in front of them.

Watching the advancing mountain of water, he opened his mouth to scream. No sound came. Icy fingers reached up into his entrails and gripped them, forming a fist.

It grew dark in the cabin. The wave towered over them now, blotting out the sky. As he looked up at it, its top edge started to curl down.

Now the scream came — and kept on coming, though hands were urgently shaking him.

"Bart! Come on, wake up!" demanded a frightened Brother William, his roommate. "It's a dream!"

"The — wave!" Bartholomew managed, pointing at the ceiling of the dark room.

"You're in bed!" shouted Brother Clement, his other

roommate, turning on a light. "In the friary. On dry ground."

Bartholomew blinked. Reality began to seep in around the edges of what he was seeing. "What?"

He looked around — at his roommates, the desk, the two sturdy double-decker bunk beds. Slowly the fist in his stomach loosened.

Clement shook his head. "It's my fault. I never should have persuaded you to come. I'm — really sorry."

Bartholomew tried to smile. "Not your fault, Clem. I didn't have to go. Shouldn't have. My father died like that, twenty years before the *Andrea Gayle* went down." He shuddered. *"The Perfect Storm* was one movie I didn't need to see. But when it came around again, after all those awards—" He shrugged. There was nothing more to say.

At breakfast in the refectory the following morning, the other monks greeted him pleasantly enough. But no one jokingly asked if he'd slept well. Or seen any good movies lately.

It must have been even worse than he thought.

The service of Lauds, which on weekdays preceded morning Mass, provided a welcome respite. He'd not always welcomed these mini-services, known as offices or hours, during which they chanted the Psalms in Latin, in the manner prescribed by St. Gregory fourteen hundred years ago. He had chafed at how they always seemed to cut across whatever he was doing, as if his time was of no importance. Gradually he had come to see that it was God's time, not his, and if this was how God intended him to spend it, then so be it.

In the robing room, he went to his peg and lifted the beige robe over his head, letting it settle evenly on his shoulders. He raised the cowl briefly to put on the appropriate surplice for the day — white for Eastertide and the great feast days, red for Pentecost and the martyrs' days, purple for Lent, blue for Advent, and green the rest of the time — then ducked his head for the chain of the small wooden cross that rested on his chest.

Carved on the cross was the symbol of Faith Abbey, a shock of wheat with a single grain at its base — a visual reference to John 12:24, "Unless a grain of wheat falls into the earth and dies, it remains alone; but if it dies, it bears much fruit."

Fingering the cross, he smiled ruefully. He'd fallen into the earth, all right, but he seemed to be resisting decomposition.

The act of robing was like a renewal of his vows, which for a monk were like wedding vows. With his first, he had relinquished the right to own, to choose, and to marry. Five years later, secure and confident in his call, he had taken his final vow, of stability and obedience. He would accept without question the authority of the Abbot or Abbess and the Senior Brother. And he would never leave. He would be buried with his brothers in the abbey's corner of the town cemetery.

As they entered the sanctuary, solemnly proceeding in a column of twos, he relaxed. Slipping on his robe was like slipping into peace. No matter how much stress he was under, or how frustrated or angry, it was as if he were entering another world. A world with no end, no beginning. Of permanence and eternity.

Was it the real world? When he first came to the abbey twenty years ago, he had wondered if he was escaping reality. He soon discovered that there was every bit as much reality within the abbey as without. But there was also a sense of abiding tranquility, which in their new basilica was even greater. As the brothers blended their voices into one, the Gregorian chant rose and fell like the ebb and flow of the sea. The thought struck him again that their 28 voices were not only blending one with another, but with the voices of monks down through the ages, who had sung these phrases in exactly the same way.

Like the smoke of incense, the chant wafted up to the distant rafters and wreathed the lofty columns, lingering in the mind long after their singing ceased.

As the last echo died away, stillness returned. It was far from empty. The basilica itself seemed to be listening — calmly but intently, noting every sound, every thought.

He smiled. The peace of God did indeed pass all understanding. Long ago he'd tried to understand it. Now he just embraced it, as probably the best part of monastic life.

Gloria Patri et Filio et Spiritui Sancto. . . . He felt at home. Cared for, by God. And this morning he wished he could just stay here, in the hollow of God's hand — forever.

After Lauds there was morning Mass, attended by the whole abbey, and after Mass there was a message for Brother Bartholomew to join Brother Anselm in the library. He found the Senior Brother in his favorite chair, by the window where he could watch the early morning sun playing on the apple trees.

Anselm had aged gracefully. The years may have grayed his hair and added a natural tonsure to the back of his head, but the brown eyes were as clear — and as see-ing — as ever. He's only twenty years older than I am, mused Bartholomew, on the verge of fifty himself.

They were alone. He drew up a chair alongside his spiritual director and waited.

There was no one he trusted more or felt closer to than Anselm, though that had not always been the case. When he'd entered the abbey's friary at the age of 28, Brother Anselm had been the novice master. He'd struck the new novice as too quick to make up his mind — and too slow to change it. "The Number One enemy of 'Best' is 'Good,'" Anselm had been fond of saying, and he'd practiced what he preached, requiring the absolute best of himself always, and assuming his young charges were doing the same.

Over the years Bartholomew had come to see that the very things he'd judged Anselm for were actually great strengths — strengths that benefited all of them. Anselm's refusal to compromise in the pursuit of excellence had in-spired the rest of them to go and do likewise.

With the passing years, the Senior Brother had mel-lowed. They all had. The average age in the brotherhood was 43, and while that was three years younger than the average of the 69 sisters in the abbey's convent, it was climbing steadily. Unless they gained some new novices. . . .

He smiled inwardly, recalling a poster that Brother Ambrose had once made for the benefit of the young men in abbey families. (Counting the children, the abbey's membership was around 350, most of them civilians.) A parody of the World War I poster of a resolute Uncle Sam pointing at the passerby and summoning him to duty abroad, Ambrose's poster featured an equally resolute, robed figure —

THE BROTHERHOOD WANTS YOU.

So far, only three had responded—none of whom had actually been born on Cape Cod, much less in the little harbor village of Eastport, as Bartholomew had.

At the bird feeder outside the window, a sparrow breakfasted while two chickadees perched on a nearby bough, awaiting the next sitting. Anselm seemed totally absorbed in this gentle drama till Bartholomew felt compelled to speak. "If this is about last night—"

The older brother turned to him. "It's not about last night—though that nightmare's grip on you is an indication of where you are."

Anselm turned back to the bird feeder. "What happened last Friday, there," he nodded toward the apple trees, "is of more concern to me. I had to wait until I could talk to Mother Michaela before speaking to you about it." Their Abbess was also the director of the choir, which had just returned from a concert tour.

"You mean, with Koli? Anselm, that was not a big deal. He—"

"You're wrong," the Senior Brother cut in. "It was—and is—a 'big deal.' And the fact that you don't know it, is another indication of where you are—or aren't."

Friday afternoon Novice Nicholas, whom everyone called Koli, had been working with Bartholomew in the apple orchard (if eight trees could be called an orchard). When Nicholas had entered the novitiate three months after his 21st birthday, he had exhibited effeminate tendencies and had admitted to having been increasingly drawn to what he referred to as "an alternative lifestyle."

Then God had intervened. To his utter dumbfoundment, Nicholas had discovered that God was real, that He loved him beyond all human comprehension, and that He had been waiting all Nicholas's life for him to realize it.

The realization had turned his world upside down, and eventually he was led to join the friary. It had been felt that he needed to be brought along by a strong, mature father figure. This would enable him to complete the father–son bonding process that had been interrupted when his own father had abandoned Nicholas and his mother eleven years before.

Brother Bartholomew had been the obvious choice for this role model, and they had worked well together. The repatterning occurred naturally, as Bartholomew, in charge of the abbey's grounds, had shown Koli how to cultivate roses, spread manure, edge and trim and mow. Gradually the novice's responses had modulated, until his previous tendencies were rarely in evidence. It was a slow process — so slow that Koli himself may have been unaware of the change taking place within him. Until Friday.

That afternoon, after several hours of pruning in the orchard, Bartholomew had commended him on the exemplary job he had done on the two trees assigned to him.

Overjoyed, and still desperate for a father's approval, Koli had thrown his arm around the older monk's shoulders and in imitation of an old beer commercial, exclaimed, "I love you, man!"

Bartholomew had frozen, then shrugged the arm off — coldly, brusquely. With no explanation.

The young novice had stared at him. Then, eyes filling, he had run off — and avoided Bartholomew ever since.

2 | devil's island

Breaking the heavy silence, Anselm spoke in measured tones. "What you did was reprehensible and inexcusable."

Bartholomew's mouth fell open. In all their years together, Anselm had never spoken to him in this fashion. He knew he should just take it. Anselm was usually right, especially in matters concerning the friary.

But he was hurt. And angry. And tired of just taking it — from Anselm, from life, from everything.

So he didn't.

"Look!" he declared. "I've always had an aversion to — " he hesitated, "to people like that. When I'm around them, it gives me the creeps. I can't help it; it's instinctive."

"No, it is not!" Anselm shot back. "You are no more a prisoner of your instincts than Koli is."

"But it's an abomination in the sight of God!" Bartholomew exclaimed, and then smiled sardonically. "Unfortunately for those who've made a religion of fairness, God is not politically correct."

Anselm refused to be drawn into debate. "I'll grant you, God does not make mistakes. He made men to be men and women to be women, and never intended them to pair off with their own kind."

He paused and looked at Bartholomew. "Let me ask you something. Does God love Koli?"

"Of course."

"Was that God's love you expressed to him Friday afternoon?"

Bartholomew did not answer.

"Well?"

Silence.

"I'm disappointed in you, Bartholomew. I'd assumed you understood what was going on here. God has been repatterning Koli's responses into something more appropriate for monastic life. We cannot live together, as we've been called to, unless we are chaste. You know that. We must embrace chastity in every aspect of our thought-life, as well as our behavior."

He sighed and shook his head. "Koli was coming into that. But your rejection of him last Friday has set that process back *months*. In fact — we may have lost him."

Bartholomew jumped to his feet. "I tell you, Anselm, I couldn't help it!"

"No!" Anselm glared up at him. "Let *me* tell *you!* If God had been in your heart to the degree He should have been, you would not have reacted that way. Now — *sit — back — down,* Brother Bartholomew! I am *not* finished with you!"

Bartholomew's jaw tightened. "Well, I'm finished with —" he stopped, in the certain knowledge that if he said one more word, he might well be finished with far more than this conversation.

He sat back down, glowering at his spiritual authority.

Almost hoping that he would give him an excuse to say—
what could never be unsaid.

Neither man spoke.

Then Anselm asked quietly, "How long has it been
since you've written anything in your spiritual journal?"

"Oh, for God's sake, Anselm! You know what our life
is like! We're on the go from the moment we wake up!
Matins, Lauds, Mass, Terce, Sext, None, Vespers, Compline, Vigils—and in between we're expected to put in a
full day's work! Plus, I've got all the grounds to look
after, and the Brothers' exercise program to run, and Illumination and Calligraphy to teach, and I'm responsible
for Koli—or I was."

Outside the window there was a flash of red. A cardi-
nal had arrived at the bird feeder. A slow smile came to
Anselm, who nodded to the visitor in red vestments.
"Whenever one of those comes, I take it as a sign of
God's presence. I believe He is here now—no matter
how unpleasant this might be for you."

Bartholomew said nothing. He was not about to admit
that that was exactly the way he felt about cardinals, too.

"In addition to all the other responsibilities you mentioned," Anselm observed, still smiling, "we're also expected to be good stewards of our personal spiritual
growth. Now, how long has it been since your last entry?"

When the younger monk didn't answer, the Senior
Brother sighed. "That's what I thought."

They both watched the cardinal. Then Anselm asked,
"What are the watchwords of Benedictine spirituality?"

No response.

The Senior Brother answered for him. "Hospitality.
Striving for excellence in all things, to the glory of God.
Internal awareness. Balance." He paused. "We're not

called to be contemplatives," and then added wistfully, "though many's the time I've wished we were."

Bartholomew nodded. And relaxed—a little. He'd been through too much with this man, over too many years, to remain flint-hearted.

"Each of us is required to press toward the mark," Anselm went on, "and cooperate with God as He prepares us to be His companions for time and eternity. We encourage the young ones to practice His presence by dialoguing with Him in their spiritual journals. And periodically we check them, to make sure they're hearing the Holy Spirit, and not the unholy one. But we older monks—we're not supposed to need supervision."

Bartholomew sat in stony silence.

"I've seen Mother Michaela," Anselm concluded, "and we feel you need an extended personal retreat. In Bermuda. Immediately."

Bermuda! He might as well have said Devil's Island. The prospect had as much appeal as being condemned to the old French penal colony.

Faith Abbey had a small work in Bermuda, where they were stewards of a 47-acre reserve known as the Harris Trust. The director was a retired priest in his 80s, Father Francis, who had once served as head of the abbey's clergy. He was assisted by four sisters from the abbey's convent. Sometimes members of the abbey went down there for R&R. Occasionally they went—or were sent—to reconnect with God. They would stay for anywhere from a few days to a few weeks—or longer.

Bartholomew grimaced. "I feel like I'm being punished, sent into exile. Why don't you just give me a leper's bell, so I can warn people I'm spiritually unclean!"

Anselm's lips tightened, but his voice remained calm. "How you choose to regard this is up to you."

The younger monk tried a different tack. "Look, Anselm," he pleaded, "I don't need to do this. I'll admit my prayer life has not been what it should be. But I can change! I can do something about it, right here. I don't need to go down there."

When he saw that the Senior Brother was not about to compromise, he asked, "How long will I have to stay?"

"God will let you know when you're supposed to come home."

"Oh, come on! At least give me a ball park estimate."

Anselm shook his head. "If I did, you'd have a finite end in mind and might be tempted to stonewall the whole thing. Just serve your hard time and come home."

Bartholomew did not answer. That was exactly what he had been thinking.

"Nothing would be accomplished," Anselm sighed. "Nothing would have changed."

The two monks looked at each other, and finally the Senior Brother softened. "Bart, you're not being ordered to do this. But we think it's right, the next step for you, and we're strongly urging you to consider it."

"How long do I have, to make up my mind?"

"We need your decision tomorrow."

Bartholomew stood up. "I'll think about it."

He did not say "I'll pray about it," because in truth, the last entry in his journal was at Christmas. Two years ago.

3 | *tu* to tango

In a waterfront bistro in the French Riviera port of Cap d'Antibes, a blond, crew-cut young man leaned close to the dark-haired woman next to him. "Let's get out of here," he murmured. "This place is too crowded."

The woman, in a tight navy-and-white striped bateau shirt and white Capri pants, raised her eyebrows. "I thought you were with your friends."

"That's the problem." He scowled and glanced at the small table surrounded by five large men drinking Heinekens. All were in white polo shirts and white ducks, even white Topsiders. And they all had white Helly-Hansen sailing parkas like the one on the back of his bar stool. One of them, seeing him looking in their direction, gave him a thumbs-up. "Any place with that bunch in it is too crowded."

She shrugged and followed as he left the bar and headed for the door, his crewmates bellowing derisive encouragement behind them.

Outside, she took his arm. "I know a place, *plus intime*. Very quiet."

He let her lead him away from the quay, through an

alley, up some steps, into a smaller café. It was more in-
timate. No Americans. No sailors of any nationality. Just
locals. The clientele spoke in low tones, concentrating on
their Pernod, Dubonnet, Aquavit. The air was redolent
with the pungent aroma of Gauloises cigarettes.

All the tables were taken, so they sat at the bar.

The young man — not much more than a boy, really —
wrinkled his nose. "Guess no one here pays much attention
to the Surgeon General's report."

The woman, seeing he was waiting for a response, realized he must have made a joke. She smiled. "Go back
to telling me about yourself," she said, ordering two double Pernods. "How did you become a sailor?"

He held up a forefinger. First, he had to finish telling her
how his tennis team had won the Ivy League championship
the year before. "The Yalie I played was ranked twenty-
seventh in the country." He paused to let that sink in,
pleased that she seemed impressed with the defining moment of his life. "I earned my 'P' *that* day!" he exclaimed,
and she laughed, assuming he'd made another joke.

She caught the patron's eye and circled her finger over
their empty glasses. Which were soon refilled.

"And how did you earn this?" she asked, pointing to
the name *Laventura* embroidered on his polo shirt, as
well as on the front and right shoulder of his parka.

"That's my yacht. Actually, it belongs to friends of my
parents. When they were visiting at the family compound
in Key Biscayne — that's in Florida — I'd admired their
boat. She's the most beautiful schooner I've ever seen."

The woman sipped the yellow liquid in her glass without comment, then turned away so he would not see her
yawn. When she turned back, her eyes were once again
bright and attentive.

"Anyway," he was saying, "as they left, they told me, 'You must sail with us sometime.' I knew they were just being polite, but—I was graduating in the spring and didn't want to settle down right away. So I wrote them and reminded them of their offer."

"And the sailing? You already knew how?"

"Well, nothing more than Lasers. But the guys showed me the ropes."

"The ropes?"

"Nautical expression. They showed me how everything worked."

"Oh," she smiled. "You like them? The guys?"

He nodded. "I'm sort of their mascot. But we're leaving for Bermuda tomorrow, and the new boy," he thumbed his chest, "is the only one who's going to score tonight. Tennis term," he added hastily, glancing at his watch. "Listen, um—"

"Antoinette," she reminded him. "Toni."

"Listen, Toni, you're about the most attractive thing I've seen ashore, anywhere in the Med. And—"

"I like you, too, Kevin," she responded, tapping his chin with a forefinger and showing him she could remember his name. "You remind me of my younger brother." She giggled. "My much younger brother."

Then, so he would not be hurt, she leaned close and beamed at him. Actually she leaned into him, so he would know there were only two layers of clothing between them. Two thin layers.

It had the desired effect. "Listen," said the boy thickly, "—Toni, I really want to *coucher avec vous*."

"*Toi*," she corrected him.

"Huh?"

"When you say what you just said, to someone close

to you, it's *tu,* not *vous.* You would say *vous* if you were speaking to *une femme de nuit.*"

"Sorry!" he stammered, chagrinned that he might have just ruined his chances.

"It's okay," she said, smiling and tossing her head, "I want to, too. Just let me go in there a moment," she nodded toward the W.C. "Then we'll leave."

"Don't be long," he whispered.

In a little while, she returned. "Let me leave first," she murmured to him. "Take your time, finish your drink, pay *l'addition.* Then leave."

"Why?"

"I don't want them to see us leaving together. I live here."

He nodded. In a moment she said good night, and he nodded, feigning dismay.

Ten minutes later he emerged and spotted her waiting in a white Renault two-door down the street. Strolling past it, he glanced around and, seeing no one, slipped into the passenger seat.

"Your place or mine?" he asked huskily.

She frowned, and then smiled; he was making another joke. "I'll take you up on the *corniche,*" she said warmly. "A place I know. *Très intime.* Very romantic."

Putting the car in gear, she took the long winding road up the side promontory overlooking the sea. There were no headlights, in either direction. They would have the *corniche* to themselves.

Abruptly she swung the wheel left, turning into what seemed to be a dense growth of brush. But there was a track through it, and she eased her way along, branches scraping both sides of her car.

All at once they were out in the open, on a little bluff, barely big enough for the car.

In front of them the vast Mediterranean stretched away under the light of a nearly full moon. It was calm; on the black mirror of the inlet, the moon seemed to draw a line straight to them.

"You were right," he said, exhaling, "this *is* romantic."

She nestled into him. "And no one even knows it's here."

After putting the car in reverse and carefully setting the emergency brake, she turned off the engine. In the silence, they could hear wavelets splashing against the base of the rocky cliff, a hundred meters below.

"Look," she whispered, nodding to their left. A mile away, a dozen yachts were moored off the Cap. Silhouetted in the moonlight, they were of all sizes and descriptions. One, larger than the rest, had three masts.

"*Laventura,*" the boy murmured, pointing her out.

"*Magnifique!*"

"So are you," he gasped, taking her in his arms.

He never felt the blow from the weighted sap strike him just behind the left ear.

"What took you so long?" the woman demanded of the dark form outside the car. "He practically had my clothes off!"

She reached over and extracted the wallet from the unconscious boy's hip pocket. Removing the money, she started going through the credit cards.

"Put it back," said the man outside.

"*What?*"

"Put it all back."

"But there's more than four hundred dollars here! And virgin credit cards—a platinum Visa, a gold Amex! I thought this is what—"

"I have something else in mind," the man said calmly. "Now—*put it back.*"

Startled at the sharp edge in his tone, she did as instructed, then looked up at him, trying to make out his face in the darkness. "Hector, you're not going to go—*strange* on me again, are you?"

When he did not answer, she prattled on with forced cheerfulness. "You were right; he turned out *exactly* as you anticipated. In fact, as he was telling me about himself, I almost lost it. It was as if he was following your script." She laughed, hoping he would laugh with her.

He didn't.

He opened the door, reached in back and retrieved the boy's sailing parka, dropping it on the ground. Then he pulled off the boy's white polo shirt and dropped it, too. After that, he removed the boy's boating shoes, adding them to the pile.

"Why are you doing that?" she asked. "You'll never be able to wear or sell—" her voice trailed off, as he came around to her side of the car.

"Take off your sandals."

"What? Why?"

"Take them off," he commanded, icy steel in his voice.

Scared now, she did it. "Hector, please! What are you doing?"

"Now the shirt. Take it off."

"No, please! I don't like this!" She started to cry.

"Do it, or I'll take it off for you."

Whimpering, she removed her shirt and dropped it beside the car. "What is this all about?" she begged, her body trembling.

"You and the American were making love," he explained, matter-of-factly. "In your ardor, one of you knocked the gearshift into neutral."

As he spoke, he reached over her and did so. "Somehow," he went on, "the emergency brake also came off." He disengaged it.

She stared at him, her eyes filling with terror.

"And then, at the height of your passion, the car started to roll."

He pushed it into motion, and she screamed. Frantically, she flung open the door and started to get out.

But he had anticipated this, too. With a swift backhand blow from the sap, he stilled her. And put her back in the car.

Straightening the wheel, he gave it a final push, and it sailed out into the night sky, nosing over and plunging down into the dark sea. It struck the surface with such force that its occupants were killed instantly—and so fractured that the blows to their crania would not raise suspicion.

The impact sent up a huge geyser. But the sea soon settled back, and the car sank quickly, until there was nothing visible. In twelve meters of water, it might not be found for days. Months.

The discarded clothing would allow the police to complete the hypothesis he had just outlined. He was about to leave, when he paused. The boy's white boat shoes were nearly new. Picking up the right one, he measured the sole against his right foot, and smiled. A perfect fit.

He thought for a moment, then threw the woman's sandals over the cliff. They must have gone wading before they came up here.

4 | the quarry cottage

Brother Bartholomew leaned his head against the back seat window of the very small, very old Mazda station wagon. Not feeling much like talking, he pretended to be dozing.

Up front, Father Francis and his Bermudian friend, Brendan Goodell, a retired AME minister, were engaged in a spirited discussion about the impact that September 11th had had on Bermuda. Seven weeks had passed, but the situation was still desperate. Bermuda's main industry was tourism, and the tourists had simply stopped coming. The Southampton Princess, normally at 80 percent capacity at this time of year, was at 12. And the Delta flight Bartholomew had come down on, which at this time of year should have had every seat filled, was flying with four-fifths of its seats empty. Restaurants were closing, hotel and retail staff were being laid off or cut back to half wages. The island was reeling.

Bartholomew didn't care. He was too busy wishing he wasn't here. After the meeting with Anselm, he'd told his roommates of his impending exile—and was taken aback at their response.

"Man, that's tremendous!" exclaimed Clement. "And it's only October. Still be warm enough for shorts and sandals!"

"It's not like I'm going down there on a vacation, Clem!"

"Well, it sounds pretty good to me," William chimed in. "In fact, it certainly was, when I was there a dozen years ago. I came home and took my final vows." He laughed. "You'll probably be in the Quarry Cottage."

"What's that?"

"On top of the hill, behind the chapel there's an old quarry with a 'cottage' in it. More like a one-room cubicle. But it's got a little bathroom, and a RadarRange and a little fridge . . . a perfect *Poustinia*."

Bartholomew was familiar with the word. It was Russian for a hermitage so small that there was room for only one occupant—and God.

But he still had an ace in the hole. His mother. After she'd retired from teaching English at Nauset High, she'd taken the job of hostess at Norma's Café. Now 74, she ran the place and enjoyed giving him a hard time whenever he stopped in, which was not infrequently, as she made the best coffee in town. Three years ago he'd sworn off the bean, having become dependent on it to get him through the day. But last spring he'd taken it up again—in moderation, of course; just two cups in the morning. He despised his weakness. Caffeine was a vile, mood-altering drug, he kept reminding himself. Yet in the early morning nothing tasted quite so good as that first sip.

For years he and his mother had been at odds. She could not forgive him for throwing away (as she saw it) the Dartmouth education she'd labored so hard to provide—in favor of a vocation that meant that there would be no grandchildren. But the two of them had battled through to where they could both accept and appreciate each other, and for the past two years they'd been genuinely close.

Her health was not what it once was (whose was?), and she would be crushed to learn that he might be going away for a long, maybe a very long time. He could imagine her pleading with him not to go, and then accusing him, telling him that his leaving was nothing short of cruel.

So out of concern for her, he wouldn't leave.

That was not how it had played out.

"Oh, thank God!" she'd exclaimed. "I've been so worried about you! I've been watching you get more and more tense. I almost called Brother Ambrose, except I knew how much that would upset you."

He was nonplused. "You think I should go?"

"Andrew," she said, calling him by his boyhood name, "It's God! I'm not into Him the way you are, but I do pray sometimes."

He stared at her. This woman never failed to amaze him!

She laughed. "I prayed He'd do something about you. I guess He has."

Never underestimate the power of a mother's prayers, he thought dourly, as the old station wagon labored up Knapton Hill.

But as the lush greenery, punctuated by red hibiscus, pink and white oleanders, and purple morning glories passed by, and the scent of cedar wafted in through the window, he had to admit there *was* something paradisiacal about the little island. No wonder some of those Englishmen whose shipwreck here in 1609 inspired

Shakespeare's final play, *The Tempest,* returned to make
it their home. When Bartholomew had first stepped out of
the airliner and onto the passenger ramp's steel steps, the
pleasant, soothing warmth had promised something that
seemed to exist only in the basilica back home. Peace.

He began to take an interest in the passing scene. The
houses were built of limestone, a material found, apparently, in endless supply. They were mostly whitewashed,
or sometimes painted in pastel shades of pink, blue, and
yellow. The roofs were white, regularly washed with lime
to purify the rainwater, caught and stored in tanks beneath the houses. On each roof were many little steps, to
keep the rain from running off so quickly it would be lost.
Rain was Bermuda's principal source of drinking water,
and while tourists might lament its arrival, the locals re-
joiced—especially at a hard, long "tank" rain. They
would cheer up their visitors the same way Cape Codders
did: "You don't like the weather? Wait an hour."

They passed an elementary school just letting out, and
Bartholomew was struck by all the children, black and
white together, in uniform. The boys wore navy blue
blazers, gray flannel slacks, white shirts, and ties in what
was presumably the school tartan. The girls also wore
blazers, white blouses, and tartan kilts. They looked
sharp and seemed happy.

"Do all the school children wear uniforms?" he asked.

Brendan nodded.

"Why?"

"The strain it takes off the parents, not having to sac-
rifice to keep their darlings in the height of teen fashion.
It's also a great equalizer. Kids from poor homes look just
as good as the ones from wealthy ones."

"*Is* there poverty?" Bartholomew asked. "I haven't seen it."

"We've enjoyed prosperity for a long, long time," Brendan replied wistfully. "Until now."

A large woman on a small red scooter took advantage of a rare straightaway and zipped past them. As a curve approached, another rider, this one on a mini-motorcycle, also passed them. Suddenly a car appeared around the corner, and Brendan had to brake sharply to allow the motorcyclist to get back in their lane.

"A little close!" exhaled Bartholomew.

"Happens all the time," replied Brendan with a sigh.

"But—he was riding one-handed. His left arm was just dangling down."

"That's the brake hand. Some young locals do that. The cool ones."

Bartholomew smiled and looked at Brendan in the rearview mirror. "D'you ever do that? I mean, in your misspent youth, before God got ahold of you?"

Brendan glanced at the mirror. "I never rode one-handed. But—I often exceeded the national speed limit, which was twenty miles per hour then, or as we now say, thirty-five kilometers."

"What was the fastest you ever made it to the airport, from where we're going in Somerset?"

Brendan hesitated. "Twenty minutes. But I wasn't driving," he hastily added. "I was on the back of my brother's bike."

Father Francis turned and stared at his friend with a surprised smile.

"My brother was so fast, the police didn't even try to catch him. They figured one day Goodie'd kill himself, and they'd go to his funeral."

Coming the other way now were four careful tourists on black scooters, closely followed by a large pastel pink No.8 Bermuda bus.

Brendan smiled. "Pink whale after minnows."

They went by a shopping center, whose parking lot was filled with late-model cars. "You mentioned Bermuda's prosperity," Bartholomew prompted him.

"Tourism's always been our mainstay. It's been dying gradually ever since the sixties, and recently its demise has accelerated. In the past fifteen years, some fifty guest properties have shut down and last year bed-occupancy was off thirteen percent. And that was *before* September 11!"

Brendan had taken the South Shore route that afforded spectacular vistas of sparkling, bright blue ocean and stretches of beach where the sand was a startling pinkish white. Abruptly he slowed for a mother duck leading a string of eight tiny ducklings.

"Where are they going?"

"Down to Spittal Pond. That's our largest wildlife preserve."

"Tell him about the flamingo," prompted Father Francis.

"*You* tell him."

The old priest turned around to face Bartholomew. "A couple of years ago, a pair of pink flamingos escaped from the B.A.M.Z."

"The Bermuda Aquarium, Museum and Zoo," explained Brendan.

"They hung out at Spittal or over at Warwick Pond, which is wide but shallow. Something happened to the male, but his mate kept looking there for him."

"We often saw her standing in the pond as we drove by on Middle Road," added Brendan.

"One day, a man noticed that she was in trouble," Father Francis resumed. "She was in the middle of the pond thrashing around, beating the water with her wings."

Brendan picked up the story. "The man went to a nearby vet, and they got a boat and rowed out to her. The poor bird's legs had gotten all tangled in kite string that must have been on the bottom of the pond. They freed her and took her back to the zoo so she wouldn't get entangled again."

Father Francis nodded with enthusiasm. "That's what I like about Bermuda. Whatever that man was on his way to do, he set it aside to rescue the bird." He paused. "He didn't just shake his head and think what a shame and keep going."

Bartholomew took that in and gazed down at the sparkling, light blue water. "Why isn't Bermuda on everyone's top-five list?"

"For a long time, it was," answered Brendan sadly. "After the war, this was a favorite spring-break destination for New England college kids — it was called Easter vacation, back then. Those who came liked it enough to keep coming back. They came on their honeymoons and as young marrieds. And then brought their kids."

He sighed. "In the sixties, all that changed. There were other spring-break places — Ft. Lauderdale and Daytona Beach, and today, Cancun. Plus, Disney World and eventually all of Orlando became a magnet for East Coast families. As tourism became an international industry, other new resorts started competing — further south."

He caught Bartholomew's eye in the rearview mirror. "We're off Cape Hatteras, remember; if you're sick of winter and want to go bake in the sun, you're going to have to go further south than North Carolina." Then he grinned. "But if you want to jump-start summer or stretch it a little, we're ideal."

Bartholomew, now totally absorbed in the plight of the island that would be his Elba, asked, "So declining tourism is your biggest problem?"

The men up front glanced at each other, to see who would field that one.

Brendan did. "No, it's drugs."

"Drugs? Here? In Paradise?"

The driver nodded, and as they passed another church, Father Francis gestured toward it. "There are sixty-two thousand Bermudians, and they have more churches per capita than any place I've ever heard of. But there's crime now."

Brendan sighed. "Our police are good. Very good. But the drug scene is stretching them to the limit."

For a long time they rode in silence, then slowed for what Father Francis explained was Somerset Bridge, the smallest drawbridge in the world. The draw part was less than two feet wide — just enough to permit passage of a sailboat's mast.

"Now we're in Sandys," the old priest announced. "The island's westernmost parish. The West End is the most peaceful, yet even here we've had a couple of drug murders recently."

Reaching the Harris Property, they turned right, into the drive and up the hill. It struck Bartholomew how rare it was to find such a large piece of undeveloped land on the island.

At the top of the hill was a tiny, whitewashed, three-pew chapel, with a breathtaking view of Great Sound and

Hamilton Harbour in the distance. It was so quaint, Bartholomew had to smile.

Adjacent to it was the ancient quarry, an area about the size of two tennis courts. The gray walls of hewn stone were eight or ten feet tall, covered with dense underbrush. The quarry floor was flat and grassy, and in the center grew a huge old poinciana tree, probably as old as the quarry itself.

The cottage at the west end was even smaller than he'd supposed. Square, squat, and blunt, it was Early Maginot Line. Grabbing his duffel bag, he followed Father Francis to the door. The latter undid the padlock, opened it, and turned on the light.

"Here's how it's going to be," he said. "We're going to leave you completely alone. Your only contact with us will be at morning Mass. And on Sunday mornings, you and I will take the bus into Hamilton, to attend Mass at the Cathedral. If you really need to talk, I'll be available."

He opened the window to let in some fresh air. "I've talked to Brother Anselm, and he's told me of your landscaping abilities." The old priest nodded appreciatively. "We can use some of that around here. You'll find everything you need in the tool shed by the main house. Do whatever you think needs doing, and the more, the better."

He opened the refrigerator and checked it, then the cupboard above, checking to make sure the sisters had left Bartholomew enough to get started. "Grocery store's up the main road, about a half-hour walk from here."

Taking out his wallet, he counted out three twenties. "This should keep you for the first week. But be careful; since everything has to be shipped in, it's twice as expensive as at home. And keep your food covered, or you'll have ants everywhere."

He turned to leave. "Well, have a good retreat," he said with a smile. "We'll be praying for you."

Bartholomew put a hand on his arm. "Wait, Father. You said 'the first week' — how many weeks is it going to be?"

The latter just smiled. "As long as it takes, my son." And with that, he left to join Brendan in the car.

As they pulled away, Brother Bartholomew imagined the great hollow *clang* of a cellblock door closing behind him.

5 | laventura

As the late afternoon sun bathed Cap d'Antibes in liquid golden light, Neil and Marcia Carrington reclined in the cockpit of their 82-foot schooner, sipping Bombay Sapphire gin and bitters and watching their crew, all in white, load the last of the supplies for their three-week Atlantic crossing.

"We can't wait any longer, darling," said Marcia, her blond hair up under a gondolier's hat. "We promised Anson we'd be there to watch him in the Gold Cup. If he's ever going to beat Dennis, he'll need all the support he can get."

She waited for her husband to respond, but his attention was given to the crew's activities.

"That's why I invited Tim and Lydia, and Stuart and Stacey to join us," she went on, "I mean, it's the least we can do." She peered at him over the top of her sunglasses. "Are you listening to a word I'm saying?"

"Anson needs all the support he can get, so you invited Tim and Lydia, and Stuart and Stacey to join us, because it's the least we can do."

"I *hate* it when you do that!" Marcia exclaimed, standing up. "I might as well be talking to a tape recorder!"

Her husband, sensing that anything he might say now would be used against him, remained silent.

Which only irritated her more. "Well, we've simply got to get going! We've lost two days, as it is! We'll be lucky to get to Bermuda before the regatta begins."

Her husband, dressed in a white polo shirt and white ducks like his crew (though twice their age and considerably thicker), at last turned his Ray-Bans in her direction. "I just don't feel right about leaving without knowing what's happened to Sterling's boy. Sterling's been my friend since London School of Economics."

Marcia tapped the teak railing with impeccably lacquered nails. She tried reasoning. "What more can we do, darling? We've told the local gendarmerie all we know. We even found a picture of Kevin for them in the ship scrapbook. And you *know* they've looked everywhere."

He nodded and stared glumly at the brass binnacle.

Suddenly she brightened. "Darling! Why don't you call Sterling! He may have even heard from Kevin by now!"

Neil rubbed his chin. "I was going to wait until we had something definite to tell him."

His wife let her impatience creep into her voice. "But darling, we *do* have something definite! He picked up a woman. A local, older than him. He persuaded her to leave. They went to another place. She left. He left. Now she's gone. And so is her car. And so is Kevin. End of story!" She shrugged and smiled. "A happy ending, I suspect, for both of them."

Holding her smile, she waited. "Oh, come on, darling!" she finally cried. "They're probably in Paris by now — or halfway to Rome!"

With a sigh, Neil capitulated. "I'll call Sterling." He disappeared through the hatch and down the ship's ladder.

When he emerged a few minutes later, *he* was smiling. "Well, darling, once again you were right."

"I was? How wonderful! How?"

"Sterling was unfazed. Apparently Kevin is given to impulsive behavior. Has a history of suddenly dropping everything and just taking off." He laughed. "Sterling wished us bon voyage."

"He did? Well then, I say anchors aweigh!"

Her husband put an arm around her. "You want some more good news? When I was below, Dieter informed me that the chef has a cousin who'd come over from Marseilles to see him. According to the chef, the man's had yacht experience and — just happens to be 'between boats,' as it were. His passport's current, and he'd be most happy to sail with us, so we won't have to go shorthanded. I gave my approval."

Marcia's brow furrowed. "I thought we made crew decisions together."

"We do, darling. But as you pointed out, we're a bit pressed for time. We can't exactly spend a few days interviewing, now can we?"

"I suppose not," she allowed, still frowning. "Does Dieter like him?"

"Obviously." Neil paused. "Although I suspect he also likes the prospect of not having to work himself and the others like dogs. They'll have a hard enough time as it is, making up the two days."

"Then I take it, it's a *fait accompli.*"

Her husband nodded. "The new man came aboard with that last load of supplies."

"Well, I trust Dieter's judgment," she mused, studying the crew as they moved about the schooner, making ready to depart. "Which one is he? These sunglasses aren't prescription."

"He's that older one, there," said Neil, pointing, "the one just going down the forward hatch."

She squinted. "He's a *lot* older, if you ask me. And frankly, darling, he looks a bit, well — rough."

Now it was Neil who was losing patience. "Darling, it's not as if we're going to be photographed for *Town & Country*. We did that *last* year, remember?"

"No need to get snippy," she countered, watching the new man disappear below. "I see Dieter was able to find an outfit for him."

Her husband nodded. "Everything but the white Topsiders, which fortunately he already had. A new pair, in fact."

"Good. Let's go; I'm bored with the Cap."

Neil did not respond. Shading his eyes, he watched a launch coming towards them. "I'm afraid, darling, there's going to be one more delay. If I'm not mistaken, that's the police."

It was. In a few minutes Inspector Roland joined them in the cockpit.

Noting Marcia's expression, he said, "I'm sure you're anxious to sail, so I'll keep this brief. I just wanted to make sure that you'll let us know if you hear *anything* of the boy's whereabouts. If he contacts you, or you hear from his family — anything at all. Otherwise, we must keep his file open."

"As it happens, I spoke with his father just before you

came," Neil informed him. "He hasn't heard from him, but he's not too surprised. Apparently the boy's done this before."

"Done what?"

"Taken off without telling anyone. He's impulsive, it would seem."

The inspector raised an eyebrow.

"Manic-depressive," explained Marcia.

"Oh." He took out a little notebook and made a note.

"Inspector," Neil asked, "what about the woman?"

"Her name is Toni Remy. She fancies herself an artist and hangs around the Cap in the summertime. I think her family sends her money from time to time."

"What makes you say that?" queried Marcia, curious to know the policeman's deductive process.

The inspector gave a Gallic shrug. "She does not sell many paintings and doesn't seem to work." He gazed at the setting sun, now a blood-red orb, bisected by the western horizon. "Toni's not a bad sort, though she has bad taste in men. She has *un penchant* for getting involved with some really *méchants* characters, the worst of whom it was my pleasure to put on ice six years ago." He scowled. "Hector Vincennes — a dirty man in a dirty business."

"What business?" asked Marcia.

"Drugs. But he was a big fish, bigger than most. He'd set up a whole new trade route for heroin, through Algeria and Morocco. Fancied himself the new French Connection." He frowned at the recollection. "Nasty piece of work. He enjoyed the killing part more than the dealing part. His victims died slowly, in as much pain as he could inflict."

Marcia shivered deliciously, eyeing the inspector with new respect. "And you were the one who put him away?"

"I should have killed him. Our system is too lenient."

The sun was gone now, and above them a mackerel sky was shading towards crimson, magenta, and purple.

"Well, I must go," the inspector said, bowing to each of them. "Perhaps in this young man, Toni has finally found someone decent."

From his launch, he called, "Be sure to let me know if you hear anything."

6 | the impossible dream

Brother Bartholomew sat on the tiny porch of the Quarry Cottage, eating his supper and trying to enjoy the gathering twilight. It was not easy because after a long day of clearing the walking paths, cutting back brush and hauling out the cuttings, he was stiff and bone tired.

And steeped in self-pity.

Solitude had a way of clarifying things. At home in the friary with all the other brothers, he used to long for it. And sometimes, when the sand flats came out at low tide, he would drift out on them for an hour or two, just to be alone.

But now his solitude was complete. And undisturbed. And unending.

And what it was clarifying surprised him; he needed people. Twenty years ago when he was a civilian, he used to go camping up in New Hampshire just to get away from them. Until Laurel, he never took anyone with him. But then, Laurel wasn't people. She was — special.

And that book was closed, he firmly reminded himself, putting down his half-eaten supper and standing up.

Best not to even open it, let alone thumb through it, however casually.

In the gathering dusk, he slowly paced the perimeter of his open-air cloister. He'd been here only three days, but they had taught him that while he might be a monk, he was not cut out to be a hermit. He missed his brothers—all of them, even Ambrose. He missed the fun, the banter and clash of opinions at supper. He missed watching sports on television with them, cycling with them, all the things they did together.

Most of all, he realized, he missed doing the services with them, filing into the basilica with them, chanting with them—good grief, he missed Latin?

Down here, Mass was the thing he most looked forward to. Not for the Eucharist, though obviously that was the most important part. Mass was the one time in the day when he had contact with others.

The first morning he had arrived at the chapel at one minute to seven, in true abbey fashion—only to find that he was three minutes late. (Patience was not Father Francis's greatest virtue.) After that, Bartholomew arrived at the chapel ten minutes early. He didn't mind; the sisters were there, setting up the altar.

When Mass was ended, Father Francis would wish him a good and productive day, and before the monk could strike up a conversation, the gray-haired priest would whirl away down the hill in his white cassock. The sisters stayed behind to do Lauds, to which he was not invited, so he went back to the cottage and had his bowl of cereal and went to work. And started looking forward to the next morning's Mass.

Tomorrow was Sunday, he reminded himself. Which meant they would be going in to the Cathedral in Hamilton, the island's one city. A really big day, he thought, mocking his anticipation.

It was almost dark now, but he decided to finish his supper, a bowl of chili and a sourdough baguette—out here, as he could not bear the thought of eating one more meal inside, staring at the wall. Now, sitting on the desk chair on the six-foot by nine-foot cement slab that served as a porch, he gradually became aware that he was being watched.

He kept spooning the chili, and without seeming to, scanned the confines of the quarry. Out of the corner of his eye, he caught a slight movement—in the brush above the quarry's north wall. There was a shadow there, darker than the shadow it was in. Frustrated by the absence of light, he could barely make it out. A cat—a small black one, with a white blaze on her chest.

Her chest? How did he know it was a female? He couldn't say; he just knew. He named her Noire.

"We've got a cat at home," he told her, keeping his voice low, so as not to startle her. "A big ring-tailed Maine Coon cat named Pangur Ban. He's named that—I named him—because he's the friary cat, and long ago in a medieval monastery, they had a cat named that."

He frowned. I'm talking to a cat, he thought. Well, so what? It was good to hear someone's voice, even if it was his own. And besides, Noire seemed interested—well, not disinterested.

"I'm a brother," he went on. "You probably couldn't tell that, because I'm not wearing a robe. Actually, this is our working habit—khaki pants, blue denim shirt. There's a cross embroidered here," and he showed the cat the small outline of a cross over his heart.

If anyone came by here now, he thought, they'd think

I'd just been released from a mental ward—a little too
soon. But it was nearly dark; no one would be walking up
here now.

"Noire, you belong to anyone? Probably not, or you'd
be home having your own supper now. You hungry?
Maybe I can find something for you."

He went in, and from the fridge retrieved a deli-pack
of smoked turkey. Peeling off a slice, he tore it in little
pieces, put it on a saucer, and went back out.

The cat was gone. He put the saucer on the ground in
front of the poinciana tree and waited. It was pitch black
by the time he gave up and went inside.

On the little, half-folded dining table next to the brown
easy chair was a clipboard with a legal pad—his so-
called spiritual journal. He'd not written a dozen lines
since he'd arrived. Tired as he was, it was too early to go
to bed. Sitting down in the chair, he took up the clipboard
and stared at it.

Then he wrote:

Why haven't I opened up a dialogue with God?

Because—I don't have much to say to Him.

And don't imagine He has much to say to me.

Or if He does, I'm not sure I want to hear it.

Because—I've got to do whatever He tells me.

I'm a monk, aren't I? His obedient servant.

He scratched that out and put:

His sometimes-obedient servant.

He sighed and put the pen down, then picked it up
again. This journal was for his most honest thoughts.
Ergo, he would pursue this, no matter how painful or
where it led. He wrote:

I loved Him once.

I must have, to have taken such a vow.

And He must have loved me,
or He wouldn't have let me take it.
Unless He really is a sadist,
as some would like to believe.

"Well, that's enough of that!" he exclaimed aloud, setting the clipboard aside.

⛵

Every afternoon at four, he would knock off work, shower, pull on his black running shoes, and go for a long walk, five or six miles. He preferred cycling, as he did at home. But walking was not so bad, once you got into it. Cycling, you had to pay attention, but walking, you could let your mind go anywhere it wanted or just dome out. Kind of pleasant. And it certainly taught patience. You might not get where you were going quickly, but you'd get there eventually. So — relax and enjoy the trip.

There was a paved-over railway right-of-way adjacent to the property, and it quickly became one of his favorite routes. Built in the 1920s, the railroad had run the 21 miles, from one end to the other. But "Old Rattle & Shake," as the locals called it, had been a disaster from the beginning, and with the coming of World War II, automobiles became a fixture on the island. The railroad was doomed, eventually becoming too expensive for the government to support.

The war ended another grand era, with the building of an airbase on St. George's known as Kindley Field. Before the war, the great flying boats of BOAC and Pan American used to land here on their way across the Atlantic or up to New York. The ultimate in luxurious travel, the Pan American Clippers boasted separate lounges for dining and cocktails, gourmet meals prepared on board, and private, Pullman-style sleeping berths for forty passengers.

Speaking of luxurious travel, Bartholomew had begun to find that the Cunard Line's famous slogan was right: Getting there (wherever "there" happened to be) was indeed half the fun.

It could be most of the fun, if you took the time to savor the medley of fragrances of the wildflowers growing along the way. Or note the amazing symmetry of a perfect spider web, diamondized by the early morning dew. Or engage a mockingbird in a dueling dialogue by imitating each of his calls. Or fill a mental photo album with images from the trip — close-ups and vistas, cloudscapes and color clusters, sun shafts and shape-shifting shadow play. . . .

This afternoon he had walked to the beach at Daniel's Head. It was deserted, the sand glistening in the late sun. Taking off his shoes to enjoy its warmth between his toes, he strolled down to where the surf ran up. The foaming slide of blue water shooed a pair of sandpipers ahead of it; then the fast-walkers became the pursuers, as the wave receded.

Watching them at their endless game, he smiled. "We have you guys at home, too," he softly informed them, "out on Coast Guard Beach." Stretching out on the warm sand, he closed his eyes and imagined himself watching sandpipers on Cape Cod.

All at once he was aware that someone had come up behind him.

"Do you talk to the trees, too?"

He froze. He knew that voice, that gently teasing Irish lilt. Getting to his feet, he slowly turned. It was Laurel.

"What—are you doing here?" he stammered.

"Taking care of business," she said with a half smile. "Unfinished business."

"But you can't be here! It's—impossible!"

She chuckled. "Never underestimate the power of a determined woman."

She looked around. "We're even on a beach. How appropriate."

"We settled this," he managed, his voice shaking. "Four years ago."

"Did we?" she said, gazing at him through lowered lashes. "I don't feel very settled about it now. Do you?"

He shut his eyes, as he had that time before.

She reached out to him, as she had before.

But this time, instead of stopping short, she touched him. And let the back of her hand caress his cheek.

"Don't," he said, starting to tremble.

"Look at me, Andrew, and tell me you don't want me."

He opened his eyes and met hers. "I can't do this."

"Yes, you can," she whispered, taking his hand and placing it over her heart.

With a groan he gathered her in his arms and pressed her to him.

⛵

When he awoke, he was still trembling. And drenched in sweat. And guilt.

"Oh, God, what have I done? That was *over*! What—is *happening* to me?"

On the half-hour bus ride into Hamilton, sitting next to Father Francis, he could not bring himself to tell him about his all too vivid dream and the sleepless night that followed it. So they made small talk.

The old priest greeted several people as they got on the bus.

"You seem to know everyone," Bartholomew observed.

Father Francis smiled. "I've been taking the Sunday 8:47 for many years."

Gradually the bus filled to capacity. Bermudians were a polite people, however, so it was possible to carry on a very private conversation in their midst. Finally Bartholomew could no longer contain what was troubling him, and their two-seat pew on the bus became his confessional.

When he'd finished relating the dream, to his surprise Father Francis laughed.

"Welcome to Bermuda," he said, keeping his voice low. "There's great light here, but there's great darkness, too. Voodoo, witchcraft—not for nothing was it called Devil's Island before it got renamed." He smiled at Bartholomew's surprise. "The dark side knows you're here, and that dream was their little welcoming present."

The monk stared at him.

"People from home have the wildest dreams, really frightening, when they first get here," the priest went on, unperturbed by the younger man's reaction. "Then they learn to get serious about their prayer life."

Bartholomew could not restrain his incredulity. "You mean, 'Now I lay me down to sleep'—that sort of thing?"

"I wouldn't take that attitude, if I were you. That little nursery prayer has kept an awful lot of people in sweet dreams." He paused. "I'll tell you something: Before I sleep, I request a guard of warrior angels around the property's perimeter."

"Father! You've got to be kidding, I mean, you're beginning to sound medieval!"

The old priest looked at him and sighed. "You haven't been praying, have you." It was a statement, not a question.

The monk made no reply.

"Well, you'd better start, my son. Or you're going to be in for some wild nights."

7 | busman's holiday

"I think you should go," said Peg cheerily, putting dessert in front of him. "It'll do you a world of good."

Dan Burke, Eastport's Chief of Police, stared glumly at the grapefruit-and-rhubarb compote she had made for him. It was low-cal, low-fat, and—boring. Gone were the days of home-made apple pie with a slice of aged cheddar alongside—*and* a scoop of coffee ice cream. Gone forever, thanks to by-pass surgery two years ago.

He had just informed his wife that his old friend Ron Wallace, one of Eastport's charter fishing boat captains, had invited him for a week's deep-sea fishing. In Bermuda. And Peg was more excited about it than he was.

For years, Ron had enjoyed a unique arrangement with a Bermuda charter captain named Ian Bennett. They were old friends, their boats were compatible, and the third week in October, when each of their seasons was pretty well over, the two captains would take a busman's holiday. They would swap boats for a week.

Usually they brought their wives, but this year the wives couldn't go. Ron's irascible mother-in-law had come to live with them until his wife Bunny could find a suitable graduated-care facility for her. So far, nothing had suited her, and Bunny pleaded with Ron to go down to Bermuda without her — anything to get him out of the house.

Nan Bennett, on the other hand, was staying home because she was worried about their son Eric, who was having serious trouble in school. Ian was still planning to come up to the Cape, though for him it would not exactly be a holiday. He was bringing four members of Bermuda's Blue Water Anglers Club, who loved the striped bass that could be caught out of Eastport. Last year, one had gotten his picture in the Cape Cod *Times,* holding up the largest striper ever caught in Cape Cod Bay.

For Ron, it was definitely going to be a vacation. He would go out when *he* felt like it, take what *he* wanted to eat and drink, and bait no one's hook but his own. He invited Dan, and they would stay at Sandys House, a guesthouse not far from Ely's Harbour, where Ian kept his 15-ton, 42-foot powerboat, *Goodness.*

But Dan was not sure. "It's been a long time since I've been away from the station for a whole week," he said to his wife.

Peg sat down opposite. "It's not like you've got anything going on right now," she pointed out. "In fact, according to Leo Bascomb, in all his years on the force, it's never been as quiet as right now." She laughed. "It's finally behaving like a village police department — where nothing ever happens."

Dan grudgingly smiled. "It *is* kind of quiet. But what about my appointment with Dr. Alexander?" The surgeon who had performed the by-pass wanted to see him annually for the next three years.

"I'll reschedule it."

"But—"

"Dan Burke! If he knew what you'd been invited to do, he'd be all for it!" She got up and started clearing the dishes. "Just watch what you eat and keep up your walking."

He laughed. "You've taken away all my reasons for not going."

"Checkmate!" she replied, but from his expression she could tell he was not resolved.

Suddenly she turned to him. "You know what your problem is? You need to be needed. All these years, you've been like a mother hen to that police department! And now—they don't need you."

"I don't think I like that analogy," he muttered, putting away the glasses.

"You don't like it, because it's true!" She came up behind him and hugged him around the middle. "You know, you really *are* getting thinner," she said appreciatively.

"Well—maybe you're right," he capitulated.

"Oh, come on! Think how much fun you'll have! You love to fish! And drink beer and tell war stories and go around with your shirt hanging out!" She laughed, and he joined her.

"You're amazing!" he said, shaking his head. "And you know what? Now that I've got my mind wrapped around it, I'm beginning to look forward to it."

"You should! You might even run into Brother Bartholomew down there."

Dan shut the cupboard door and hung up the towel. "I'd forgotten he's there. I called the friary to see if he wanted to do some fishing, and they told me he was down there. Maybe we can get him out on the boat." He paused. "No, probably not."

"Why?"

"They said he was on some kind of personal retreat or something."

On Saturday afternoon, four days later, Dan and Ron got off the plane in Bermuda. It was 3:15 by the time they checked in at Sandys House, overlooking Sandys Cove in Sandys Parish.

"That's pronounced 'Sands,' by the way," Ron explained, as he filled in the guest card for the day manager, "not the way you'd think from its spelling." He smiled. "The British enjoy doing that."

"Doing what?"

"Mangling pronunciations."

"You mean, like Wooster, for Worcestershire?"

"Yeah," replied Ron, "or Lester, for Leicestershire."

"Aloowishus for Aloysius."

Ron was stumped for a moment. "Chumley for Cholmondeley."

Both men laughed.

The first thing they had to do, announced Ron, was line up motor scooters at Oleander Cycle. There were no rental cars on Bermuda, only scooters. If you were going somewhere beyond walking distance, you took taxis or buses or ferries. Or rented a scooter.

The manager called the cycle shop, which offered to bring two over on a truck. But Ron said no, they'd come over and pick them out.

"The newer, the faster," he explained to Dan on the way.

"Well, we certainly want the fastest," the Chief agreed with a laugh.

"Oleander specializes in Ergons, from Taiwan. Young locals tell me they're the best."

Ron picked out two candy-apple-red Ergon doubles. They were made to carry two people, or one large man. Ron and Dan were both in the latter category. There was a little practice track — a good thing, because Dan's machine took some getting used to. But once they got out on the road, he found he could keep up with Ron. The trick was getting used to staying on the left.

As they roared past Ely's Harbour, his friend signaled for him to pull over. Dan pulled up alongside, and Ron pointed out *Goodness* at her mooring and then extended his arm to the sun, cupping his fingers.

"What are you doing?"

"Old Indian trick," Ron explained. "There are still four fingers between the sun and the horizon. We've got about an hour before it sets, and maybe twenty minutes of usable daylight after. Let's go over to the Bennetts' and see if we can take *Goodness* out. Just to check out her rig and tackle, you understand."

"Of course," said Dan, understanding.

They motored over, and found Nan expecting them. She gave Ron a hug and said, "It's *good* to see you."

Before he could mention the boat, she said, "I expect you'll be wanting to take *Goodness* out."

He grinned, and threw a knowing glance to Dan.

But Nan wasn't finished. Lowering her voice, she asked, "Ron, would you mind taking Eric out with you? He's the reason I'm not up on the Cape with Ian."

"What's the problem?"

"That's just it; we don't know. His headmaster called us in a couple of weeks ago. Eric had been on track for an outstanding senior year, after which Oxford was a possibility."

She looked quickly around, to make sure her son was not within hearing distance. "Suddenly he's not paying attention, dropped off the football team, and has started having 'unexplained absences' in the middle of the school day."

Ron looked concerned, but had nothing to offer. Dan shook his head. He had a hunch what it might be and did not want to pursue it. They were down here on a vacation, he reminded himself.

"We've tried to talk to him," Nan concluded. "It's no use. It's like he's not even there." Her voice broke, and she bit her knuckle.

"Of course, we'll take him, Nan. No problem."

Actually it was Eric who took *them* out. The blond, blue-eyed, rail-thin seventeen-year-old handled the boat with consummate skill, though to Dan he did not seem to be particularly enjoying himself. He had, in fact, a haunted look about him — a look Dan had seen from time to time on other kids. . . .

"Eric?" Ron called from the cabin, where he had taken the wheel, "help my partner understand the finer points of game-fishing."

The boy came back to familiarize Dan with the finer points of a big ocean reel and fighting chair. "You hook a marlin, you're going to have your hands full," he said with authority, as if he were a charter captain addressing a client. "You put the brake on here, and you keep the tip of your rod elevated — *always* — up in the air, so it bends. Like this," and he demonstrated the rod's extreme flexibility.

Pointing to the swiveling socket in the middle of the chair, he said, "And you keep the butt anchored here — *always* — and keep both hands on the rod, at all times. The last thing you want to do is lose a $1,500 rod and reel."

"You got that right!"

Eric smiled — for the first time since they left the harbor. "Mom said you're from Cape Cod — whereabouts, exactly?"

"Well," said Dan, extending his arm and bending it up at the elbow, as if signaling for a right turn, "if my ear were Boston, and this elbow's Chatham, we're right here on the inner crook — little village called Eastport."

Eric nodded. "I know what he does," he said, nodding toward Ron in the cabin. "What do you do?"

"I'm the chief of police."

Eric froze. Then quickly unfroze, hoping that Dan hadn't noticed.

But he had. "Don't worry, son," he said with a smile. "I couldn't be more off duty. Anyway, Bermuda's a little out of my jurisdiction."

Eric didn't smile and soon found a reason to go into the cabin.

"Hey, Dan," Ron called back to him, "You want to try her?"

"You go ahead; you're doing fine."

"Yeah, well, you're not getting a free ride here. You're going to have to drive, while I'm landing the one that's going over my mantel. So you'd better get in here and see how she runs."

Dan laughed and came in, taking the wheel. He tried a

few turns and was surprised at how responsive the boat was. "She seems awfully"—he sought the right word—"agile. And powerful."

"She's hot, all right," Ron nodded. "Hotter'n *Lucinda,* my boat," he explained. He paused and added ruefully, "Kinda makes me wish I had a spare hundred thou."

Eric emerged from the hold and went quickly aft to stow the gear.

Watching him, Dan said quietly to Ron, "His mother's right to be concerned."

"I know," Ron murmured, nodding. "What do you think's the problem?"

"Tell you later."

They stayed out till the sun went down, then headed back to Ely's Harbour. As they approached, Eric took the helm and guided them to the mooring, maneuvering adroitly to avoid two boats parked nearby. At the last moment, he reversed engine and backed down, so they just glided in to the buoy.

"You know," Ron said to him, as they got in the dinghy, "You're probably the best driver your age I've ever seen. Your dad's taught you well. He must be proud of you. I don't imagine it'll be too long before he'll have you taking your own charters out on *Goodness.*"

The boy said nothing. But Dan noted the tears that came before he could turn away.

8 | the white horse

As Saturday afternoon dissolved into Saturday evening in the harbor town of St. George at the other end of the island, Ian Bennett's younger brother Colin sat at the bar of the White Horse Tavern. He preferred the outside bar in back, but a cold snap had brought everyone indoors.

Normally he would be at one of the small round tables, flanked by mates who were adding to the forest of empty green bottles on the table. But on those rare occasions when he chose to be alone, he took the stool at the end of the long bar, with its back to the front window. This afternoon — and evening — he preferred his own company and was working on his fourth "Dark 'n Stormy." Made with Bermuda's Black Seal rum, it was the drink of choice among local sea-faring types, when they weren't knocking back Heinekens.

He cast an eye around the place. With the exception of the six guys over by the fireplace, it was quiet. They were the crew of the big schooner that had come in earlier that afternoon, *Laventura,* out of Newport. All in white, right down to their Topsiders, they seemed like decent sorts. No Rolexes, though. Gentleman sailors.

Except one. Even with four drinks in him Colin possessed a sailor's eye — that could pick up the slightest hint in wind or weather that might presage a sea change. One of the six was older than the rest. And didn't seem really comfortable in their company.

Grateful for the momentary distraction from what had brought him here to drink alone, he observed the man. He did not move with the graceful ease of the others. And he forced himself to smile, when the others were laughing. The thought crossed Colin's mind that he was not really a sailor at all. Studying him now, he noted the hardness around his eyes.

All at once the man looked up, caught Colin eyeballing him, and gave him a malevolent stare that made Colin's blood run cold. He was definitely not a character one would want to encounter on a dark night! That reminded him that his glass needed refilling, and he signaled Mike for another Dark 'n Stormy.

Normally on Saturday night the White Horse would be rocking. But the *Norwegian Majesty* had just sailed from the terminal on Ordnance Island and taken with her most of the tourists who'd been wandering the town. The White Horse regulars were not sad to see her go. Her departure signaled the approaching end of the cruise ship season. In two more weeks, they could come in here and count on getting a table and not having to wait half an hour for their food.

The other reason for the quiet was that tonight was the beginning of Race Week. Over in Hamilton, the matchrace regatta known as the Gold Cup was about to get underway. Tonight there was a posh reception at the Bacardi

Building in honor of all the skippers who had just arrived, and every nautical type who could wangle an invitation was there.

Colin had two invitations, actually. But he was in no mood to party. On the bar in front of him was a legal document of several pages. He started to scan the top page, then stopped; reading it again wasn't going to change what it said.

Well, if he had to be miserable, it might as well be here. Sailors, captains, mates, boatyard workers, sailmakers, pilots — all regarded the White Horse as their place. The only reason to go anywhere else would be for a little privacy or to impress a potential client, in which case they might go up the wharf to the more upscale Carriage House, or to San Giorgio's, whose Italian cuisine was superb and not too pricey.

Mounted above the tavern's fireplace was the rear end of a wrecked police boat. The ceiling over the bar was festooned with buoys and old sailing caps, and the walls were covered with photos and graffiti that meant a great deal to regulars, and nothing at all to visitors. The former were remarkably tolerant of the latter, however, knowing how much the island's economy depended on their cash.

They were especially so, if the visitors happened to be young and female and reasonably pulchritudinous. Indeed, local mariners were not averse to investing a fair amount of time and Heinekens, convincing them of their seafaring charm. Occasionally it actually paid off — just often enough to keep the ball in play.

Colin never had to buy more than one round for visitors of that persuasion. His flashing dark eyes and dazzling smile qualified him as what women considered "cute." Men never knew exactly what constituted "cute," but women always did — and Colin was its definition.

He was not feeling particularly cute tonight, though; he was well on his way to feeling nothing. For the moment, all he felt was devastated. The documents in front of him were divorce papers.

Amy, his wife of eight years, was suing him, from her family's estate in Georgia, where she'd taken their eight-year-old son Jamie. He'd been staring at the papers for two hours and still couldn't believe it.

"You finally got to her, didn't you," whispered Colin bitterly, waving to Mike for yet another. "And now you've got her."

His father had been a charter fishing captain, and his mother had inherited just enough for them to keep the family home in Somerset and send their two sons to good schools off-island. Colin, who had just turned 30, had followed his older brother to a prep school named Deerfield Academy. But he'd not followed Ian to Williams College, as after Deerfield had come Lawrence Academy and Tabor Academy (twice).

Williams might still have been receptive to an application from Colin, as his combined SAT scores were 1470, and his older brother had compiled a sterling record. But he was more interested in ocean racing than college. In the cockpit of a 12-meter America's Cup challenger, his concentration was absolute and sustained (as it had never been at the various academies). All things being equal, he was one of the finest sailors the island had produced, and Bermuda, like New Zealand, was renowned for its sailors.

In the days when Rolex used to sponsor the America's Cup, they traditionally awarded each member of the winning crew a stainless steel Submariner. In the back of Colin's desk drawer was a green presentation box containing a Rolex he'd won but never worn. The other was on his wrist.

His father had died suddenly of a massive heart attack when Colin was 21. As lung cancer had taken his mother six years before, there was a modest estate. Ian got the house and his father's boat, *Goodness,* both of which were heavily mortgaged. Colin got the money — $82,000, all that was left after the tuition bills. With it he bought the boat of his dreams — a Venus 34.

Designed and built in Bermuda, the broad-beamed, gaff-rigged Venus was a superb ocean sailor. Other transoceanic sailing vessels that dropped anchor at St. George's Harbour might be bigger, but in heavy weather, none did better than a Venus.

Colin paid top dollar for her and named her *Care Away.* He maintained a one-room apartment in town, which he used mostly as an office, or a place to live when the boat was out of the water. The rest of the time, it was mainly convenient for stowing stuff, plus it had a shower, which the boat didn't.

When it came to fitting out *Care Away,* he decided to go for minimum maintenance rather than authenticity. Stevie Hollis, one of the few sailmakers left on Bermuda, might have brown "tan-bark" sails on his 34-foot Venus, but Colin's were white. And his bright work was polished stainless steel, not bronze.

Similarly, following the advice of another captain friend, Stuart Lunn, he decided to go with the best radar, radio, GPS (Global Positioning System), and autopilot money could buy. As Stuart said, "If you're going to put in technology, don't skimp. When it saves your life one day, you'll be glad you didn't."

But Colin also had a good brass sextant aboard. In the event of a lightning strike, all electronics would be fried anyway—even the handheld, backup GPS unit in a drawer under his bunk. If that happened, he could still get across the Atlantic the old-fashioned way, using his Rolex (which gained seven seconds a week), as a chronometer.

He'd spent the last of his inheritance on the tools he would need to support himself as a shipwright. For Colin had a real knack for putting broken boats back together again. Whatever nature messed up, he would set right again, and he gradually earned a reputation that would ensure he always had work if he wanted it—which most of the time, he didn't.

Except during hurricane season, roughly September through November, when he would work nonstop with relentless intensity. Wherever a major weather event knocked boats around, Colin could be expected to arrive in its wake. His prices were high, and while the boat owners and marina managers might object, they always paid. When Colin Bennett fixed them, they stayed fixed.

After that, he took the rest of the year off—dropping down to the Caribbean in January when Bermuda got too cold or beating up to Bar Harbor in July, when it got too hot. The rest of the time, St. George's was just fine. Unless or until the spirit moved him to go somewhere else.

He liked to think of himself as a gypsy of the sea. And then, along came Amy.

9 | the *gleama*

It was her roommate Pam's fault. Amy would never have gone to Bermuda on spring break; Bermuda was where their parents used to go. *Their* friends all went to Barbados that year.

But her roommate had this thing about Bermuda. Her parents had fallen in love at the Coral Beach Club, dancing under the stars to the calypso music of the Talbot Brothers. Pam felt compelled to go there, and she could be extremely persuasive.

It turned out better than Amy expected. A lot better. They, too, stayed at the Coral Beach Club, and while there were a number of old fuds around, and a layer of younger fuds, there was also a younger, with-it group. They played tennis (well) and swam and did the beach thing, and scootered everywhere — and included Pam and Amy. It was surprisingly fun.

Two days before they were due to leave, they'd been to Hamilton, done the shops, spent a day at the Dockyard and another at Horseshoe Bay. The only place they hadn't gone was St. George. But that was a long haul, out to the east end of the island. "You go ahead," she begged off. "I'm going to hang here by the pool."

But Pam had insisted. The Bermuda experience would not be complete without St. George. With a sigh, Amy tugged on her white windbreaker and tied a white kerchief over her short blond hair. Donning her Jackie O's, she followed her friend's scooter out of the car park.

By the time they took the obligatory pictures of each other in the stocks in St. George's public square, the sky was beginning to darken. They ducked into the White Horse for a quick bite. By the time they'd finished their club sandwiches and were ready to leave, there was a serious downpour going on outside.

For once, it was Amy who took charge. Unzipping the rolled-up hood in the collar of her windbreaker, she put it over the white kerchief, and was about to lead the way out into the elements, when the young man at the end of the bar spoke to her.

"Not a good idea," he said, giving her a full-wattage smile. He was so cute that Amy immediately distrusted him, proceeding toward the door as if she hadn't heard him.

Pam had, though, and seeing him, she'd hesitated, dazzled by that incredible smile.

"You really don't want to ride in this downpour." He said to Amy, still smiling but emphatic.

She ignored him, and held the door open for Pam who was hesitating. "You coming?"

Pam was torn.

"Let's get going!" Amy declared. "We're not going to melt! And I don't feature waiting here all afternoon."

The young man stood up. "Don't be dumb!" He nodded towards the window. "It's the first rain in several days. It'll bring the oil up out of the pavement, and the combination will be so slick, it'll make anything on two wheels feel like a pig on ice."

Pam frowned. "Amy, maybe we'd better—"

"*Will you come on?*" Amy snapped, and glared at the *gleama* (their code word for a mega-cute), as if to convey that his was the lamest pick-up line she'd ever heard.

The young man, not smiling now, held up his right arm and pointed to an ugly scar that extended over his elbow. "I got this on a scooter on a day like this, when I went out with exactly the same attitude."

Now it was Amy who hesitated. Glancing out the window, she saw torrential rain sweeping across the square.

With a sigh, she capitulated.

He bought the first round. They bought the next, and the third—long after it had stopped raining and begun to dry.

His name was Colin Bennett. He was an ocean racer. He had been to practically every exotic port they'd ever heard of. And now he had a new boat and was living aboard it. When he offered to show it to them, Pam wasn't sure. Until Amy pointed out that it, too, was definitely part of the Bermuda experience. Amy, it turned out, could be as persuasive as Pam.

So the next afternoon (their last), Colin and his captain friend, Stuart, who had a car, took Amy and Pam to the Hogpenny Pub in Hamilton for lunch. It became an all-afternoon lunch, after which they repaired to *Care Away*. The boat was big enough to afford the couples some privacy, if the girls were prepared to go as far as the guys were prepared to take them. They weren't, and the evening ended pleasantly. Bermudians could be gentlemen when circumstances called for it.

As Stuart drove them back to the Coral Beach Club, Pam nattered away next to him about how wonderful Bermuda had been, just like it had been for her parents, and how she really loved his island and wasn't just saying that but really meant it.

In the back seat, Amy let Colin kiss her. To her surprise, she found herself kissing him back — and meaning it. In fact, it was all she could do to keep the brakes on.

As they said goodbye, Colin asked, "Look, uh, give me your address. Maybe, you know, I'll write you or something."

She wrote it out for him. "Well, if you do, maybe, you know, I'll write you back." They both laughed.

To her surprise, he did write. Mostly about his boat, and where he was going. The moment she opened it, she turned to the end, to see how he signed it. "Cheers." Pretty non-committal. But he *did* write.

So, she did the same. She told him about her upcoming finals, and how strange it felt to be almost done with school forever, and how Pam was bugging her to do the Grand Tour with her, five-star hotels in all the capitals of Europe, just like her grandparents had. She had no intention of going, though it might be fun to see Rome.

When she got to the end, she chewed the tip of her pen. Then signed it, "*Ciao*," as a modern Roman might.

He wrote back, with a very funny description of the cruise ship passengers in the White Horse, and said at the end that he'd like to see Rome someday himself. And signed it, "Yours."

She wrote back and told him how awful exams were, and how her whole family was coming for graduation, and how Pam was really putting pressure on her, and her father said he'd give her the trip as a graduation present, but she really didn't want to go. She signed it, "*Arrived-erci*."

He wrote and lightly, offhandedly suggested that if the prospect of grand touring bugged her that much, why didn't she come to Bermuda, instead? He signed it "Luf" — a jokey substitute for "Love." Except — was he just joking?

Normally she'd run it past Pam, her best friend and confidant, as well as roommate. But Pam was miffed at her for stalling re the GT. So she wrote Colin back and lightly, offhandedly said she'd consider Bermuda as an alternative. At the end of the letter, she practically chewed a hole in her pen. And finally signed it, "with fond remembrance." Warm but obscure. Wistful but noncommittal.

She mailed it before she could change her mind.

Twenty minutes later she did change her mind. Good grief! "With fond remembrance" sounded like something on a funeral home card! But her fond remembrance was already winging its way.

Not having Pam to check things with was a megabummer. It was time to make up with her roomie.

But when she told Pam she was thinking of going to Bermuda instead of Europe, her best friend just stared at her. "*Bermuda?*"

"Why not?" Amy shot back. "It was good enough for your parents, wasn't it?"

Pam looked at her, her eyes widening. "It's not — that *gleama*, is it?"

No answer.

"It *is!*"

Silence.

"Ames!" Pam shouted at her, "you can't be hung up on

a guy that looks like he stepped out of a Lands' End catalogue!"

Amy nodded and threw a rueful smile. "That's why I've got to go back. To see if he's more than just a *gleama*."

And so, to Pam's, and Colin's—and her own—surprise, she did.

He met her at the airport, but instead of going straight to the Coral Beach Club, they stopped off at the Swizzle Inn, where the owner, Jay, was an old friend. On the island, Colin explained, that usually meant that the families were old friends, someone having married someone way back. But Jay was a regular guy, and he ran the best place west of the White Horse.

Fortunately a table was available on the upper verandah. Colin ordered lunch for them — Fish & Chips and swizzles — and they talked lightly about the weather and the oppressive humidity that was about to descend, ending the tourist season.

"Is that tough on people like Jay?" she asked.

"Not really. The ones who depend on the tourist trade," he nodded towards their host, greeting another table of returnees, "have been busting their humps for the past three months. They're ready for a break. But after three months of summer, they'll be rested up and ready to go again."

He offered her a shaker bottle of clear liquid, "Here, try this on your chips."

"On my fries? What is it?"

"Vinegar."

"*Euw*," she gasped, wrinkling her nose.

"Brit trick. It works. Try it."

She did, frowning, and then, tilting her head, she smiled. "Mm, not bad. Know any other Brit tricks?"

"Maybe," he murmured, flashing her that full Lands' End smile.

"Are you flirting with me, sailor?"

"Aw, shucks, ma'am; you caught me."

"Well, don't," she said, smiling, too, but half serious. "I'm not sure I'm ready yet."

"Would you like another swizzle?"

She had to laugh. "Candy's dandy, but liquor's quicker?"

"*The Golden Trashery of Ogden Nashery.*"

"You know Ogden Nash?"

He smiled. "My checkered academic career, such as it was — or wasn't — exposed me to many things. Some of the oddest bits seem to have lodged in the backeddies of my mind."

She smiled. "You *are* a man of many layers."

He stopped smiling. "I'm not sure how to take that. Truth is, I'm actually not that good at playing games — unless, of course, I'm running the table."

The waitress came up and asked if they would care for anything else — another swizzle, perhaps?

He raised his eyebrows.

She shook her head.

He shook his head, and the waitress departed.

"If you're not running the table, who is?"

"I wish I knew," he said with a shrug, adding, "All I know is, the stack of chips in front of me is small and getting smaller." He scrutinized the imaginary stack in front of her. "While yours is tall and getting taller."

"Thurber?"

"Sort of." He frowned and looked at her, one eyebrow raised. "Now you wouldn't be gamin' a poor sailor, would you, ma'am?"

She raised her hands in mock innocence.

"'Cause if you are—I'm not sure I'm ready yet."

They laughed. Then laughed again.

"Can we back up a little?" she pleaded.

"No prob. X.O., take her up to periscope depth." He leaned back. "So, what'll you do now that you're done with college?"

She told him how her father was training her to take over the family business, managing several thousand acres of Georgia pine.

He told her how he'd gotten involved in ocean racing—almost as a lark at first. But it gave an adrenalin rush like nothing else, so you got hooked on it, real quick. Only the love of a good woman, like *Care Away,* could ever cause you to leave full-time racing.

Her turn. Trying to think of something to say, she noticed a few small, white scars around his knuckles and remembered him telling her before about his solo voyages across the Atlantic. "The last time you went, the time to the Med—how long did it take?"

"Thirty-eight days. But I had good westerlies; it can take longer."

"Thirty-eight days!" She shook her head in wonder. "What was the first thing you saw?"

"My landfall? Gibraltar. Northern Pillar of Heracles."

"Did you break out champagne?"

"I never drink at sea."

"Not even a beer?"

He shook his head.

"Why?"

"Too risky. You run your boat right—good seaman-ship—not much is going to go wrong. But when it does, it happens quickly. You've got to be sharp, make the right decision immediately."

"Were you ever—frightened?"

"Nope."

"Not even by a hurricane?"

He thought for a moment. "Well, if I know one's com-ing, obviously I'm going to get out of its way."

"You listen to the radio for warnings?"

"If I have a reason. You build up your intuition out there. Develop a sixth sense. I keep a log. Every two hours I note the cloud conditions, sea conditions, heading and reckoned speed. And the barometer. If it's falling fast, and the high cirrus are beginning to fan out, you bet-ter believe I'm going to tune in WWV! At six past the hour, they give the Atlantic warnings. I also use their time tick to reset my watch, for the sextant."

She shuddered. "I don't think I'd like solo sailing."

"You never know till you do it," he shrugged. "It's overcoming the last fear barrier. You find out what you'll do when your life depends on the sum of your decisions." He smiled. "It does anyway, but it's much more obvious when you're alone out there. Or climbing above eight thousand meters. Or going up a rock face without a rope."

She frowned. "You're a thrill junkie."

He thought about that. "I suppose so. I'm hooked on racing, that's for sure."

"But *Care Away* isn't a particularly fast boat, is it?"

"Is she," he corrected her. "*Care Away* is a person—a

very likeable lady, once you get to know her. She's also my home. And I want my home comfortable, a good cruiser I'm happy to spend all my days in."

Amy frowned. "I still don't see how you can—"

"Do both? In my apartment over on St. David's, which I use mainly for keeping stuff—I've got two bikes—a skinny-tired one for going fast, a fat-tired one for cruising. All depends on what I feel like."

There was indeed more to this *gleama* than met the eye. Best to find out how much more. "Thirty-eight days," she marveled. "Ever get lonely?"

He looked at Grotto Bay, barely visible in the distance. Then returned his gaze to her with a half smile. "Not lonely, exactly. *Care Away's* good company. The best. And there's always something that needs doing. But some days, when there's not much wind—"

She finished it for him, "You wouldn't mind having someone to talk to."

"Yeah," he admitted. "I suppose so."

"But then, after the doldrums, you'd have to put up with them."

He laughed. "Exactly!"

She circled her finger on the table. "Was there ever anyone you—felt really good about having on board?" She paused and thought, now he's going to think I'm getting personal. She took a deep breath. Well, I am.

But to soften it, she quickly added, "I mean, on a really long trip."

He carefully chewed the last of his fish before replying. "I took my nephew out for a few days, a year ago. It was my brother's idea; Ian thought Eric should get to know his Uncle Colin." He smiled sadly. "I don't think he counted on the boy having so much fun. We had a ball!

He was only nine, but I've never seen *anyone,* any age, learn faster than he did." He shook his head at the memory.

In her mind she could see him teaching the young boy. She liked what she saw.

"That's the thing," declared Colin, warming to his subject. "If someone really likes what I really like, I'll teach them as fast as they can learn. Eric loved sailing—the boat, the life, the whole thing. And you know what? When the trip was over, it was hard to see him leave."

"He never went again?"

Colin shook his head. "He loved it too much. Told my brother he wanted to grow up to be a sailor, like Uncle Colin." He sighed. "His father had other plans for him."

The waitress returned and asked if they would like coffee. They would.

"And so," Amy summed up, "other than someone like Eric, you prefer your own company. Just you and Lady *Care Away.*"

He looked her in the eye. "You got it."

Well, he might be blunt, but he was honest. And his message was unequivocal: No woman could ever persuade him to put her before the boat. Amy shivered. Time to get back up to periscope depth again.

"So the solitude never gets you down."

"Not really. Time does a funny thing out there," he mused. "I'll think of something I need to take care of, a project that might take most of next morning. I'll resolve to do it, but when morning comes, I'm sitting there in the cockpit under a clear sky and—it doesn't get done. Nothing does. But I'm content."

He laughed. "That's probably the most valuable skill a sailor can have—the ability to just sit."

She smiled. But when she'd first asked, she thought she'd seen him start to remember something, then shy away from it. So she asked again.

He hesitated. "There *was* one time. . . ." His voice drifted off, and he looked out at the bay again, his eyes narrowing. "Sometimes a school of flying fish will run with you awhile, jumping alongside. Occasionally one will land on the boat. If you can reach it in time, you throw it back in the water. If not," he shrugged, "you just kick it over the side. Or if you're hungry, you cook it and eat it. They're quite good."

He did not take his eyes off the distant water. "One perfect afternoon, sunny, rolling sea—I'd been out about a month—the wind was moderate, and I was making three, three-and-a-half knots. All at once, this school of flying fish kind of adopts me. You could see them shimmering, silvery blue-green, just below the surface, blending with the broken pattern of the sun's reflection. Every so often—for sheer joy, it seemed—one would arc up into the air like a mini-dolphin and dive back in. Then another would show that he could do that, too. And another, and another."

He laughed. "Hey, I cheered them on! They were having fun, and they were fun for me." He paused. "Somehow I think they knew that. More and more of them broke the surface, and it was like we were on parade!"

He stopped smiling. "I didn't notice that a young one, not more than three inches, had landed on the deck. He was in the sun, and he was still. But his scales still glistened. Moving fast, I scooped up a bucket of seawater and started trying to revive that little fish. 'This is crazy,' I told myself, 'just pop it in the skillet.' But I kept at it for half an hour, moving it in the seawater, bawling like a kid."

He shuddered and fell silent, and she reached out and touched his hand.

"So," he said, his voice rough, "I guess the solitude *can* get to you." He turned away quickly before she could see what was in his eyes.

But she saw. And wanted to comfort the little boy she saw in him. Whoa, girl! Lighten up!

"Had you ever thought of taking an animal with you?" she asked lightly. "A cat, maybe?"

He smiled. "You're not the first to suggest that. And you know, I *have* thought about it. Ian even offered me a kitten, a gray-and-white female from their cat's litter."

"Why didn't you take her?"

"Nearly did. Even had a name picked out: Esmeralda. I imagined her napping in a little box next to me in the cockpit, sleeping on the end of my bunk at night." He paused. "But then I made myself think about the dark side. And realized that Ezzie wouldn't have a clue how dangerous an environment a boat is, and wouldn't have her mother to teach her. I couldn't watch her all the time. She might be up in the bow, playing with a knot in a line, and a swell would cause her to lose her balance and go over the side. If I didn't see it, she would be gone. And if we'd grown close, as we were sure to, that would be—devastating."

He smiled at her, shaking his head. "You suppose we could talk about something else?"

She nodded and smiled brightly; yes, there were more layers to this one than met the eye. But she couldn't think of anything to say.

Nor was he helping. He just sat there, studying her, a

half-smile on his face. And that smirk, if that's what it was, was beginning to annoy her.

Finally, eyes twinkling, he observed, "You're in a bit of a bind, aren't you?"

She frowned but said nothing.

"I mean, you came all this way to check me out, and now you feel a bit foolish because you don't know exactly how to go about doing that."

"Do you *always* speak what's on your mind?" she snapped at him.

"Why not?"

She had no answer.

"Amy," he said gently, using her name for the first time since she'd arrived, "either it was a good idea for you to come or it wasn't. I happen to think it was."

She was not ready to agree.

"Look," he said, catching her eyes with his, "we can go on playing games if you want to. But honestly — why waste the time?"

Now he was infuriating! Coming here was *not* a good idea! It was the worst idea she'd ever had! She could be in Roma right now, on the *Via Veneto* sipping a Belini with Pam at Harry's American Bar.

She glared at him, and he impassively returned her gaze. Neither turned away.

Oh, he was *really* making her angry! So sure of himself — well, we'll see.

She decided to take him on. Straight on. *Mano a womano.*

"All right!" she declared. "From now on, we play by Bermuda rules. We say *exactly* what we think. No more, no less. No game-playing. And we say it, no matter how romantically incorrect it might be, even if it sends me back on the next plane. Because you're right: I didn't come here to play games! I came to see if," she hesitated and then played by the new rules, "I wanted to make any emotional investment in a–gypsy of the sea."

In that instant, Lands' End vanished. Colin did the sort of split-second re-evaluation that women would never understand. But men understood perfectly. If she's the one, and you *know* it, then you go after her—and move heaven and hell to get her.

"Deal." It *was* a done deal, as far as Colin Bennett was concerned.

It took Amy a little longer. But once she admitted to herself that he *might* be the one, things did seem to come together rather quickly. They ate breakfast together, lunch together, supper together, talking all the time, finding new subjects they mostly agreed on.

After a few days, the talking subsided. They knew they felt the same way about the sunset, or the two Long-tails cavorting over the cliffs at Horseshoe Beach, or the young boys playing soccer (he called it football) in the late afternoon at a school in Somerset Parish, the sun limning their lithe forms and creating halos around them.

They said nothing, because there was no reason to speak.

When she asked about going out on *Care Away,* he put her off. Too cloudy or too windy. He wanted her first experience with the other lady in his life to be just right.

She believed him, but she wondered if it might also be–that he was afraid it wouldn't work out. Because she was afraid of the same thing. According to Bermuda Rules, she should say what she was thinking.

But there was one subject that by mutual unspoken assent neither of them had mentioned. Them.

And somehow *Care Away* was in the midst of them.

Inevitably the day came, when conditions were ideal. "We're going," he announced at breakfast.

"When?"

"Soon as you can get your kit together."

"My kit?"

"Whatever you're going to need—windbreaker, deck shoes, sun-screen." He looked at her red knees. "Long-sleeved shirt and pants. You don't want to fry out there. The sun reflects off the water—"

She cut him off. "I *have* been on boats before, you know."

She was ready in fifteen minutes.

11 | two ladies

It had been calm at breakfast, scarcely a breeze. But the wind had picked up, and now there was distinct chop in St. George's Harbour as he rowed them out to *Care Away,* in the Convict Bay anchorage.

Amy eyed her rival and had to admit she was — stunning. Her hull was royal blue, with a thin red line of trim at the waterline, matching the red Bermuda ensign at her stern. Her deck was teak, her bright work polished stainless steel. Her rolled mainsheet was covered with a tight canvas sheath, also royal blue.

Amy's heart sank. How could she possibly compete against this — nautical *gleama*?

Colin tied the dinghy to the mooring buoy, then swung easily aboard her and put down a three-step ship's ladder for Amy. When she, too, was aboard, he cast off, and they were under way.

At first, she loved it — the wind in her face, the broad white sail on its gaff rig, the sound of the waves thrumming against the bow. Best of all was watching the shoreline recede swiftly behind them, smaller and smaller. They, too, were Longtails, leaving all cares behind.

Once they had cleared St. George's Channel, he headed her south in the Narrows, running before the wind. As the sun rose higher, the breeze moderated, and he put on all her canvas — mainsail, staysail, jib, topsail, mizzen — showing her off, in all her glory. Under full sail they were soon surfing atop each wave that passed.

It was fun, at first, whooshing along, and then settling a bit, only to be picked up by the next wave. Such fun that she looked around, half-expecting a school of flying fish to adopt them.

But this was not a ride in an amusement park, which was over after a few exhilarating minutes, setting you back on *terra firma*, laughing about how much fun it had been. This ride kept going. And going.

And after half an hour of whooshing and settling, she began wishing she'd had something sensible for breakfast. She could feel the greasy fried eggs and two shiny sausage links sliding around down there and sloshing up the walls of her stomach.

Think of something else! She concentrated on the knotted end of the mainsheet, dangling from the stainless steel grommet, as it swayed with the motion of the boat, this way and that. Find something else! She turned away, but a little burp brought up the brown taste of sausage.

She closed her eyes, and guessed she'd be able to keep eggs and sausage down for five more minutes, then she would be puking her guts out over the boat's leeward side. She'd prefer the privacy of the tiny head, but then she'd have to clean up the mess afterward, and — Oh, God! This was a terrible mis–

"Amy," he said gently but firmly, "open your eyes. Keep them on the horizon."

She did as she was told, and smiled weakly.

She concentrated on the horizon. Hard. And burped. Sausage again, but this time some orange juice, too.

"It's not working," she gasped.

"Then come over here. There's one thing that always works," he said cheerily, adding under his breath, "if anything's going to."

He hadn't meant her to hear that, but she had. Nevertheless, she did as he instructed, taking the place he'd just vacated, at the tiller.

"Now keep her headed roughly one-six-five," and he pointed to the compass floating in the gleaming binnacle.

Once she got used to pushing the tiller in the opposite direction of where she wanted to go, she found that the boat did not respond to the helm as quickly as a car. So she over-corrected. And then overcorrected again. Behind them, their wake, which had receded in a straight line, now resembled the track of an alpine skier.

"Relax!" he called to her, grinning. "Give her time. She'll come to your heading eventually. Just be patient with her."

She did relax. And took a deep breath. And relaxed some more. And found that only very minor corrections were needed to keep her on a heading in the general vicinity of 165°.

"Now you're getting it!" he cried. Turning to *Care Away,* he asked, "What do you think?" He listened. "Yup, I agree!" He turned back to Amy, beaming. "Hey, Ames, she likes you!"

She giggled, feeling ridiculously pleased. How did he know her nickname?

He taught her how to tack, come about, and avoid jibing. How to close haul and keep her mainsail taut, reading the telltales. How to take a reef in the mainsail, when the wind reached 15 knots or more and started kicking up whitecaps. And each new thing he taught her, he only had to tell her once.

He really is a wonderful teacher, she thought, breakfast long forgotten. And he makes it fun. No wonder his nephew had such a good time.

After four sun-dazzled hours, he headed them home. "Steady her up on zero-three-zero," he called.

"Aye-aye, cap'n."

The waves were now coming at her off the port bow. Following the imaginary line she could see through the swells forming ahead, she guided this magnificent blue sea creature effortlessly through them, like a skier negotiating moguls.

"Ames!" he cried, overjoyed. "You're a natural! I didn't even tell you how to do that!"

"I love this!" she called back. "This could be the most fun I've ever had!"

A rogue wave, out of pattern with the rest, suddenly loomed to starboard. Deftly she fell away before it, then neatly rounded it, and resumed their heading.

"Amend that!" she shouted, laughing. "This *is* the most fun I've ever had!"

He let her have the helm all the way back, taking over only as they approached his mooring. She caught the buoy, first try.

At the end of the day, tired, sun-baked, smiling, they sat drinking Heinekens at the White Horse. He looked at her over the little round table. "Bermuda Rules, right?"

She nodded.

"You're the best first-time sailor I've ever seen! Man or woman."

"Even better than Eric?" she teased him.

"Well," he said, not quite willing to go that far, "he was only eight."

"We're going tomorrow, right?"

"Of course."

"No matter what the weather is?"

"No matter what."

"Okay," she declared, putting her bottle firmly on the table. "Bermuda Rules. After a day like today, if I had my way, I'd spend the rest of my life sailing."

Both were stilled by what she had just said.

As she looked at him, studying his steady dark eyes, she was thinking of the one thing they hadn't shared. They'd kissed briefly, careful to keep it casual. Held hands briefly, parting naturally.

She knew she had never met anyone she enjoyed being with more. Nor had she ever imagined finding anyone she could share silence with. And when she wasn't with him, she didn't feel whole. She would wake up in her room at the Coral Beach Club and wish she could drag time forward, till he came to collect her.

"I want to move aboard *Care Away*," she announced. "Tonight."

"You're sure?" he asked softly.

She reached out and covered his hand with hers. "I'm sure."

12 | to the table down at sandys

Saturday was turnover day in Bermuda's hotels and guesthouses. Not all guests came or departed on Saturday, but enough did that places like Sandys House held a weekly welcoming party for new guests late Saturday afternoon before dinner. Often they served Planter's Punch because it was such an excellent icebreaker.

Sandys House was essentially an upscale Bed & Breakfast. But the owner, St. John Cooper-Smith, had an arrangement with a retired chef who didn't mind cooking on the weekend. This meant that in addition to breakfast, he could offer his guests a modified plan, featuring a sumptuous evening repast at the end and beginning of most stays, Friday and Saturday evenings.

Ron Wallace and Dan Burke arrived back from their orientation trip aboard *Goodness,* barely in time for a glass of punch before the well-welcomed guests went in to dinner. The dining room had a bay window at the far end, facing west. This meant dinner guests could appreciate some truly spectacular sunsets as they ate at the long cedar dining table, at the head of which, his back to the view, sat their host.

Joining him this evening were seven guests who had elected to take advantage of the modified plan, including "our two fishermen from Cape Cod," as he welcomed Ron and Dan to the table.

"By the way," he concluded, when he'd finished the introductions, "do call me by my first name, which, for those of you who are first-timers, is pronounced — Sin Jin."

Dan chuckled, suspecting that the day manager had related their banter about the English mangling of names. Speaking of names, no sooner had Dan been told everyone's, than he started forgetting them. Lucky thing that Chief of Police was an appointed, not an elected office, he thought; he'd make a lousy politician. Focusing on the table conversation, he tried to pick them up in context.

On their host's left was Maud Brown, a retired stockbroker from Anaheim. Dan put her age at "indeterminate seventies," though nowadays with fitness and exercise so much a part of growing older, it was hard to tell anyone's age for certain. Fitness was of no particular concern to Maud, though. Before they came in, she'd been smoking a pencil-thin cigar.

In the place of honor at their host's right (and Dan's left), was Maud's distant cousin and frequent traveling companion, Margaret Chalmers from Philadelphia. Unlike her cousin, Margaret ("Oh, call me Mags; everyone does") helped herself sparingly when they went to the buffet on the gleaming cedar sideboard behind him, avoiding frivolous calories. She had high cheekbones and short-cropped silvery hair, favored tailored slacks, and carried herself with an almost regal self-assurance. Except for the no-nonsense, steel-rimmed glasses, she reminded him of Katherine Hepburn in "The Philadelphia Story."

Ron was across the table from him, and next to him were Jane and Buff MacLean from Sewickley, Pennsylvania, who were embarrassed that everyone could tell they were on their honeymoon. Jane was a special-needs teacher, taller and older than her new husband. Normally she was quiet, she assured them, even a bit shy, "but these Planter's Punches certainly have a way of putting *that* in the closet."

Seeing their smiles, she assumed they didn't believe her. "Seriously! My nickname at Sewickley Country Day was Plain Jane Tremaine." She paused and giggled. "Oh my goodness! I never thought of that! I guess now I'm — Plain Jane Tremaine MacLean!"

Everyone laughed. So did Jane, who was having a wonderful time, liking all these new friends, adoring her husband. There was nothing plain about her tonight, thought Dan. All the world loved a lover, and tonight she was radiant, happy as a clam at high tide, as they said back home.

Too bad the same could not be said of her bridegroom. Buff MacLean, proprietor of a fitness center known as Buff's Bods, had long blond hair, blow-dried and sprayed, with sideburns at the length currently dictated by GQ. Dan guessed that the well-defined pecs and abs under the tight Ralph Lauren Polo shirt (white, to show off his tan) required two hours a day of heavy lifting to maintain.

That's just jealousy, he rebuked himself. He might be getting thinner, but alongside Body Beautiful over there, he felt as shabby as Inspector Colombo's old raincoat.

What was sad about Buff was that he was trying so

hard to be happy — or at least give the appearance of being happy.

The sunset had been a disappointment, obscured by a low layer of approaching clouds. And now, as it grew darker outside, the window on Dan's left began to act as a mirror. In it, he could see the reflection of the real mirror over the sideboard behind him. Which meant that he could see Buff's face without the latter realizing that he was being observed.

Buff's expression, when no one was looking in his direction, became worried, impatient, almost tortured. Whatever was on his mind, it was not the joys of wedded bliss.

The last guest, to Dan's right, was Laurent Devereux. The Frenchman, sixty-ish, was director of an import-export firm headquartered in Paris. Next week he would lead a seminar at a global communications convention to be held at the Southampton Princess. He had left the City of Lights a week early, he told them, because he was *très fatigué.* And what better place to rest and mentally prepare for *la bataille,* than this *charmant pied-à-terre,* so far from the Princess, where he would be instantly *engagé,* and rest would be *impossible.*

To Dan, *Monsieur le Directeur* did not appear all that tired, but perhaps the French gauged fatigue differently. There was no denying his Gallic charm, and to judge from the sidelong glances that the older ladies present were throwing him — what, jealousy again? No. Well, maybe. Put Brian Dennehy next to Louis Jordan, and who would any woman look at?

Well then, did he harbor an aversion to *Les Français*? *Mais non, pas du tout!* He took his wife to every subtitled movie she wanted to see. He liked the old ones; *films noirs,* Peg called them. Their gritty realism had it all over Hollywood, and their tough guys—Gabin, Montand, Belmondo—seemed a lot tougher than the homegrown variety.

But the last French flick, a *Palmes d'Or*-winning attempt at bringing Marcel Proust's life to the screen, had been deliberately obscure, something Dan considered obscene, the height of French *hauteur.* Watching it, he had tried to imagine anything more painful, like sticking needles in his eyes.

Feeling a twinge of guilt over where his thoughts had gone, Dan turned to Devereux. "Did you, by any chance, see the new Proust movie?"

With an expression of faint distaste—as if he'd just sampled a vintage he would ask the *sommelier* to return to the kitchen—Devereux shook his head. "I'm afraid," he said with a charming smile, "I'm really too busy for the cinema." And he turned back to his plate.

Nice put-down, Frenchie, thought Dan. Maybe, after all, he was a bit of a Francophobe.

It was not long before the guests became friends—not unusual at Sandys House, where the return rate was 95 percent.

More details began to emerge. Their host's modified RAF moustache really was an RAF moustache. Barely 20, Flight Lieutenant Cooper-Smith had interrupted his Oxford education to fly with Transport Command in the Burma Theater. Ms. Brown, the stock broker from Anaheim, had anticipated every major downturn of the market—including the present one. Her grateful clients referred to her as "The Unsinkable Maudie Brown."

Margaret Chalmers had rowed at Wellesley, as had her daughter. Her brother had rowed with Grace Kelly's brother when they were members of Philadelphia's Vesper Boat Club.

Ron Wallace told about his boat-swapping arrangement with Ian Bennett, to which St. John observed, "I went to school with Ian's father."

Dan revealed he was the Chief of Police of a village not much bigger than Somerset, which had become so quiet that he'd not thought about it once down here.

Jane MacLean was a birdwatcher with a life species list of more than two hundred, to which she'd added six entries in the short time they'd been here.

When attention shifted to her husband, he perked up and informed them that membership had increased 30 percent since he'd opened his fitness center four months before. But, as noted Dan in the window/mirror, the moment the spotlight was off him, the smile vanished. Indeed, in the past hour he'd begun sneaking glances at his watch.

Stop it, Dan chided himself; this is a vacation, not a stake-out! But it was no more possible for him to stop than for a bird-dog to ignore a scent. And Dan's nose was telling him something was awry here.

Abruptly Buff got to his feet and announced, "I've got to — take care of something."

"What, darling?" asked Jane, startled.

"Just — something!" He tried to smile, as if it might be a surprise for her, and departed into the night.

The others quickly resumed conversation, to minimize his bewildered bride's discomfort.

Their host now turned their attention to Laurent Devereux, and Dan wondered what pearls the Frenchman might cast before them. But Devereux was saved by the bell, or more precisely, the electronic melody of *Für Elise* on his cell phone. Holding it to his ear and frowning at the poor reception, he excused himself and went outside.

"Why don't people leave those things in their rooms!" exclaimed Maud.

"Look who's talking!" jibed her cousin.

"What do you mean?"

"Maudie, dear, you took three client calls outside!"

"Well — that's different!"

Everyone laughed, and the dinner party, for that's what it had become, went merrily on. Dan was tired. He imagined others were, too, but no one wanted to miss the fun. It was 10:30 before they finally got up from the table.

He wondered if anyone else had noticed that neither Buff nor the Frenchman had returned.

13 | once in love with amy

Alone at his end of the White Horse bar, Colin Bennett was slowly sinking into the slough of despond. Idly he watched the group in white, as one of them, the older one, detached himself and went outside to use his cell phone. In the mirror behind the bar, Colin could see him out there, making his call. No, he was no ocean sailor. In a few moments he came back in and rejoined his group, glancing at Colin, who quickly averted his gaze.

Colin signaled the bartender, Mike, for another; six ought to do it. But so far, instead of blurring the past and blotting the pain, the rum seemed to be sharpening the eight-year-old images.

There had been a succession of girls before Amy, each convinced that she would be the one to change him. Get him to give up his vagabond ways, settle down, raise a family, act responsibly. Put her before the boat. Each had given up in despair.

Amy Baxter was different. Fiercely independent, the daughter of a Georgia paper baron, she'd known nothing about boats. And turned out to be a natural. She'd gone with him up to Bar Harbor, where they'd whiled away the summer, and she'd become a first-class sailor. In late August, as the first tropical depression formed and began heading west along the Tropic of Cancer, they'd dropped down to Bermuda to see which way the wind was blowing, as it were.

Here in the White Horse, he'd tried to give her the option of not accompanying him further. "From here on in, it'll be all work and no play. I'm at it, soon as there's light to see by — a good hour before you even think about getting up. And I keep at it till the light's gone. And it'll be that way for three straight months." He paused for emphasis. "I usually drop ten, twelve pounds."

She'd listened solemnly, because he was being solemn. But it was obvious she wasn't buying it.

He tried harder. "And getting there — wherever there is — will be no fun at all. I'm not hunting hurricanes exactly, but I do intend to 'git there, fustest with the mostest,' as it were."

She smiled. "Nathan Bedford Forrest."

He looked up, surprised. "How'd you know that?"

"I majored in history — *Southron* history," she said, tilting her head. "What I want to know is, how'd you know?"

"I'm familiar with your Civil War. Or should I say, the War for *Southron* Independence?"

"Call it what my granddaddy did: the War to Repel the Northern Invader. But you didn't answer my question."

He closed one eye and squinted at her out of the other, like Robert Shaw playing Teddy Tucker in "The Deep." In a rum-soaked brogue he muttered, "Aye, girl, Bermuda was the main rendezvous of the blockade runners." He shrugged. "My granddaddies kept your granddaddies in the fight."

"I never knew that."

"Then you probably didn't know how close Britannia came to intervening on your behalf. Had she done so, she would have based her Atlantic fleet here, at her wee outpost off the Carolinas."

He shook his head. "But ye've distracted me, girl. I was telling you why you didn't want to come with me on my next venture. If I'm going to where a hurricane's just been, I'm going to have to cut close behind it — *very* close behind it."

She was trying not to smile, but her round blue eyes were dancing at the effort.

"Look," he acknowledged, a slight edge in his voice, "you've become a sailor. A fine one. But we've never gone through any heavy weather. Never had any reason to. Now. . . ."

Her eyes narrowed. "Colin Bennett! Are you trying to send me home? 'Cause if you are, I'll be out of here so fast, it'll make your—"

"Whoa, Nellie! I didn't say that! I'm just trying to warn you what it's going to be like. If you wanted to go home and see your family, this would be the time to do it, that's all."

She thought about that — for all of four seconds. "I'm coming."

A slow grin spread across his face. "Good on ya, mate!" he'd exclaimed, imitating his Aussie friends. "But don't say I didn't warn you."

She never did. On their way down to Eleuthera, which had taken a direct hit, they went through some of the foulest weather he'd ever seen. Once they'd gotten there, instead of sitting around all day while he worked, she asked if she could help. He'd been reluctant, but she'd persisted, and he started showing her how to fix things. Funny thing, just as with her seamanship, she turned out to be a natural.

After Eleuthera they'd gone on to St. Kitts, Tortola, Martinique. Finally, around American Thanksgiving, they'd called it a season and returned here. And had come to the White Horse, famished for someone else's cooking.

He'd been sitting on this very stool, and she next to him, when she'd told him.

"I'm pregnant."

He'd stared at her. Then exclaimed, "Good on ya, mate!"

They'd both laughed.

Marriage was the only thing they'd never discussed — perhaps because neither wanted to risk what so perfectly suited them.

"How long have you known?"

"Two weeks. I kept hoping I was just late."

"Well," he said, taking her hand, "what do you want to do?"

She pulled the hand away. "What are you asking?"

"Not that!" he recoiled, hurt that she would even think — he pointed to her stomach. "That's *us* in there!"

"Then what *are* you asking?"

He shrugged. "You want to get married?"

"What do *you* want?"

He laughed. "I asked first." Then he grew thoughtful. "I'd like him to have my last name. Legitimately."

"Him?"

"Well, if it's a her, I suppose that'll be all right — long as she takes after her mother."

She looked at him, her head tilted. "I thought you were never one for commitments."

"Thought so, too. But—I've never met anyone like you."

Abruptly he slapped the table with his palm, causing the green empties to jump. "Then it's settled!"

He adopted his Shaw/Tucker brogue. "Reckon ah'm gonna do the right thing, m'am. Make an honest woman of ya. And the bairn?" He bent over close to her midriff and spoke softly to it. "Aye, yer not gonna be born outa wedlock, and that's fer sure, matey!"

They went to Georgia to see her parents, tell them their news, get married as quickly as possible, and enter into happily-ever-after time.

Only one person was unhappy with this Princess Bride ending—so unhappy, that he would have preferred Colin do the wrong thing. In fact, he would have even preferred his daughter do the hideous thing. It would have been preferable to her tying herself down for life to this winsome loser.

Amy's grandfather, who had gone to the Citadel and retired from the Army as a colonel, had left everything to his only son, Avery, who so liked the sound of "Colonel Baxter" that as soon as his daddy died, he instructed the servants at *Live Oaks,* the family's shooting plantation in Thomasville, to call him that, too.

Amy's mother loved her, but not enough to stand up to her father. Nobody stood up to Colonel Baxter. After years of being abused and neglected, Mrs. Baxter had developed a quiet but enduring fondness for the attentions of a gentleman caller, a White Russian nobleman named Stolichnaya. In the privacy of her sewing room, he would come calling every afternoon about four. If her husband was aware of the Russian's existence, he didn't care. It kept his wife manageable—and in his mind justified the things he did with a certain lady over in Valdosta.

Avery Baxter had another daughter, Agnes. Four years older than Amy, she did not bother to hide her dislike of their father. As soon as she was out of Randolph Macon, she married a biologist who taught there. Her husband might not be the brightest bulb in his department, but Agnes didn't care. They lived comfortably on the income of the trust that her grandfather had set up for her, and returned to *Live Oaks* as infrequently as possible. Agnes did love her mother though, and on those occasions she would slip away at teatime to the sewing room, where together they would enjoy the pleasure of the Russian gentleman's company.

Having no sons and a daughter who despised him, Avery Baxter's hopes for the future centered on Amy. Having already instructed her in the ways of the family business, he intended to turn over much of the running of it to her, once she graduated from Randolph Macon. And then she had thrown her future away on Colin.

14 | amy's story

Amy's mother, delighted at her news, had immediately begun planning the wedding one afternoon, while *Live Oaks'* manager was showing Colin around. "We'll invite all our plantation friends—"

"Mother," Amy gently cut in, "those people are not our friends. We hardly know them."

"Well, they will be after this wedding," her mother went blithely on. "And you'll wear your grandmother's gown. Did you know the veil has a thousand seed pearls sewn into it?"

Amy nodded and smiled. "You've told me many times." Then she frowned. "Should I—be wearing white?"

Her mother chuckled. "Honey, you have no idea how many of my sorority sisters' first-born children were 'premature.'"

They both laughed.

Her father saw nothing amusing about her condition—or any of the rest of it. When her mother had gone up to "do some sewing," he asked her to come into the den—and close the door behind her.

He took the captain's chair behind the great oak desk,

and waving her to the chair opposite, got right to the point. "I've had your lover investigated."

"Daddy!" she exclaimed, staring at him in disbelief. "That is so — tacky!"

His knuckles whitened as he gripped the edge of his desk. "As I suspected, he has no visible means of support." He indicated the manila folder in front of him.

"I could have saved you the money," Amy declared, nodding at it. "He fixes boats. He's good at it, so he works when he feels like it. He's a gypsy of the sea."

"Mighty fancy name for it," her father muttered, opening the folder. "He's been kicked out of some excellent schools," he observed, reading the file, "and has never earned a regular paycheck."

When she did not respond, he looked up. "You've heard of ski bums and tennis bums? Well, honey, your fiancé's a boat bum. That's all he is."

Leaning forward, she glared at him. "That may be, Daddy, but he's *my* boat bum, thank you very much!"

"You really ought to read this," he went on, unperturbed. "There's been a regular procession of young ladies who've been — *guests* aboard his boat. Were you aware of that?"

"Yes, Daddy," she said acidly. "He's told me about all of them."

"And you don't mind being the next in line?"

"I intend to be the last."

He tapped the file. "I wonder how long you two would have lasted, if he hadn't knocked you up."

She stood up. "This conversation is over! Colin and I are getting married, here or in Bermuda, and you can be part of it, or not!" And before he could reply, she left the den, slamming the door behind her.

They held the wedding in Thomasville, because it would have broken her mother's heart if they hadn't. Agnes came down from Chapel Hill to help with the preparations, and the three of them immersed themselves in the details with abandon. Pam and Aggie would be Maid and Matron of Honor, and three sorority sisters would be bridesmaids. Colin's brother Ian would be Best Man. Anson, his racing mate from Marblehead, was coming down, and Stuart, Stevie, Daniel, and Geoff were coming over from Bermuda to be his ushers.

Amy's mother had such a good time with her girls that she seemed to grow younger and more vivacious with each passing day. Her husband went the other way, balking at the astronomical wedding expenses, until Aggie invited him into the den for a little close-the-door-behind-you talk. She simply told him that unless he wanted all of Thomasville and Albany to know exactly what he was up to over in Valdosta, he was going to put up and shut up.

It was a perfect wedding. Everything went off as if it had been planned for weeks, not days. After the ceremony, the dancing, graceful waltzes at first, grew quite spirited, fueled by a punchbowl of Dark 'n Stormies, courtesy of the White Horse Troop, as they called themselves. It was such a good party, in fact, that the bride and bridegroom were loath to tear themselves away, though they were flying to Rome that night.

When the grandfather clock chimed six o'clock, Amy realized that they really must be going. Where was Colin? No one seemed to know. Then she noticed her father was also absent, and with a sinking feeling she went to the den. The door was closed, but not tightly; she could hear what was being said inside.

Her father was speaking in a light, bantering tone.

"You're the first boat bum I've ever met. What a pity that's all you'll ever be."

"It's all I want to be, sir," replied Colin, matching his easy tone.

"Yes, and that's the pity of it. My grandson will have you as his role model."

Colin laughed. "As it happens, we are hoping for a boy. Of course a girl would be fine, if she turned out like her mother." He paused. "It's amazing how Amy turned out, considering she had you as a role model."

Her father was no longer amused. "Best be on your way, lover boy."

"Mr. Baxter—forgive me for not calling you Colonel, but you didn't earn that—you've made a big thing out of my having no money. But money's all you do have. No friends. No one who's glad to see you. No way of supporting yourself, if you ever had to."

"Get out of here!"

"Now me, on the other hand," Colin went on, "I take what nature or man's carelessness has broken and put it back together again. Which means people are always glad to see me, and I'll always be able to support my family. And—I have mates who would go through fire for me." He laughed. "So, I wonder which of us is really the richer."

At that, Amy burst in and took Colin's arm. "Come on, Mr. Bennett," she said, her eyes shining, "we're out of here!"

As they left the den, she refused to say goodbye to her father or even look at him; in fact, she fully intended never to set eyes on him again.

In subsequent months and years, Amy would hang up when her father called, throw his letters away unopened. To her, he was dead. And so he reciprocated, disinheriting her and leaving her — them — with only the income from the trust that his father had set up, which he was powerless to revoke.

They regarded the trust money as emergency funds and lived off what Colin made in the hurricane season. He did extend his work time an extra month, but he didn't mind. Indeed, it truly was happily-ever-after time aboard *Care Away*.

Four months after the wedding, Amy's mother died of liver failure. Amy was able to get to *Live Oaks* two weeks before she passed away. Aggie was there, too, and the three of them would spend the afternoons together in their mother's bedroom, having as much fun as they could, until she was too tired.

The Russian gentleman was there, as well — there was little reason to exclude him now — and he was a boon companion, inviting them to call him Stoli, as his friends did.

Amy's father was never part of their gatherings. Aggie told her sister that after the wedding he must have said or done something so horrible to their mother that she moved into one of the guest rooms and seldom came downstairs again.

They spoke to him as little as possible, and after the funeral they went away for good, leaving their father all alone on his grand plantation.

Eight years passed. Then three months ago, Amy's sister had called. Their father had just undergone quadruple bypass surgery.

"So?"

"Well — he's different."

"How?"

"He's sorry for what he's done and wants to make it right."

Amy chuckled. "Sounds like a death-bed conversion, if there ever was one. Maybe he got a little glimpse over the edge, and saw what was in store for him."

But Aggie was serious. "This may be for real. He wants to see us, ask our forgiveness before he dies."

"He's about to die?"

Aggie laughed. "I don't think so." She paused. "But he seems serious about wanting to get reconciled. Especially with you. He's reinstated you in his will."

"Well, isn't that special!" said Amy, with dripping sarcasm. "Did it ever occur to him that I might not be ready to forgive him?"

Silence.

"Sorry, Ags, no point killing the messenger. Have you seen him?"

"Yes."

"And?"

"He's—different."

Amy sighed. "All right, what do you think I should do, older, wiser one?"

"Why don't you just come over? If he's changed, fine; if he hasn't, split. But if you don't come, and something does happen to him, it could be on your conscience for a long time."

Amy knew she was right. "I'll come tomorrow. Don't tell him; I want to take him off guard."

"Whatever you say, younger, dumber one." Then she remembered. "If you agreed to come, he wanted to get you the ticket."

"No. No obligations. I'll use the trust money."

"It'll be good to see you, Ames."

"You, too."

Outside her father's hospital room, Amy paused to brace herself for the sight of him, head wan and pale on the pillow, tubes running out of him everywhere, an IV drip suspended above him. Taking a deep breath and putting on a smile, she entered.

Her father was sitting up in bed, doing the New York *Times* crossword. In ink.

"Thanks for coming, honey," he said, putting the paper down. "I guess it's too much to expect a hug."

"It is," she replied, taking the visitor's chair.

"Did Aggie not tell you why I wanted you to come?" He smiled at her, looking sincere. "I've got a lot to ask your forgiveness for."

Amy clenched her jaw. "Too bad you can't ask Mom," she said, not bothering to hide her bitterness.

"It is too bad," he agreed. "I've asked God to forgive me, over and over."

Amy stood up. "Yeah, well, that's great, Daddy, and I'm sure it makes you feel better. But frankly, it's a little late! And *quite* frankly —" she almost said it. Almost left.

But if there was anything to this, anything at all, she could not in good conscience abort the process.

She sat back down.

And stayed two weeks, long enough to get her father home and settled on the road to recovery.

When she finally got back to Bermuda and aboard Care Away, she and Colin had a fight. A horrendous, unprecedented fight — in which things were said that could not be taken back. Things that made it impossible to remain on the boat a moment longer.

She had taken Jamie with her. To Georgia.

15 | fathers and sons

That Saturday was Brother Bartholomew's birthday. His fiftieth birthday. The worst birthday of his life.

Sitting in the chair in the one-room cottage that measured ten feet by eighteen feet, staring at the lintel of the door on which he had just struck his head, Brother Bartholomew wondered if he had ever been so miserable. Not even as a corpsman in Viet Nam, and certainly not in nearly twenty years in the friary. This was the worst.

This was — *wretched*.

In a way, that doorway summed up everything. The cottage had been built two centuries earlier, when the height of the average Bermudian had been five-foot-four. Bartholomew was six feet. As long as he remembered to duck, he was fine. The trouble was, he kept forgetting.

And that bed! He glared over at "the rack." He called it that, not as a colloquialism left over from his Marine Corps days, but as a medieval instrument of torture. Nor could he blame the rack on eighteenth-century Bermudians; it was a thoroughly modern invention, a bed that could be folded in half to masquerade as a sofa, if he ever had any company. Which he never did.

Like the door, it was just under six feet tall, with arms at both ends. Which meant that anyone his height or taller could not lie out straight on it, even if he slept diagonally. Plus, there was a hard ridge down the middle, where the fold was. If he was exhausted, he might get three hours of sleep before the rack contrived to awaken him.

He would have simply put the mattress on the floor, were it not for the cockroaches. If there was one creature on earth that Bartholomew purely loathed, it was the cockroach. To him, they were worse than snakes or spiders; they seemed the embodiment of evil. They came out only at night, and no matter how many you killed, there was always one more.

"Happy Birthday!" he exclaimed aloud, to break the silence. That was another thing: In the cottage the silence was so total, it actually seemed to have a ringing quality to it.

The sad part was, his birthday had not started off that badly. When he had returned to the cottage from a morning of edging grassy footpaths, he found that the sisters had left some ripe oranges for him, picked from the property's little citrus grove. With them was a manila envelope with his name on it.

It was a fax from home, from the young people in the calligraphy guild. They had composed and beautifully lettered a greeting in Latin:

Diem Natalem Age,
Frater Bartolomeo,
tibi Deum precamur

—Happy Birthday, Brother Bartholomew, we're praying for you.

He could have cried.

Homesickness, like breaking surf, had washed over him before. Yet he'd always been able to regain his footing and shake it off. But this was a tidal wave — and for once, he gave in to it.

In his mind he was back in the friary's *Scriptorium,* on a sunny Saturday afternoon. Through the open window wafted the indolent sounds and smells of summer, while on the window seat beneath it was curled the friary cat, Pangur Ban — basking in the sun, supremely confident that all was right in his world.

His young charges were perched on stools in front of the five drafting tables — two boys and three girls, high schoolers, from abbey families. In front of each was tacked a clean sheet of white paper. Playing softly on the stereo was a recording of the abbey's monks singing Gregorian Chant, the notes echoing off the stone of the basilica, evoking a timelessness well suited to the ancient craft they were about to practice.

At the blackboard stood the master calligrapher, his chalk held horizontally, in imitation of the square nib of a lettering pen. He deftly drew a large capital R and smiled at them. All was right in his world, too.

"Like everything we've covered so far, adding a swash is not as easy as it looks. After you've formed your basic R, start lightly here," he said, beginning to duplicate the swash, "apply pressure — here, and begin your lift-off — here."

With a graceful gesture he lifted the chalk from the board. "You see?"

He nodded to them, confident they would be able to do what he'd just demonstrated. And they hesitantly nodded back.

Hands clasped behind his back, he moved slowly behind them, pausing to murmur a suggestion here, an encouragement there.

"Now again."

They drew another. And once more he passed behind them, offering the help that each needed. His smile never wavered—and gradually theirs gained confidence.

Finally, tall, willowy Kate, in an exaggerated Rex Harrison accent, exclaimed "I think we've got it! By George, I think we've got it!"

Bartholomew beamed. They had indeed.

Now, gazing down at their elegant birthday effort, he missed them terribly.

He got up. He'd send them a reply, something light and cheerful. Glancing at his watch, he saw that it was twenty minutes to noon. If he went down to the main house right now, he could get a fax off before they started lunch.

He went down the path, composing one as he walked. He'd commend their Latin, and their fine hand (probably Kate's). He was just imagining their delight at hearing from him, when he arrived at the kitchen door. He asked if he could use the fax machine, and the sister at the stove gave him the office key. Letting himself in, he dashed off the note, popped it into the fax, and for once it went through without balking.

Returning the key to the kitchen, he was suddenly assailed with the aromas from not one but several simmering pots. All four sisters were in the kitchen now, tossing a salad, slicing a loaf of homemade bread, getting out the dinner plates.

Noting his expression, the sister at the stove seemed to

read his mind. "Happy Birthday, Bart!" she exclaimed. "You'll stay for lunch, of course!"

"We have plenty," the bread sister assured him.

"These are Greek olives and Feta cheese," added the salad-making sister. "I'll set a place," said the fourth.

With the salivary juices already building in the back of his mouth, Bartholomew murmured, "Well, perhaps I—"

Father Francis came in. "He's not staying!" he announced flatly. "He's here on personal retreat. He'll eat up at the cottage. Alone."

The sisters were crestfallen, but none more than Bartholomew. He trudged back up the hill, and sitting morosely on his little stoop, he chewed his cold, dry turkey sandwich and added Father Francis to the list of things he loathed about Bermuda. At the top.

⛵

The list grew longer later that afternoon at the grocery store. Purchasing the ingredients of his solitary birthday supper, he reached for what would be its *pièce de résistance,* a pint of Rum Raisin ice cream.

And stopped. He had the distinct impression that God did not want him to have it. He knew why; his cholesterol had gotten high enough that the abbey's doctor in residence had recently cautioned him to avoid high-fat foods or face serious trouble.

He reached for it again, only to receive another interior warning, clear and unmistakable.

"But I *always* have Rum Raisin ice cream on my birthday!" he declared under his breath, not caring that he'd now joined the ranks of those who muttered to themselves as they pushed their carts through supermarkets.

Or that he sounded, even to his own ears, like a petulant child.

By the time he got through the checkout counter, he was so angry that he retrieved a discarded *Royal Gazette* from the trash bin by the door, though on a personal retreat one was not supposed to read newspapers or anything else that would bring back the world he was supposed to be retreating from.

That evening after supper, he read the old paper from cover to cover, even the endless descriptions of distant cricket matches. He went to bed at eight o'clock, an hour earlier than usual, just to be done with the worst birthday of his life.

He did not say good night to God. He had not spoken to God since the ice cream incident, not even to return thanks before his meal.

He fell into a deep and dreamless sleep, until awakened by the creaking rack at eleven. Which made him angry — even angrier than he'd been three hours before. He lay there in the darkness and steamed.

But while he was not on speaking terms with God, it seemed that his heavenly Father would have words with him.

Get up, came the thought. *I want to talk to you.*

Well, I don't want to talk to *you,* Bartholomew thought back.

Nevertheless, he got out of bed, pulled on a sweater, and slouched down in the chair. From the table next to him, he took up his clipboard and wrote down what it seemed God was saying to his heart:

Is this the way friends treat friends?

Under it, Bartholomew wrote:

Who says we're friends?

I do.

Bartholomew hastily responded:

Saint Teresa was right when she told you: "If this is the way you treat your friends, it's no wonder you have so few of them."

It hurt when she said that. It hurts now, when you say it.

Good! Now you know what it feels like!

I know.

All at once, another thought came to him, hard and cold: You are crazy, thinking you're talking to God. You're just imagining what He might say to you. It's nothing more than "Let's Pretend."

He considered that. It made sense: The psychiatric explanation would probably be that this was some form of mild, schizophrenic self-delusion, or, taken to the extreme, a multiple-personality disorder. Bizarre, perhaps, but explicable.

And yet . . . the Bible did say that anyone filled with the Spirit of God should be able to hear His still, small voice within. Believers had been doing it for centuries. And not just saints or mystics. Look at Tevye, in "Fiddler on the Roof."

He smiled at that. And besides, even if he *was* imagining it, or making it up, was his imagination not inspired by the Holy Spirit? At the very least, he was giving voice to his conscience.

He decided to continue the exercise.

All right, Father, what do you want of me?

You can stop behaving like a child.

That stung. You're right, he admitted. I have been. Forgive me, Father, for I have sinned.

Do not be sarcastic with me. And give up your self-pity. It is merely anger, denied an external focus.

That sounds like it came off a Salada tea-bag, he wrote. Then, abashed at being so smart-mouthed, he added: What am I so angry at?

What do you think?

You?

Yes. Who else?

Father Francis.

My son, he was only speaking for me. It was difficult for him to do, because he is fond of you.

Bartholomew thought about that. Then he wrote:

Now that you say that, I can see it. I was lonely and— in self-pity. I really wanted to have lunch with them!

Why?

He thought about that and wanted to write something else in response, other than what was coming to him. But if this was— what he thought it was— there was no point in being anything less than excoriatingly honest. So he wrote:

Probably to release the pressure that's been building in me these past two weeks down here.

Probably?

All right! I *was* trying to get out of the pressure cooker, if only for an hour or so.

He paused and added: And all Father Francis was doing was keeping the lid on. Your lid.

Yes.

The poor guy was only trying to do what you were calling him to.

Yes.

And it cost him.

It usually does.

Well, you know what? Now—I love him!

Good. He is my gift to you, my son.

Bartholomew yawned and glanced at his watch—and was astonished to see that an hour had passed. Once again, he asked:

Father, what do you want of me?

You already know.

If I knew, I wouldn't be asking.

You know.

Feeling himself getting angry again, he wrote:

I suspect you want me to say "Surrender." But I already have! Look what I've given up for you! I'm not allowed to earn a living. I'm celibate. I'm under obedience. What more do you want?

Your opinions. Your will. Your independence.

Why don't you just say my essence and be done with it!

Your essence.

Bartholomew threw down the pen, which skittered away under the bed. He got up and with difficulty retrieved it.

This is ridiculous! he wrote. When did anyone ever win an argument with you? And Jacob doesn't count; he was only wrestling an angel.

He sighed and laid the pen down. Then picked it up again:

What's the point of going on with this?

It is important for you to write down what is in your heart, my son. For while I already know what you are going to say, you do not know what my reply will be.

They spoke in this fashion for another hour, and gradually Bartholomew's heart softened. Finally he wrote:

You know, I enjoy this, just talking with you, one on

one. In fact, I think I enjoy it more than anything you and I have ever done.

Why?

He thought for a moment, then wrote: I was only seventeen the last time I saw my earthly father, and he was never one for talking much. So I guess somehow this—talking with my Heavenly Father—is finishing that.

Your father was a good man, my son. He loved you very much.

Me, too. I never told him. And it's a little late now.

He is here with me now, my son. And he knows.

Bartholomew wiped his eyes, to keep the tears off the pad.

This is weird, he wrote, when his emotions had calmed down. Really weird. But—it's also the best birthday I've ever had.

Another wave of emotion swept over him, and he covered his eyes with his hand, his shoulders shaking.

Then he wrote: Thank you, Father. I love you.

I love you, too. Now get some sleep. There is more we must cover tonight.

16 | a miserable saturday afternoon

Everyone, it seemed, was miserable that Saturday afternoon. Amy Baxter Bennett sat in the paneled den of her family's plantation house, gazing out the window where her son Jamie had been playing with Blitzkrieg, one of her father's pointers.

Shivering, she drew the beige cashmere cardigan closer about her shoulders. And sneezed, adding another wadded-up tissue to the small pile beside her chair. Her cold had blossomed into a full-fledged case of the flu. Her head throbbed, her energy level was zilch, and her father had gotten his doctor to prescribe a potent antibiotic and an even more potent antidepressant. Most of the time she was halfway to la-la land.

She shivered again. It *was* cold in here, despite the fire Eustace had laid in the hearth. She looked up at the portrait of her father above the cherry wood mantel, next to the huge Hagerbaumer of a covey of quail breaking cover in the early morning. Avery Baxter was resplendent in his red Abercrombie & Fitch tweed shooting jacket and chamois vest with its shotgun-shell buttons. He was standing in a pine grove alongside a horse-drawn shooting wagon, with his prized Holland & Holland cradled in his arm. Seated at his feet, looking alert, were his two German shorthair pointers, Panzer and Blitzkrieg.

"You're such a snob," she murmured at the portrait. If it were just that, she thought, smiling sadly, she could probably endure this penance vile, to which she had sentenced herself and Jamie. But the side of her father that had always chilled her, despite his efforts at genial behavior, was beginning to show again. He always got his way eventually, and it was beginning to look like he had, once again.

A small noise behind her, made her turn. It was Jamie, in from playing. "Mommy? I miss Dad. I miss our boat."

"I know, dear."

The boy looked at her, head tilted. "We are going home soon, aren't we?"

"I don't know, darling; we'll see."

"I hate it when grown-ups say, 'We'll see.' It's such a cop-out! They want to say no, but they don't have the guts!"

"Stop talking like your father."

"I miss him."

"You said that."

He frowned at her. "Well, I want you to know it! I want you to *consider* that, when you make your decision."

"What decision?"

"About what's going to happen to us."

She sighed and shook her head. Their thirty-year-old, eight-year-old. "What are you talking about?"

"I heard you guys."

"Heard — what?" she asked, suddenly dreading the answer.

"The fight, about what was going to happen to me."

"Jamie!" she exclaimed, reaching out to enfold him in her arms. "I'm sorry!"

He pulled away. "You guys never fight. Then you did, and now we're here."

She was at a loss for words.

Her son wasn't. "I just want you to know: This place sucks!"

"That's an ugly expression."

"Dad uses it. A lot."

She sighed. "It's almost supper time. Why don't you go play computer games."

Scowling, he nonetheless turned and went down the hall. Avery Baxter had done a shrewd thing in anticipation of their coming. He had hired an electronic games consultant to fill a room with the games young people played — all the latest, all the best. And Jamie, in spite of himself, had been impressed.

But he still thought the place sucked, she reminded herself. How did *she* feel about it?

It's a little late to be wondering about that, she rebuked herself. I mean, since you've just done something that will make this "home" for the rest of your life.

Oh, God, if only he would call!

Down the hall came Eustace, gently bonging the four dinner chimes with the padded mallet.

"What did you do this afternoon, Jamie?" asked his grandfather, when they were all at their places.

"Played computer games."

"All afternoon?"

"No, sir," said the boy, poking his peas, "after I'd played with Blitzen."

His grandfather smiled. "His name is Blitzkrieg."

"Blitzen, Blitzkrieg, whatever." The boy shrugged and did not look up.

"It's an important distinction," his grandfather went on, with a patient smile. "One is the name of a reindeer, the other is a concept that revolutionized modern mechanized warfare."

"Oh," the boy responded, still not looking up.

"Oh?" his grandfather persisted.

Jamie slammed his fork down, sending peas in all directions. "Okay, I'm sorry, all right?" he blurted out. "I won't play with Blitzen any more."

He turned to his mother and shouted, "You remember what I told you about this place? Well, it does! Big-time!" And with that he ran from the table.

Her father took a bite of fat-free salad and chewed thoughtfully. "What did he say about this place?"

Amy sighed. "He just misses his father. He'll get over it."

She did not tell him the exact quote, because she was beginning to believe that Jamie might be right.

17 | the beater

The White Horse's chief bartender came down to Colin's end of the bar. "Phone's for you," he said, nodding at the kitchen end of the bar.

"Who is it?" asked Colin.

"How should I know?"

"Aye, me sainted mother, God rest her soul, warned me never to talk to strangers." Colin squinted at his friend. "Michael, me lad, now tell me: Is it man or woman?"

"It's a man," said the bartender, wiping his hands on a bar towel. "Take the call or I'm hanging it up."

"I don't care to talk to a man. I want to talk to a woman. One woman. My wife."

Mike relented, knowing as all the White Horse did, that Amy had left him, and that was why he was in here, tying one on. "Well," he added with a smile, "it sounded like there was a party going on behind him, if that makes a difference."

"Makes all the difference!" exclaimed Colin, grinning, as he walked down to the phone and picked up the receiver.

It was Anson Phelps. "Colin! I've been looking all

over for you, man! You must have your cell phone turned off. Called your apartment, called the harbor master to find out if you were on your boat — why aren't you over here?"

Colin could hear the band at the Bacardi reception. Under any other circumstances. . . .

"I asked them to send you an invitation; didn't you get it?"

"Didn't check my mail," he lied.

"Well, come on over!" cried Anson. "It's a great party! Everyone's here — Dennis, Murray, Magnus, Neil, Neville, Chris — they're *all* here! And they're wondering why you're not."

"They are?" Colin was touched that his mates from Australia and New Zealand wanted to see him.

"Yeah, man! The Aussies and Kiwis only get here once a year. They want to see their main man in Bermuda. Where's the Beater, they keep asking."

Colin chuckled. The nickname had originated with his nephew, when Eric was six. He'd taken the boy along on a fitted dinghy race, which he'd won. "Uncle Colin!" cried the delighted boy. "You're the beater! *I* want to be the beater when I grow up!" The crew in his dinghy and the adjacent dinghy had heard this, and he'd been "The Beater" ever since.

He decided he owed him the truth. Anson was one of his ushers, and the Rolex in the drawer was the result of his picking him for his crew ten years ago.

"Amy's left me."

"Oh, man! That's not good. I thought you guys were forever."

"So did I."

Anson thought for a moment. "Look, I was going to

talk to you about something important, and—well, maybe it'll help. At least, to get your mind off things."

Colin gave a rueful laugh. "Let's see if I can guess: You want me to crew for you next week."

There was a pause. "You're amazing!"

It was not so amazing. Each year in October, the best ocean racers in the world met in Bermuda for the Gold Cup—five days of one-on-one match racing, until on Sunday afternoon (a week from tomorrow) only one captain was left standing. Since the boats—International One Design—and sails were provided by the Royal Bermuda Yacht Club, the Gold Cup was the closest thing to a test of pure skill that it was possible to find.

Eight skippers were invited, usually those with the highest international ranking. For them, entry fees were waived, but that was the only inducement. No appearance money was needed to draw them. They came because, if you were convinced that the captain did not exist who could beat you in a fair race (and all considered the Gold Cup to be the fairest, best-run regatta on the planet), then Bermuda was the place to prove it.

Sixteen other captains, unseeded, had to pay for the privilege of battling it out, to see, after a round-robin of match-ups, which of them would face the seeded captains. For the unseeds, this was their entry into the game. If they did well, the world would know that there was some hot talent coming up. And sometimes an unseed won, beating the best of the best (that year).

Invariably one IOD hull might be a shade faster in heavy wind, while another might have the edge in lighter conditions. Therefore, each day's contestants drew lots to see who would be in which boat. There was also a weight limit—which resulted the previous year in the heaviest skipper riding around the island in a rubber suit, to sweat off enough pounds to keep all three of his crewmates.

No one was supposed to have an edge, but of course, everyone tried for one anyway. And there was a way. Two years ago, Dennis Connor had persuaded local ace Paula Lewin, a skilled captain in her own right, to set aside her own ambitions and join his crew. He wanted someone familiar with the capricious, unpredictable, knock-you-down winds that bedeviled Hamilton Harbour, where the two-buoy course would be laid out.

This year Anson wanted the same edge. The stakes were enormous — infinitely higher than the $20,000 first-prize money. Most of the seeded captains, who would be competing against one another in the upcoming America's Cup, were also the chief fund-raisers for their respective syndicates.

Anson Phelps, who had won one Cup and would be one of the favorites in the next trials, had already raised $60 million for his Marblehead syndicate. That was enough to put one newly designed hull in the water. But to be truly competitive, they would need a second boat, a stalking horse to race against in preparation. That, plus crew, plus all expenses for two years, would take another $30 million — and it would have to be fresh money from unknown sources, since the syndicate's members were tapped out.

It was up to Anson to find that money. And since all of them were beating the bushes for new backers (sometimes the same bush), if he did well here, it would obviously make his job much easier. That's why he wanted the edge that Colin could give him.

Colin had given up ocean racing to concentrate on his

family. Except — at the moment his family was on the verge of extinction.

"Colin?" Anson's voice came over the phone. "You there?"

"Oh, yeah, sorry, man."

"Well?"

"Got to think about it."

"You're still the best, man. Still the Beater."

Encouraged by the fact he'd not said no, Anson sweetened the pot. "Come with me, and I'll make you crew chief for the next Cup."

Colin could feel his competitive juices starting to run. He may have given up racing, but racing had clearly not given up on him. Still, he hesitated.

"All right, Colin!" exclaimed Anson, playing his ace, "come with me next week, and if we win, and I can raise the dough for a second boat, you get her. You can have her wheel."

Colin's eyes widened. If he'd ever dreamed of skippering an America's Cup contender, this was the next step. "How long before I have to let you know?"

Anson roared with laughter. "That got you, didn't it! Figured it would! Come on over here, and we'll have a drink on it."

"Give me your cell phone number. I'll call you in an hour."

Anson gave it to him. "Don't take any longer than that, man. There's half a dozen onions around here who'd give their right arm for the chance. But I want the Beater."

"I'll call you, man," said Colin, hanging up.

Behind the bar, Mike was about to make him a fresh drink, but Colin shook his head. "Nope, got to think now."

What he wanted to do was call Amy, and ask her what she thought. He went out into the night, to use his cell phone.

He started to dial the number for *Live Oaks,* then stopped, frozen by the memory of The Fight.

It happened ten days ago, the night after she'd gotten back from settling her father at home, after his bypass surgery. At first, it was just a squall on the horizon, no bigger than a man's hand. If only he'd thought to look at the barometer. . . . But he was just glad to have her home. She'd never been away for two weeks before, not even to see her mother at the end. Jamie spoke for both of them, when he cried, "Yay, Mom! Swiss Family Bennett's back together again! Let's take *Care Away* out for the rest of the day to celebrate!"

Colin grinned and turned to his wife. "Honey?"

Amy was not smiling. "I've got a wicked cold." She frowned. "Why isn't he in school?"

"He asked if he could stay home to welcome you, and I thought that was about the best reason for missing school I'd ever heard of!"

"Better than your reasons, when you kept skipping school?"

"Huh?" Colin looked at her, surprised.

"I don't think he should miss school if he's not sick."

Colin sighed. "Okay, bad call. You want to go sailing, or not?"

"Not."

That was how it began. It ended after Jamie had gone to bed.

"Honey, what's the matter? You've had your knickers in a twist ever since you got home."

She glared at him. "I hate that expression! It's a crude,

vulgar cliché—like a lot of the things you say. Just because we live on a boat, doesn't mean you have to sound like—"

"Like what? A boat bum?"

"I don't want to talk about it."

"Well, I think we'd better," he said evenly, studying her. "It's your father, isn't it."

"If we're going to talk," she went on, ignoring what he'd just said, "I want to go back to this business of school. We've got to take Jamie's schooling seriously if he's going to have a chance to go to prep school off-island."

"Off-island? Why on earth would he want to do that? You want him to go to college? He can get in any college, in England or the States, right out of Hamilton Academy. But all he wants is to become a sea captain as soon as possible."

"Like you."

"What's wrong with that?"

"He's only eight! Most boys grow out of their boyhood fantasies, like wanting to be fighter pilots."

"Or boat captains?"

"Or boat captains."

Now he was mad. And hurt. "It was good enough for you once!" he shouted, then caught himself. "Ames, what *is* it?"

She took a deep breath. "It's just that I see things—differently now. Maybe I had to get off this boat, to get some perspective, after eight years."

"Eight pretty good years."

"They were good," she admitted. "But maybe they could have been better. Much better."

He was beginning to suspect where this was coming

from. He sought her eyes. "Why do you want him to go to prep school off-island?"

She would not meet his gaze. "Because maybe he needs some perspective, like I did. And the sooner, the better."

"You want him to go to Deerfield, don't you."

"Why not? You and your brother did."

"Yeah, and we both wound up captains, like our father."

"Well, maybe he won't. Maybe he'll want something better."

That really hurt, and she knew it. He did not trust himself to answer.

She did not feel the same compunction. "I just think he should have the same opportunity you had, even if you booted yours away."

"Well, we're getting downright bitchy, aren't we!" Again he caught himself. "Amy," he pleaded, "this isn't you. It's your father talking. And he's filled you full of his—" he narrowly avoided the crude, vulgar cliché that leapt to mind.

"He may have talked to me," she cut in sharply, "but what he said makes sense!"

Colin sighed and shook his head. "He gotten to you, Ames; can't you see that?"

"All I can see is someone who's too selfish to give his son the same opportunity he was given."

Colin flung the rest of his coffee over the side. "Oh, I see where this is going! To save the kind of money it would take to send him to Deerfield, I'd have to work all year long."

"You mean, like everyone else?"

"You're hittin' pretty hard there, ducks!"

"You said Sandy Harrison offered you a partnership in his boatyard."

"Is that what you want?" Colin shouted. "Me to spend all winter scraping barnacles off rich people's yachts, and all summer teaching their brats how to sail?"

"Well, how *did* you expect to pay for Jamie's education?"

"Never really thought about it," he replied honestly.

"Well, if you had?" she asked, her eyes narrowing.

"Don't know," he shrugged. "Guess it could come out of the trust fund."

"My trust fund," she corrected him. "You want to spend *my* money on *our* son's education, because *you* don't want to work hard." She looked at him, her head tilted. "You know, you really *are* a boat bum!"

"Well," he said standing up, "you don't want to live with this boat bum any longer? Fine! Go back to Georgia!"

"Maybe I will."

He spat out a string of crude, vulgar clichés, and she left that night, taking Jamie with her. That was ten days ago, and now the divorce papers had arrived.

He stared down at the cell phone and decided to make the call. No matter what she might say, she could not make him more miserable than he felt right now.

Shivering in the night air, Colin stared down at the illuminated face of his cell phone. The number for *Live Oaks* was on the screen, but the strength of the signal left something to be desired. When he tried walking south towards the water, it grew even weaker. He went in the opposite direction, and it improved—enough to make the call. He pushed the talk button, the phone rang, and Eustace answered. "Baxter residence."

"May I speak to Mrs. Bennett, please?"

"Who?"

"Amy."

"Whom shall I say is calling?"

"Eustace, it's Colin," he said, fighting not to lose patience. "I need to talk to my wife."

"One moment, please."

He wondered how long her father had worked with poor Eustace, to get him to answer the phone that way. He was nothing if not persistent, and eventually he got his own way.

But not this time, Colin thought, gripping the phone. Not this time.

As he waited for Amy to come to the phone, he noted that the signal was getting weaker again, so he walked further north, in the direction of the signal tower. When it was as strong as it was going to get, he found himself on York Street, standing in the shadows.

From where he stood, he could see the steps leading up to St. Peter's, the oldest church on the island. And then he noticed something really odd: Someone in a white parka and white pants was going up them with a duffel bag, even though the church was locked. In the old days, churches could be left open at night. But with the insertion of drugs into the island's fragile social fabric, anything of value had to be kept under lock and key.

Watching from the deep shadow where he waited, Colin could see the man stop at the church's main door, look carefully in all directions, and start working on the door's lock. In a moment, the old mechanism yielded, and he slipped inside, closing the door behind him.

Colin was mystified. What could he possibly think he was going to put in that duffel? After a few acts of vandalism, the church had been careful to keep its chalices, patens, and anything else of value, in the old safe in the back.

"Hello?" said a voice into the phone in his hand. It wasn't Amy; it was her father.

"I want to speak to my wife," Colin informed him coldly.

"Oh, lover boy! Good of you to call!" said Baxter, adopting his amused, bantering tone. "I was wondering when we'd hear from you, once you'd received that little FedEx we sent you."

"I want to talk to Amy! Now."

"Well, now, that's a real shame," replied Baxter with

oleaginous concern, "because, you see, she's made it most emphatically clear that she does not want to talk to you, under any circumstances."

"Let her tell me that!"

"Oh, it's true, I'm afraid. She asked me to get rid of you if you called, and to tell you not to bother writing. Any letter from you will go into the trash unopened — as mine used to."

"I want to talk to my wife!" shouted Colin, losing it.

"Sorry, old sport; that's just not going to happen."

"You miserable —" Colin salted the air with invective.

But Baxter was enjoying the moment too much to be goaded out of it. "You saw that the hearing is set for next Tuesday?"

"Yes."

"Are you planning to attend?"

"No! This whole thing is bogus! All I need to do is talk to Amy and —"

"We won't go into that again. As far as the hearing goes, it matters little whether you come or not. The judge is an old friend."

"You think you've won, don't you," Colin muttered.

"Oh, I don't *think*. I know! The hearing will take place in Thomasville, where my daughter was born and raised. And was married — to an irresponsible, unstable foreign indigent. I doubt you will even be granted visitation rights."

Colin was speechless.

Not Baxter, who had saved his best shot for last. "Oh, I almost forgot. I've got my daughter back now, and my grandson, too. But I'm not quite finished with you. I'm going to hurt you where you live, just the way you did me." He paused. "I'm going to get your boat."

Before Colin could ask how, the line went dead. In a daze he made his way back to the White Horse, scarcely noticing that the man who had gone into St. Peter's was waiting outside the White Horse now, and his duffel, instead of being fuller, now appeared empty. As Colin approached, he saw it was the older crew member from the *Laventura,* the one who'd gone outside to use his cell phone.

Just then a black car — larger than most on Bermuda — pulled into the square and stopped alongside the man with the duffel. He got in, and the car drove swiftly away.

Colin shrugged and went into the White Horse.

"Over here, mate!" Mike called to him from the kitchen end of the bar, holding up the phone receiver. "It's Anson Phelps. Says he's been trying to reach you on your cell."

Mike looked around at the raised eyebrows and appreciative expressions. "Yeah," he told the crowd at the White Horse, "Anson Phelps! The man himself!"

Colin took the receiver from him. "Anson? Deal me in."

19 | a cask of amontillado

The black limousine, a little larger than the size most Bermudians were allowed, crossed the tiny drawbridge and soon pulled into a long, circular drive, stopping at the front door. The dark shutters of the large house were all closed, though Bermudians seldom shuttered their homes for less than a full gale.

The front door opened. A gentleman emerged, wearing a navy blazer, an old school tie, dark red Bermuda shorts, and dark knee socks — acceptable formal attire on the island. Greeting the white-clad crewman warmly, he informed the driver that his services would no longer be required. The car left, and the man of the house ushered the crewman inside.

"How was your crossing?" he asked, showing him into the living room.

"Uneventful."

"The best kind."

"Yes."

"Care for a drink?"

"That would be nice."

"What can I offer you?"

"Anything but Heinekens," the crewman replied. "That's all they drank, all the way across. And what do they order when we get ashore?" He shook his head in disgust.

The other man smiled. "Well then, how about a Gray Goose martini?"

The crewman sighed. "Perfect."

In a few minutes the man of the house returned with two stemmed glasses and a silver shaker, coated with frost. Oiling the rim of each glass with a twist of lemon peel, he carefully filled the glasses to the rim. "Shaken, not stirred," he said, placing one in front of his guest.

The crewman took a sip. "That," he said smiling, "is the best thing I've put in my mouth since Marseilles. My cousin calls himself a chef, but that is hardly the title I would bestow on him." He paused and sniffed the air. "It would seem, however, that we might have a real chef on the premises."

The man of the house smiled. "There is no one here but me."

The crewman raised his nose, now studying the fragrances emanating from the kitchen. "Garlic . . . shallots . . . sautéed mushrooms?" He looked at the man of the house and raised an eyebrow.

The latter nodded. "My friends tell me I have a culinary gift. Tonight in celebration of your completing this phase of your mission, I have prepared *escargots* and *bouillabaisse,* with a '95 Montrachat."

The crewman took another sip. "I look forward to it."

"And afterwards, an English dessert — Stilton cheese with red currant jelly, and the ideal complement, a dry Lustau Amontillado."

The crewman took another sip. "I look forward to it."

He studied the clear liquid in his glass. "You know, I must commend you — and your partner. Your concept is brilliant. Possibly even more brilliant than the one you and I worked out long ago."

"Times have changed," said the man of the house.

"Yes, to make that kind of money today in heroin, you have to use a forklift!"

The man of the house now eyed the crewman's small duffle, mildly surprised. "You have everything — in there?"

"No."

"It's not still on the boat?"

The sailor shook his head. "It's ashore."

"Where?"

"In a safe place."

The slightest frown passed across the other's brow. "Why didn't you bring it?"

"I thought we needed to settle something first."

"What's to settle?" The tone was still pleasant, but the eyes were no longer warm.

The crewman set his glass down and fixed the other with his gaze. "My compensation."

"What do you mean?"

"A tenth of what I brought is not appropriate."

"Two. Million. Dollars. Is not appropriate?"

The crewman, not in the least intimidated, explained. "I went to Bangkok to get the formulae and laboratory plans. I went to Sri Lanka to get the two thousand starter pills. I went to Zurich to get the twenty million. And then, at the Cap, I killed a man to take his place on the yacht that brought me here."

The man of the house said nothing.

"So far, I have done all the heavy lifting. And I will be

doing all of Phase Two's heavy lifting. I chose my yacht with great care. *Laventura* is scheduled to call at Nassau, Port au Prince, Montego Bay, Charlotte Amalie, Port of Spain—practically every place on your list. There could not be a more perfect cover."

The man of the house nodded. "A masterstroke, I must admit." He paused, reflecting on it. "What do you think would be appropriate compensation?"

"A third."

"A *third?*"

"Of projected net revenue."

Despite his sangfroid, the man of the house recoiled. He needed a moment before he could answer. "You want, in other words, to be a partner."

The crewman nodded. "A *full* partner."

"I see," said the man of the house, tapping his fingers together. Then he smiled. "Well, you have certainly made a convincing case. I will have to consult my partner— our partner—in the morning, but I don't think there will be a problem. Not when I explain all you have accomplished—and what you are so perfectly situated to accomplish this winter."

With a smile, he stuck out his hand, and with a smile the crewman accepted it and shook it.

"Welcome to our firm," said the man of the house with abrupt warmth. "Now we have even more to celebrate."

He showed the crewman into the dining room, where two places were set, went into the kitchen and soon returned with two small trays of snails simmering in garlic butter, with toasted slices of sourdough baguette on the side. He poured out two glasses of wine and sat down.

The crewman ate with gusto. "You did these well," he observed.

"I do everything well."

Little additional conversation passed between them.

The man of the house arose to clear the trays and disappeared into the kitchen. When he returned with a large tureen of stew, the crewman's eyes were wide, his mouth open. He was gagging, saliva sliding out of the corner of his mouth. With great difficulty, he managed to get to his feet, steadying himself with both hands on the table. "What—have you done?"

"It must have been the snails," replied the other man with mock concern. "I suspect one may have been just a bit off."

The crewman collapsed to the floor.

When he came to his senses, he was on his back in a bathtub, in eight inches of salt water, his legs bound together and his arms secured to his side by duct tape. Two full, six-gallon water cooler bottles, filled with more salt water, sat on his chest and abdomen, making it impossible for him to move.

The man of the house stood at the other end of the tub, his hand on the faucet. "Ah, I see you have rejoined us. You really need to tell me where you have sequestered our—property."

The man in the tub muttered an oath in French and clamped his mouth shut.

The other man turned on the water, till the one in the tub had to arch his neck up to breathe. The man outside the tub came to the opposite end and pushed his head under, holding it there. A minute passed, then an explosion of bubbles indicated the man in the tub had exhaled the breath he had been holding.

The man outside the tub raised his head, until he gasped and blinked and sputtered. And shouted.

"This is an old house, Bermuda limestone. Make all the noise you want; no one will hear you."

The man in the tub stopped yelling.

"Where is our property?"

No answer.

Down went the head again. This time it was not brought up after the air burst. It was brought up only when the head's eyes bugged, and the body went into spasm.

The man outside the tub forced a stiff plastic tube down the other's throat and blew into it. Several times. Which revived him.

"Indicate by nodding that you will tell me what I want to know, and I will remove the tube and allow you to speak. I cannot release you until I've recovered our property, but then I will. I'm afraid it's out of the question for you to become our partner, but we can certainly proceed with our former arrangement, as if none of this — unpleasantness — ever happened."

The man in the tub remained silent, following his tormentor with eyes filled with hatred.

"You are thinking that if you tell me, I will simply kill you," said the man outside the tub. "Believe me, all of this is most distasteful. You may have killed in your line of work. I never have." He shuddered. "And I cannot bear the thought of going through life as — a murderer. So, I will keep my word."

Still no answer.

The man of the house sighed. "Time for another dip."

Putting a thumb over the end of the tube, he plunged the head under the surface, holding it there as long as before, then using the tube to revive him.

"You have amazing strength of will! You would die

before giving me what I want." He smiled. "But your body's survival instinct is just as strong. Each time I blow air into you, you recover. So we will go on with this exercise all night, if necessary."

It was not necessary. After seven more dunkings, the man in the tub nodded, and the man outside the tub removed the tube.

When the former had told the latter what he wanted to know, the man outside the tub pushed his head under and held it there, till the air exploded, the eyes bugged, the body spasmed, and a string of tiny bubbles exited the corner of his mouth.

20 | give ... and forgive

Three hours later Brother Bartholomew was awake again. He got up and went to the chair. In the margin of the legal pad on the clipboard, he made a note of the time: 4:30. Two hours before it would start getting light out.

He said the Our Father, and listened inwardly. God (if it was God) came right to the point.

There is still unforgiveness in your heart.

I am not aware of any, wrote Bartholomew. I've forgiven everyone who ever did anything to me. Mentally put it all on the altar during Mass. Also went to those I could, and wrote the others.

And you've forgotten what they did?

I certainly don't dwell on it.

Have you forgotten?

Pretty much.

But not the way you want me to forget the sins for which you've sincerely repented.

I see what you mean. He thought a moment, then added:

There *are* times when I imagine what will happen to them after they die and go through that tunnel towards the light — you. I imagine you reviewing the movie of their life with them. Each time they need to reflect on the hurt they did, intentionally or unintentionally, you'll hit the pause button. Pause, pause, pause — I imagine them growing so revulsed at what they did — who they *are* — they start vomiting uncontrollably. . . .

He paused, and wrote:

That doesn't sound much like forgiveness, does it.

No.

What should I do?

Write down everything grievous that has ever been done to you.

He did. When he finally came to the end, it was getting light out.

Of all those who'd wronged him, the worst was the master sergeant in charge of the division's corpsmen in Viet Nam. The man had absolute power, and it had corrupted him absolutely.

Bartholomew — Lance Corporal Doane, back then — had not been afraid of him. So the sergeant had singled him out and broken him, reducing him to tears — and had almost convinced him that he'd done it all for Doane's soul's sake.

God spoke to his heart.

I want you to forgive them all. By name.

He did.

I want you to pray for each one by name, seeing each face, every day.

Bartholomew felt the resistance rising up in him. I can't, Father.

Can't? Or won't?

Don't want to. Why?

Why do you think?

Because—my prayers might make their day for that moment a little brighter. So—I still haven't forgiven them.

Not if you don't want their temporal suffering alleviated.

All right, Father, I surrender. I'll pray for them, individually, every day.

Even the master sergeant?

Even him.

Good.

Bartholomew yawned, got up and stretched, and looked in the little fridge to see if there was enough milk for cereal. There was. Then he remembered he was going to Mass at the Cathedral that morning, and decided to wait until afterward.

He was about to get dressed and go outside to greet the day, when God spoke again to his heart.

Come back to the chair, my son. We are not finished.

Sorry, Father, I thought we were.

I want you to go back through your life and write down every incident where you did grievous harm to someone else, and why.

I'm not sure how much I'll be able to remember.

If the memory has faded, ask me to refresh it for you.

Bartholomew started with Novice Nicholas, then Brother Ambrose, and his mother, and Laurel, and then incidents from his schooldays and childhood. As promised, God brought to mind details long forgotten.

When at last he could recall no more, he told God:

I detest the person who has emerged from these acts. I am sick at my soul to see who I truly am in the depths of my being, save for your grace.

Good. I want you to remember who you are, in your

unredeemed nature — if necessary, refer to these pages — any time you are tempted to think more highly of yourself than you ought, or to hold someone else in unforgiveness.

Bartholomew groaned aloud, flinging the pad away from him.

Go take a shower, said God to his heart, you need one. And hurry; you don't want to keep Father Francis waiting.

As soon as they were seated on the bus, Bartholomew told the old priest of what had happened to him in the past 24 hours — all of it, leaving nothing out. "It feels like it's been a week!" he concluded.

Father Francis just nodded and smiled. "You're having a good retreat, Bartholomew." He chuckled. "Finally."

"So now what?"

The old priest smiled, as he gazed out the window of the bus. "Build on the foundation you've laid. Stay close to God. And when you go home, ask Him to give you renewed love for Novice Nicholas and all your brothers."

Bartholomew turned to him. "Will that be — soon?"

Father Francis laughed. "A lot sooner today than yesterday!"

They watched a flock of people in shorts and T-shirts, running along the side of the road for some good cause.

"God will tell you when it's time to leave. I shouldn't think it will be that long now." He looked at the younger man. "And when you do, it will be with a heavy heart."

Bartholomew nodded. "I know. I can't believe it, but I've grown fond of the cottage."

The old priest had one more surprise for him. As they

were walking up the hill to the Cathedral, he said, "I want you to take this afternoon off, starting as soon as the Mass has ended. Just drift, wherever you sense God's Spirit leading. Don't leave Hamilton until the three o'clock ferry."

He reached in his pocket and pulled out his wallet. "Here's some money for lunch and the ferry." He gave him $30. "Let Him guide you. Practice His presence." He smiled. "The two of you spend the afternoon together."

They had reached the Cathedral's main door. "Remember," murmured the old priest, *"Vaya con Dios."* And with that he entered, leaving Bartholomew nonplussed.

21 | flawed paradise

In the high pulpit, the bishop in his red vestments paused before commencing his sermon. To Bartholomew, looking up at him, he was an imposing figure, like Orson Welles in "Moby Dick," playing a Puritan minister/ship captain, casting a weather eye over his flock of whaling families.

Had he ever met a bishop? He seemed to recall a retired one years ago, a friend of Father Francis, as this one was.

But the man in the pulpit was far from retired. Black, mid-fifties, heavyset—Bartholomew smiled; *pontifical* fit perfectly. But not pompous. For all his gentle, self-deprecating wit, this bishop imbued the office with immense dignity and a quiet, deep spirituality.

"No man is an island, unto himself," he began. "John Donne wrote that four centuries ago, in one of his best sermons. It fits this one, since we are an island people. Some English adventurers around Donne's time came here accidentally. But they came back on purpose. They'd found paradise—or as close as they were likely to get on this side of the veil. And perhaps the other."

The bishop smiled at the ripple of laughter. "But my

friends, it is a flawed paradise. Happily God seems to have drawn a curtain over the flaws, so our visitors are unaware of them. But we who live here are all too aware of them. And the principal one is drugs."

People nodded. "What are they doing to us? We're an island family—a large one, but family, nonetheless. We used to trust one another. But there's only one way to support a drug habit." He shook his head. "Members of the family are now stealing from other members, doing things that were unthinkable when I was a boy. And the victim of this national tragedy is Trust."

More heads were nodding. "We're beginning to distrust one another, to become apprehensive. And to start withdrawing from one another." He paused. "Race is becoming more of an issue between us."

He let that sink in, then smiled. "But God has an answer. *He* is the answer!" He spread his arms to the congregation. "Look around, my friends, and see our great strength: half of us are white, half black. That's not integration. That's unity. Family unity."

He caught the eye of some of the children in the congregation. "You know what? God doesn't care what color paper the present is wrapped in. He wants to see what's *inside*." As the children giggled, he turned to their parents. "What color is it in your heart? Is it light? Or is there darkness there? That's the only color He's interested in."

Again he paused. "My friends, we are strong because God's Spirit has drawn us together. Given us caring concern for one another. Made us a church family. It's the unholy spirit who would divide us, instill fear, plant seeds of distrust."

He smiled. "He can't get away with that in here. But

we need to keep our love for one another on the front burner. And sometimes that's going to cost."

It grew quite still in the cathedral. "Sometimes we wonder if we would die for our faith, as the martyrs were required to. 'Of course!' we say. But we won't know till that moment comes." He sighed and smiled. "I pray for all of us, it will never come."

He grew solemn. "But there's another kind of death. Death to pride. Death to self. Death to preoccupation with the approval of others." He looked from one to another. "Friends, God may require one of these lesser deaths of you, if you are to remain true to your faith."

He put his hands on the lectern and smiled. He was finished. "And so, friends, in the words of John Donne, ask not for whom the bell tolls. It tolls for thee."

The Mass was ended, and Father Francis went to join the others in the fellowship hall for coffee, and to pay his respects to the bishop and the canon. Bartholomew elected not to accompany him, preferring to linger in the now-empty cathedral. Its walls, bathed in sunlight from the southern clerestory windows, exuded soft, golden warmth.

For a long time he sat there, enjoying the stillness and the peace. Gradually he became aware that he was not alone. There was a young man at the back of the nave, staring at a notice on the bulletin board. He was not a walk-in; Bartholomew vaguely remembered him being there during the service. Nice-looking kid — 17 or 18, thin as a rail, blond hair long but combed, coat and tie.

At length, the boy drew a deep breath and headed resolutely toward the corridor that led to the clergy offices. But just as he was about to go there, he stopped, slowly turned and went back out the main entrance and disappeared.

Curious to see what had transfixed the boy's attention, Bartholomew went back to see. It was not hard to find; the headline was arresting:

YOU DO NOT HAVE THE RIGHT
TO REMAIN SILENT

"Not where drugs are concerned," the flyer went on. "If you know something, you have to tell someone."

Bartholomew wondered what the boy knew. Was he on his way to tell someone, when he lost his nerve?

He looked at his watch; almost one o'clock. Time to drift. He went out into the sunlight and ambled down the hill toward the waterfront. At the door of the Hogpenny, he paused. He'd heard the food was good in here, and it would be a blessing to have a meal prepared by someone other than himself.

Are you hungry? came the thought.

Not particularly

Then don't eat.

I have the money.

Save it for now.

Where are we going?

Nothing came, so he continued down the hill. Arriving at Front Street, it felt like he ought to go west, so he did.

For no reason, he paused in front of a large yellow building on the waterfront.

Go in.

He looked up. A sign identified the building as Shed #1. Had he heard correctly?

Go in.

He did. Bermuda's annual cat show was in progress. About a hundred hopeful cat-owners had brought their household pets to be judged in different breed categories. Bemused, Bartholomew bought a ticket, went upstairs, and entered the hall.

There were rows of cages, with the owners, mostly very young and accompanied by parents, sitting beside them. Wandering down the rows, Bartholomew suddenly felt homesick, specifically for Pangur Ban. The friary cat had preferred the bottom of his bed at night, but he had booted him off enough times that he'd finally chosen another.

Listen, you dumb cat, Bartholomew told him in absentia; you want to sleep on my bed when I get home, you can.

How on earth could the judges pick prizewinners without crushing those owners whose cats weren't chosen?

He soon found out. A judge, plump and gray-haired, looking dapper in his hound's-tooth sport-coat, stood in the middle of a semi-circle of ten cages, each with a feline finalist awaiting his assessment. In front of him, sitting on four rows of folding chairs, was an audience of perhaps forty, comprised mostly of hopeful young owners, parents and friends.

One of the cages behind him was open, and with both hands he held up and extended its occupant — a large, tawny, ring-tailed male — for the audience to admire.

"Now this is a fine specimen of the Maine Coon breed. His eyes are clear, his muscle tone is firm, his coat is full and rich. Whoever is caring for this animal is doing a splendid job!"

In the front row, a little girl in pigtails positively

shone. Her mother, sitting next to her, happily patted her shoulder.

"This excellent cat is my eighth choice," said the judge, returning him to the open cage.

Bartholomew was surprised. From the generous praise, he had assumed the cat would get at least the red ribbon, if not the blue. Then he realized that *all* of the finalists would be similarly commended—and all ten owners would be similarly delighted.

In the foyer, he strolled among the booths and displays, stopping at one called BFAB, the Bermuda Feline Assistance Bureau. A lady explained that they trapped feral cats—cats that had been either discarded or born in the wild—had them spayed or neutered, gave them shots against distemper and feline leukemia, and returned them to their natural habitat. In this way, they were doing what they could to help control the feral cat population.

Bartholomew told her he was staying on the Harris Property and had seen several feral cats as he was cleaning out brush there.

"Nell?" the lady called to an associate, two booths away. "This gentleman's staying at the Harris Property." She turned back to Bartholomew and explained, "That's Nell's territory."

In a moment Nell came over. "We took seven from there just a week ago."

Bartholomew looked at her. "By any chance was one of them black? With a white blaze on the chest?"

"And two white socks on the front feet?"

Bartholomew smiled. "That's the one."

"Oh, yes," nodded Nell. She's a beauty, that one." She tilted her head. "You've made her acquaintance?"

"Well, we dined together once — almost. I named her Noire."

"She'll make a good companion, if you have the time and patience."

"Listen," said Bartholomew, reaching in his pocket, "I'd like to help your work."

"Why don't you buy a cap?" suggested Nell.

He looked at the navy blue ball cap with the BFAB insignia. "How much are they?"

"Fifteen dollars."

He took it. Holding back four dollars for the ferry, he would have two left over.

As he left Shed #1 with the cap on, he was the happiest he'd been since he'd come to Bermuda.

There was still a little time before the ferry. He continued drifting west, and turned left toward a little park, next to the Royal Bermuda Yacht Club. Beside him was an ice cream and notions shop.

Go in.

He did.

Ask if they have Rum Raisin ice cream.

They did.

Licking the best-tasting cone he'd ever had, he emerged from the shop and retraced his steps to the ferry terminal. He got aboard, taking a seat on the upper, open deck. As the ferry left, he gazed at the receding skyline of Hamilton. Like the houses, the office buildings were either white or pastel shades of pink, blue, and yellow. And above them on the crown of the hill, like a mother watching over her children, was the square, gray cathedral.

Bartholomew leaned back in the sun and closed his eyes. For the first time in years, he knew *perfect* peace.

Your retreat is ended, my son, came the thought.

I don't want it to end.

It does not have to. You can take what you have learned home with you, and you can remain as close to me there as you desire.

Does this mean I'll be going home now?

Soon. I have need of you here for a few more days.

So be it. Father, one thing puzzles me. The ice cream — yesterday it was not all right; today it was.

Whose idea was it yesterday?

Mine.

And today?

Yours.

He thought about that. In other words, if I give to me, I am both giver and receiver. But if the gift comes from you, then I receive it as love, and respond with love.

That is the surrendered life, my son.

Clouds sailed across an azure sky, driven by a northwest wind that raised whitecaps on the surface of the harbor. In the distance off the port bow, two sailboats, side by side with spinnakers in full bloom, one red and one blue, jockeyed for position as they approached a buoy.

Perfect peace — it really did pass all understanding.

22 | knock you down

Perfect mayhem described the scene aboard the boat with the red spinnaker.

"Stand by the jib!" cried Anson Phelps, his hand on the tiller. "Buoy in thirty seconds!"

"Jib leader's jammed!"

"Well, *unjam* it, Kerry!" shouted Anson, letting fly a stream of invective. "Twenty seconds to buoy! Colin, where's the wind going to be, when we round her? You don't know?" He ripped off another peal of epithets.

"I don't care if it's just changed! That's why you're out here! Now give me input on the other boat! Kerry, jib ready? Good! Ten seconds! Colin! Where's the other boat? Input, man! All right, Alex, down spinnaker in five! Four . . . three . . . Watch the boat! *Watch the boat!*"

Bam! The two boats collided as they rounded the buoy together. The impact threw Alex off balance, and he lost the spinnaker line. Like a suddenly deflated balloon, the spinnaker collapsed, draping the bow, dragging in the sea, stopping them dead in the water.

Anson was in a white-knuckled rage. A litany of the crude and the vulgar poured from his mouth, until he started to lose his voice. Since that was a luxury a captain could ill afford, he fell silent. But he was no less angry.

"All right," he muttered, "that's it for today!" He spun the wheel and headed for the yacht club. "In all my 33 years, that is the worst piece of seamanship I have ever encountered! Novices on Sunfishes could do better!" On and on he went, until they reached the assigned berth at the RBYC docks.

Later, after they'd showered and cleaned up and were out on the covered terrace, Anson ordered a Heineken for Colin and a Foster's for himself. He led them to a table over to the side, where they would not be disturbed.

"Where were you out there, man?" he asked Colin, not unkindly. "Because you sure weren't in the boat with the rest of us."

Colin didn't answer. He just shook his head slowly.

"Look, man, I'm counting on you! Not just to read gusts before they knock us down, but for leadership! There's nothing wrong with Alex and Kerry. They're young, but they're good. And they handle stress well— like the kind I dish out. They just need to be steadied down, and you're the one who can do that."

Anson waited, but there was no response. Finally, frustration mounting, he exclaimed, "I need the Beater out there, man! Tell me he's going to be there tomorrow!"

"He'll be there," said Colin quietly.

"Well, good!" sighed his friend, relieved. "Because tomorrow we start racing for real! And I don't ever want to go through that dog's breakfast again!"

As the ferry headed for Somerset Bridge, it passed through the shadow of the towering cruise ship *Crystal Harmony,* parked at anchor in Great Sound. On her fantail, for the pleasure of any passengers who had not gone ashore, a solitary bagpiper was playing "Bonny Dundee."

The skirl of the pipes made Bartholomew homesick — for the first time in several days. The abbey had two pipers who led their outdoor processions, like last year on the anniversary of their basilica's dedication. That was a gorgeous day — all of them in their robes and white surplices, following tall banners with colorful streamers and Latin exhortations — *Benedicamus Te, Laudate Dominum, Laetantur Caeli.* Led by two pipers in full kilted regalia.

Brother Dominic had questioned whether bagpipes were appropriate at a religious occasion, but to Bartholomew they were clearly descended from an obscure tradition of Celtic Christianity. Besides, he'd loved them ever since his father had taken him to see "Gunga Din." Just when it appeared all was lost, the beleaguered heroes heard the faint skirl of pipes in the distance, signaling the approach of the rescue column of Highlanders and Bengal Lancers. No wonder the English had once banned their playing in Scotland and Ireland! That sound would inspire anyone to fight like a lion!

He was jolted back to the present — literally, as the ferry docked at Somerset Bridge.

It was four o'clock. He was about to walk back on the Railway Trail, but he'd walked it so many times during the past two weeks that he decided to go by the road, even if meant climbing Scaur Hill. He'd just reached the top when two men on scooters motored past him.

Abruptly one of them braked and stopped. The man

looked familiar. He couldn't make out the face under the helmet and behind sunglasses, but there was something. . . .

"Brother Bart!" the man cried. "Is that you?"

"Dan?" Bartholomew could not believe it. "What are you doing here?"

"We're fishing! Staying at Sandys House." Through the narrow cut in the rocky hill, cars whizzed past. "Look, this isn't the best place to chat. Climb on, and I'll take you to our place."

Dan scrunched forward on the saddle, leaving barely enough room for his monk friend behind. As they leaned into corners and buzzed around slower moving vehicles, it was exhilarating — but hardly an experience Bartholomew looked forward to repeating.

Eventually they turned left into the well-landscaped, circular drive to Sandys House. In the cycle park, Ron was waiting and wondering what had happened to Dan. He knew Bartholomew from Eastport and was surprised to see him there.

The three men repaired to the bar, where a number of the guests had already gathered. Dan steered them to a corner table. "Peg thought I might run into you. Gather you've been on some kind of personal retreat."

The monk nodded and smiled. "It's pretty much over now."

"Say," said Ron, "we're taking Nan Bennett — Ian's wife — and her son Eric out to dinner tonight. The Chief bagged a four-hundred-fifty-pound blue marlin this afternoon, and we're going out to celebrate! Want to come?"

Bartholomew hesitated. The retreat was over. Dan was a good friend. It would be nice to eat with company, for a change. . . .

Seeing him on the fence, Dan seconded the motion.

"Come on, we're going to the Frog & Onion, which sounds a lot like Gordie's back home."

Ron nodded. "You'll think you're back in Eastport."

"Well—"

"Eric will be here to get us any minute."

But as badly as he wanted to go, it didn't feel right. "Let me take a rain check," Bartholomew said with a sigh. "And I mean that; I'd like to go any other night. Just not tonight."

"A deal," said Dan. "I'll check with you tomorrow."

Just then, Angela Atkins, the cheerful social director for Sandys house, came up to Ron and Dan. "I don't suppose either of our Cape Cod fishermen would be interested in a bit of snorkling tomorrow morning? Roger Thomas, our local naturalist, is taking anyone who'd care to check out the reef at Sandys Cove, at ten o'clock."

One look at their expressions made her laugh. "No, I suppose not."

"Come on, Dan," his monk friend teased, after she'd gone on to the next group, "how long has it been since you've used a snorkel and flippers?"

The Chief scowled at him. "Some things you don't do at my age. And close to the top of that list is appearing in public in a bathing suit."

The three men laughed. Ron looked out the window and nodded towards it. "Eric's here."

They got up—Ron and Dan to leave, Bartholomew to say good night.

As Eric entered, Bartholomew realized with a shock that he was the boy in the cathedral.

Suddenly the boy's eyes widened, and he ran out, jumped in the car, and roared out of the driveway, leaving the three of them stunned.

"Well," observed Dan, "Nan's been really worried about him. Looks like she's got good reason."

"I'm going to call her," said Ron, leaving to find a phone.

Dan was looking carefully at his monk friend. "You've seen the boy before, haven't you?"

"He was in the cathedral today, at the eleven o'clock Mass."

Dan's eyebrows rose. "So that's where he was. We had to wait an hour for him—but it was worth it."

Bartholomew looked out the window. "I got the impression he was wrestling with something pretty heavy."

"Yeah," Dan agreed, "I talked to him a little on the boat yesterday. I haven't told Nan yet, but I've got a feeling it's drugs."

Bartholomew nodded and told him about the flyer the boy had been studying, and how he'd almost gone back to the clergy offices.

Ron returned. "Nan doesn't want to go out tonight. She wonders if we could come by and stay with her until Eric comes home."

Wishing them good luck, Bartholomew walked back to the Quarry Cottage.

Twilight was gathering when he got there. But he could see that he had a visitor—in formal attire, black with a white blaze on her chest. In the center of the quarry was an old poinciana tree—possibly as old as the cottage itself. In front of the tree was an old stone bench, covered with lichen. His guest was sitting on it, exactly in the middle.

"Good evening, madam," he greeted her, bowing slightly. "May I show you a table for one?"

She gazed at him impassively.

"I'll be with you in a moment," he said, ducking into the cottage. He returned with two saucers, one with milk, one with a slice of deli turkey, torn into small pieces. He set them on the grass, half way between her and him.

"Please do begin; don't wait for me." He went back in, put together a sandwich, and bringing the desk chair, came back out.

The light from the open door behind him fell on the two saucers. She had not touched them. But neither had she gone away.

"You waited? What lovely manners!"

He returned thanks — for this meal, for the whole day, and for Noire.

23 | man with no name

At 10:30 Monday morning, like a mother duck leading ducklings into a pond, Somerset's resident naturalist, accoutered in face mask, snorkel, and swim fins, led eight intrepid adventurers, similarly equipped, into the clear, calm waters of Sandys Cove.

As there were only four takers from Sandys House — Maud and Margaret, plus the honeymooners, Jane and Buff — their number was augmented by four guests from the Red Lion Inn down the road toward Ely's Harbour, just before Willowbank.

Their guide had briefed them on the coral reef they were about to explore — "Go near it, but don't brush against it; it's sharper than it looks." And he'd alerted them to the fish they were likely to encounter — red snapper, bright blue and yellow parrotfish, and myriad jacks, groupers, and eels. Now he was leading them out a hundred meters or so, to the optimum diving location.

But before he could give them the signal to commence, one of the Red Lion guests — a blonde, strong of chin, body, and opinion — demonstrated that she was also more independent-minded than the other ducklings. Having informed them that, thanks to spinning, she could hold her breath for at least a minute, she simply up-tailed, up-finned, and disappeared.

She wanted to be the first on the reef, she reported later, to see something special, before the others arrived and maybe drove it away.

She got her wish.

It was a priceless minute. She saw yellowtailed damsel fish, whitebonded butterfly fish, parrotfish and red snapper. But she was intrigued by a little green fish, following it down into a wide cleft in the reef. It was on its way to join another, which was feeding on something under an outcropping of pink coral. Curious, she swam closer. But her shadow startled the little green fish, and they darted away.

What had drawn them? It appeared to be something shiny and round, like a brown marble in the fine, white sand. A marble? Curiouser and curiouser, she reached down to retrieve it. But it was lodged in something under the sand.

Running out of breath—and patience—she brushed the sand away. The air in her lungs exploded into her facemask, as she screamed. The "marble" was an eye, in the face of a man.

Bursting to the surface, she tore off her face mask, screaming hysterically. The naturalist went to her immediately, trying to ascertain what had happened. Had she encountered a Portuguese man-of-war? A moray eel?

She just kept screaming and screaming. He tried to assist her to shore, but she pulled away from him and made it to the beach on her own. Once she was out of the water, her hysteria began to subside. Enough to tell him and the others, "There's a man down there! A dead man! The fish

were eating his eye! I thought it was a marble and —"
suddenly she doubled over and retched over the swim-fin
clad feet of Buff MacLean, who was doing his best to
calm and comfort her.

Inspector Harry Cochrane came out from the downtown headquarters of the Bermuda Police to head up the
investigation. He was a medium man — medium build,
medium brown hair and eyes, medium disposition.

But that was all that was medium about Tidy Harry, as
his fellow officers dubbed him with grudging respect. For
unlike the cinematic inspector of the same name, made
famous by Clint Eastwood, this one went by the book. Always. He had, in fact, written the book, at least the part
on procedures that was taught at the academy.

Accompanied by Sergeant Tuttle, he quickly set up a
situation room at the Somerset Police Station. By the
time police divers had retrieved the body and sent it on to
the hospital pathologist, clerks, phones, and computers
were in place. All information having to do with the
crime would be processed through this room.

But so far, there was little to process. All clothing had
been removed from the body (Caucasian male, early
fifties, no distinguishing marks or features other than a
twice-broken nose and four old puncture scars, probably
knife wounds). Fingerprints had been taken and wired to
Scotland Yard and the FBI, which by the end of the day
had sent word back: Neither organization had any record
of him.

The pathologist's report indicated that the body had
been in the water not more than two days, three at most.

From the salt water in the lungs, it was clear the man had died by drowning. But he had obviously not wedged himself under the corner of the reef and covered himself with sand before expiring. This was murder, of the premeditated kind.

And there was nothing to go on. In the past two days Inspector Cochrane had interviewed everyone who had been on the snorkeling party, then everyone who had been in the vicinity of Sandys Cove in the last three days. No one had seen or heard anything out of the ordinary.

So, late Tuesday afternoon, Harry Cochrane went for a walk. Nowhere in particular, just out and about. It's what he did at the beginning of a case. Just took what he had and went for a walk with it. No point to the walk, really, except it kept his mind relaxed. And he wanted it that way, not leaping to conclusions that would later be like Rorschach inkblots. Once you saw them as two butterflies kissing, you could never see them any other way.

He walked the Railway Trail behind the police station, hands in his pockets, listening to the distant buzz of noise-making kites, enjoying the shifting pattern of the late afternoon sunlight through the trees. Letting logic and intuition lightly arrange and rearrange the pieces, until one or two began to fit.

The utter absence of clues was in itself a clue, of sorts. This was no amateur's doing. An amateur would have left something behind or overlooked something. There would be a contusion, a scratch, a sign of struggle — something.

He paused to admire the boughs of Queen Anne's Lace that formed a canopy of green stained glass above him.

This was not just a murder, he mused. It was an execution — improvised, perhaps, but carefully thought out, nonetheless. The discovery of the body had been a fluke.

The perpetrator had every reason to believe that it would not be discovered for months. Years.

Which meant that he — or she — or they — were, in all likelihood, still on the island. They would have no reason to leave.

The pathologist's report had mentioned a couple of things, intriguing enough for Cochrane to give him a call. On the wrists and ankles were found traces of adhesive. Presumably the victim had been bound with — what? Duct tape, probably. Had he been drowned while trussed up? Possibly. Except, why bother to unwrap him?

Because, Cochrane glanced up at the yellow kiskadee scolding him, whoever did it assumed that the body would remain underwater for so long that when (if ever) it was found, the remains would be skeletal. And might even be regarded as having arrived there by natural causes.

Of one thing they could be reasonably certain: The drowned man was not your average Bermuda tourist. The old knife wounds, and the nose that had been broken twice a long time ago, indicated that the victim had been no stranger to trouble. Quite possibly he had received the knife wounds in prison.

Yet if that were true, the Yard or the FBI would have him in their database. He seemed to be a crook without a country. . . . Unless — he was a Euro. Cochrane smiled and made a mental note to have Tuttle wire the prints to Interpol first thing in the morning.

Was the murder drug related? Probably. There wasn't much else on Bermuda that would attract a hard-case who'd done hard time.

How long had he been on the island? No way of knowing. Nor had anyone missed him. The only recent miss-

ing person report involved a cruise ship passenger who'd
been left behind by the *Norwegian Majesty*. (She'd tried
to get the cruise line to pay for her flight home, but the
long-suffering captain pointed out that he had delayed the
ship's departure nearly an hour and sounded the whistle
four times. Turned out she'd been in Trimingham's — in
Hamilton, because the branch store didn't have her size.)

As for the whereabouts of the murderer, it was safe to
assume that whoever did it was still on the island. Only
six flights had left since the victim was presumed
drowned, and no cruise ships. The names on the mani-
fests of the departing flights had all been checked and
matched with ticket-holders' arrival cards and photo IDs.
Since September 11, at least this part of their work was
easier. All were accounted for, and all appeared to be le-
gitimate tourists or business persons.

Cochrane smiled. Murder was no more difficult to
commit on Bermuda than anywhere else. The tricky part
was getting off their tight little island. There were only
two ways. If they had an idea whom they were looking
for, and he was not a local whose cousins might hide him,
all they had to do was put people at the airport and the
cruise ship terminals and wait.

If they had an idea whom they were looking for.

24 | a froggy would a-wooing go

Late Tuesday afternoon a fire crackled in the hearth of the dark, rough-timbered pub known as The Frog & Onion. When Bartholomew asked how the pub got its name, Ron explained that the original owner had been a Frenchman who'd fallen in love with a Bermudian. Or maybe it was the other way around.

A favorite hangout of West End locals, much as East Enders favored the White Horse, it had lighting so dim that the fire was the best illumination for reading the menu. But as Dan and Brother Bartholomew squinted at it, Ron assured them everything was good.

Anything would be good, as far as Bartholomew was concerned. He could not believe how much he was looking forward to this. Dan had remembered his promise of a rain check, and now they were here. He could already taste the rack of lamb.

"Did you hear about the murder?" Ron asked him.

"Hard not to," he replied with a smile, "what with the police cars and the ambulance over at Sandys Cove. Father Francis filled me in when he told me about Dan's call. He said that one of the guests at Sandys House had found the body."

"Actually it was someone from the Red Lion," Dan said. "A young woman, down for a quickie vacation."

Ron smiled. "Some vacation."

Bartholomew looked at Dan. "What do you think?"

Dan smiled. "I'm glad it's someone else's problem."

They both laughed, recalling the wild ride they'd had two years before. And the year before that.

Momentarily puzzled, Ron smiled. "Oh, yeah, you guys were involved in that diamond thing over on East Bluffs." His eyebrows rose. "*And* the thing at Teal Pond!" He looked at the two of them with new respect. "Holmes and Watson! Which of you is Holmes?"

Dan and Bartholomew each pointed at the other, and they all laughed.

"Not even a little curious?" Bartholomew teased his friend.

"Nope. Just glad to be down here fishing." Dan raised his pint of Bass Ale to Ron.

"Well, I am," admitted Bartholomew.

"Am what?" asked Ron.

"Curious."

"Thought you were on a personal retreat."

"I was," the monk admitted. "It ended yesterday."

"So you're open for business?"

"You mean, back to normal?"

Dan nodded.

"Well, I'm sitting here, aren't I?"

His friend thought for a moment. "When are you going home?"

"I'm not sure," Bartholomew answered honestly. "Soon, I think."

"You want to come out with us tomorrow?" asked Ron.

Bartholomew hesitated.

"He likes fishing," Dan explained. "He just doesn't like small boats."

Ron frowned. "How can he like fishing, and not—"

At that moment the waitress arrived with their dinner. Short and slight, she nonetheless handled the tray with well-practiced ease. "Careful of the plates," she warned them, "they're hot."

Bartholomew looked at his entree and started to laugh.

"What is it?" asked Dan.

"You've no idea how much better this is than what I've been eating!"

"You haven't tasted it."

"Don't have to." He took a bite, chewed, and sighed.

Dan chuckled. "I was going to ask you if you wanted to ask the blessing, Friar Tuck, but since you seem to have your mouth full—" he glanced up at the dark ceiling. "Thank you, for this, for us, for everything."

"Amen," agreed Ron.

"Mmm," concurred Bartholomew.

Later, as they were finishing dessert, Bartholomew asked Dan, "I really am curious; what's your take on it?"

"Are we back on the murder?"

Bartholomew nodded.

Eastport's Chief of Police reflected. "Well, they're doing it by the book. Just what I'd do, interviewing anyone who might have seen anything."

"Did they interview you two?"

"You bet," offered Ron. "Soon as we got back. An Inspector Cochrane."

"What did he ask?"

Dan turned to Bartholomew, mildly surprised. "I thought you were the reluctant dragon when it came to crime-solving."

Bartholomew smiled. "That was only when I was afraid it would interfere with my call."

"Your call?" asked Ron.

"Being a brother."

"And now?"

"Nothing can interfere with that now."

Dan smiled. "Sounds like a good retreat."

"The best. Ever."

Ron, who'd been watching the door, now softly exclaimed, "Oh, no! Don't look now, Dan, but M&M have just arrived."

"Who?" asked the Chief.

"You know, Maud and Margaret from Sandys House." He groaned. "They're coming this way." He turned his gaze to the fire and studied it.

"Hi," said Dan politely as the two ladies approached. "Nice fire," he added, nodding towards it. He pointedly did not introduce their guest or invite them to join their table. They took the other table near the fire, and the men went back to their conversation.

"What did the inspector ask you?" Bartholomew persisted.

"The usual," replied Dan, with a shrug. "What were we doing, why had we come, how was the fishing. And had we seen anything at all unusual in the last couple of days, particularly at night."

"What did you think of the inspector?"

Dan assessed him from memory. "He's good. Didn't waste any time. Covered everything. And — he was watching us all the time as we answered, to see what our bodies might say beyond what our words conveyed."

Bartholomew smiled. "Like you do."

"Yeah," smiled Dan, "I guess."

Bartholomew turned to Ron. "Our Chief conducts all interviews himself, if possible." He turned back to his friend. "So, he is good."

"Yup," admitted the Chief. "And he saved the key question for last, almost as an afterthought. He's a pro."

Ron frowned. "Which reminds me: Why anything unusual at night?"

"Because you can't very well haul a stiff out there and stuff him under a reef in broad daylight."

They all laughed.

"Not too easy to go stiff-stuffing at night, for that matter," noted Dan. "He — or they — must have used one of those underwater lights that scuba divers strap on their heads for hands-free work."

Bartholomew, gazing into the fire, did not seem to hear him. "There *was* something unusual Sunday afternoon," he mused.

The Chief looked at him. "You mean, Eric taking off like that?"

Bartholomew nodded, and the Chief turned to Ron. "What did you make of all that?"

"You mean, when the boy finally came home? I thought he looked — strung out. And I've never seen a kid get from the front door to his room faster, with fewer words." He paused. "Except my own kid."

They laughed.

"You think there's a connection between Eric and the murder?" Bartholomew asked.

The Chief frowned and slowly nodded. "I've been

wondering about that. I get the feeling he may be involved with drugs. And if the murder turns out to be drug related. . . ."

"Is there anything either of you can do for him?"

Ron sighed. "I'm going to call his father. If it was my kid, I'd want someone to call me."

"I'm sure Nan's been talking to him," Dan observed.

"Yeah, but you know how men discount what their wives tell them." He smiled. "I don't mean you and Peg. Anyway, I'm going to call Ian first thing in the morning, before he gets those Blue Water Anglers out on the bay."

Dan noticed Bartholomew had not taken his eyes from the fire. "There's something else, isn't there," he asked softly.

Bartholomew nodded. "When he came into the bar Sunday — it seems like a week ago — he was fine, at first. Then he saw something, and it spooked him. And he took off like a bat —"

"Some-*thing*? Or some-*one*?"

They were startled; the question had come from the next table.

"Maudie!" hissed her friend, scandalized.

"Well, *they're* talking about it, and *we're* talking about it. Why don't we talk about it together?"

Margaret turned to them, genuinely embarrassed. "I'm sorry, I can't do a thing with her when she gets this way."

"Gets what way?" Maud snapped at her. "Everybody eavesdrops in restaurants; I'm just honest about it."

Margaret shook her head. "I'm really sorry."

"And stop apologizing for me! I can apologize for myself, if it's called for." She turned to the other table. "I want to know what that one thinks," she declared, pointing at Bartholomew. And sensing the resentment emanating from the group of men, she added, "And *I* saw something yesterday morning that I think *you'll* be interested in. I was there!"

That got their attention. "You were one of the snorkelers?" asked Dan.

"We both were."

With a sigh, Ron waved to the two women to come join them, and ordered a round of Fra Angelicos.

"What's that?" asked Maud.

"Trust me."

"All right, ladies," said Dan, when they'd pulled up their chairs, "let's hear it."

"Boys go first."

"Maud!"

"I'm just being funny." She turned to Bartholomew. "But I do want to hear what you think."

He turned to Dan, who simply shrugged. So he said, "I think there was something — or someone — in the room that freaked him out."

Maud nodded. "I think so, too," she said. "And I think I know who it was."

That *really* got their attention.

When all eyes were on her, Maud opened her purse and extracted one of her very long, very thin cigars. Ron, who smoked, flicked open his Zippo and lit it for her. She inhaled deeply, and then slowly let the smoke out. This was her moment, and she was milking it for all it was worth.

Then in meticulous detail she related the morning's adventure. Which was interesting but hardly arresting, until she got to the part about the girl being sick.

"You remember I said that the other two from our place were a honeymoon couple?" she asked Bartholomew, who nodded. "Well, the bridegroom, Buff MacLean, puts his arm around the girl from the Red Lion's shoulders to comfort her. And he leaves his arm there — a little longer than was necessary."

Margaret turned to the men and said, "She's got an imagination like the Dismal Swamp."

"And how often does it turn out I'm right?" Maud scowled at her friend. She turned back to the others. "This Buff character's been married, what, all of two days? And all of a sudden he's hitting on this other woman. With his new bride standing right there! Or maybe —" she stopped to take another deep drag on her super-slim cigar.

At which point the waitress arrived with five snifters, cradling a honey-colored liquid. More delay. Then Maud exhaled into her snifter, filling it with a cloud of smoke.

"Or maybe — what!" Ron almost shouted.

"Or maybe — he already knew her. Which could explain why he was so antsy to get out of there, Saturday night." She turned to Dan. "Yes, Chief, I noticed it, too. He'd left the table about half an hour before he actually got up and left."

Dan nodded. "And never came back."

"And we stayed with his poor bride long after you two went to bed," chided Margaret. "Finally, we saw her to her room. He wasn't there, either."

"He'd told her he was going to get a surprise for her. Some surprise!" snorted Maud. "If you ask me, he was down the road at the Red Lion, romancing Miss I-can-hold-my-breath-for-a-minute. Or maybe —" she took a swallow of the liquid. "Hey, this is good!"

"Or maybe — *what*?" shouted Ron. He looked around and was relieved to see no one else in earshot.

"Or maybe — he was busy murdering someone and sticking them in the cove."

They all thought about that.

"Why would he go snorkeling there the very next morning?" asked Margaret. "Wouldn't that be the last place he'd want to be?"

Bartholomew traced the rim of his water glass. "Not if he was interested in establishing an alibi," he said thoughtfully. "Of course, he'd be hoping the body would never be found. But if it *was,* that would the last place anyone would expect the murderer to be."

Maud looked at him. "I like you. You have a devious mind. What do you do in real life?"

Dan shook his head. "You'd never believe it."

Bartholomew didn't answer, asking her instead, "You think — it was this MacLean fellow that Eric saw in the bar? And that the boy knew something that connected him with the murder?"

Maud sighed. "It does sound a little far-fetched, doesn't it?" She looked around the table. "But no one's fetched anything less far."

Later, as they were leaving The Frog & Onion, Dan took Bartholomew aside.

"Someone else left the table that night and never came back," he murmured, "And I don't think he went a-wooing."

Then he remembered something else. "And he, too, was in the bar, when Eric came in."

25 | the new french connection

Harry Cochrane could not remember ever being so tired. He stared at the Interpol report on the desk in front of him. It had arrived by fax an hour ago. What time was it now? He looked at his watch: ten o'clock. Was that ten at night? Or ten in the morning? The situation room had no windows; he could not see if it was light or dark out.

Why was he so spaced? He'd pulled all nighters before. Missed three nights sleep, in fact, and hardly noticed it—until he crashed. You're 57 now, he reminded himself. A bit old and creaky. No longer the button-bright crime-fighter of yore. You're going to retire in three years.

But if he was honest—and he always tried to be, at least with himself—he had to admit the case was getting to him. A brutal, execution-style homicide—in paradise. He had been trying, by sheer force of will, to *make* a break happen. The effort had cost him last night's sleep. To no avail. There were no clues. No witnesses. No mistakes. Nothing.

Until now.

He focused on the Interpol report. Hector Vincennes.

Murderer. Drug king-pin. A list of charges dating back 42 years — all his adult life and most of his youth. Early release from maximum security prison five weeks ago.

At the bottom of the sheet was the name of the arresting officer: François Roland, Inspecteur, Préfecteur de Police, Cap d'Antibes. On an impulse he reached for the phone, then stopped. It was four in the morning over there! How would he like to be called at four? But if he waited till it was office hours, it would be two or three in the morning here. And if he wasn't asleep by then, he would be worthless.

He picked up the phone, and with the help of several operators, reached the office of le Préfecteur — and eventually a very sleepy, very resentful Inspecteur Roland. Who became not at all sleepy or resentful when he heard why Inspector Cochrane had called.

"His early release took me by surprise," said Roland. "I thought we had him on ice for at least four more years." He paused. "We had a missing person situation here last month, a young man aboard an American yacht who took off with a former girlfriend of Vincennes. We assumed it was *l'amour.*" Pause. "If I'd known Vincennes was back in circulation, I would have assumed something far darker than —"

Cochrane interrupted him. "The yacht — what was its name?"

"*Laventura.*"

"It's here!"

"That's right! Bermuda was on its itinerary! And practically every major island in the Caribbean — *Oh, mon Dieu!* It all fits!"

"What fits?" demanded Cochrane.

"Yesterday morning, a flying squad of Bangkok police

raided a methamphetamine lab—and shut down Thailand's entire meth supply! The best part? For once, the meth cartel's eyes and ears in the police force failed them. There was no advance warning of the raid—and they got all the top people! Now the chemical engineer who set up their lab—and designed the labs in Singapore, Rangoon, and Sri Lanka—is telling all he knows, to keep his neck out of the gibbet!"

"Sounds like a big story," Cochrane replied. "How come we haven't heard about it?"

"Because for once, things are breaking our way. Bangkok is playing it close to the vest. Interpol wants to net as many of the big fish as they can."

"But they told you, because—"

"Vincennes is one of the biggest. And since I know him better than most, they wanted me in, as it were."

All thought of fatigue had vanished from Harry Cochrane's consciousness. This was the best news in—so long, he could not remember when he'd had better. "Then you know what he was up to. Tell me!"

"I will, inspector." Roland lowered his voice. "But I must ask you to tell no one else, not even your most trusted personnel. We have to keep this as quiet as we can, for as long as we can. The ones we are trying to hook have so much money they can buy anyone."

"Tell me about Vincennes," Cochrane prompted.

"According to our new friend, the engineer, Vincennes had done a deal with him. He had purchased twenty sets of plans for meth labs and twenty thousand starter doses. Apparently he intended to set up labs throughout the Caribbean. He was going to franchise them, like MacDonald's!"

Cochrane swore. That was all Bermuda needed!

Cannabis and cocaine were everywhere, Ecstasy had arrived, heroin was making a comeback — and now this!

He recalled what little he knew about meth — speed — mostly from the police bulletins. It had been big in the States in the sixties, when designer drugs like LSD first appeared. It had pretty much died out, but had exploded out on the Pacific Rim, where the booming economy had produced a new middle class, with discretionary income to spend on recreational drugs. That was the danger: Meth, like cocaine, was perceived to be psychologically but not physically addictive, like heroin. If you were careful, used it only at parties, or on weekends. . . .

He swore again. The Caribbean had its own emerging middle class. Which was well established on Bermuda.

To Roland he said, "Well, something seems to have derailed the meth express. Your man was eliminated by someone here. You have any idea what went wrong?"

Roland thought for a moment. "One — he'd mentioned to the engineer that he was going to Zurich from there. Perhaps he was picking up funds. Someone else's funds. Who, *peut-être,* did not appreciate his attitude."

"What attitude?"

Roland chuckled. "Well, during my last *engagement* with Hector, it emerged that he had *une plus grande conception* of himself. He saw himself as the new French Connection."

A dense growth of red-blossomed bougainvillea hid the palatial, hilltop domicile from the eyes of anyone below. Yet the view of Hamilton Harbour from the sky-blue marble terrace that surrounded the white marble pool was spectacular. Particularly in this last hour of sunlight, when all the houses nestled below were bathed in golden hues.

Normally the owner took comfort in this view from his terrace at this time of day, knowing the truth of what his friends assured him: that of all the magnificent homes in the parish, his was the jewel in the crown.

But there was scant comfort in the information that René Dupré, also known as "Laurent Devereux," had just related to him this Tuesday afternoon.

"Do you realize," he said to the Frenchman, "that this is the first—unpleasantness we've encountered, since our serendipitous meeting in Monte Carlo two years ago?"

Dupré waited.

With a wistful smile, the owner stared down at the harbor. "I often think about that. How on a whim I decided to drop down to Monte because it had grown so oppressively hot in Paris. How I thought I would try the *chemi* table, and I don't really care for *Chemin de Fer.* How you played so skillfully I invited you for a drink afterwards. We had dinner together."

Dupré nodded. "You informed me that the bottom had fallen out of the coffee market, and the income from your farm in Kenya and the plantation in Jamaica had dropped to a third of what it had traditionally yielded. Also, the growing unrest in Kingston had forced you to double your security force — which was already the largest private army on the island."

His host looked at him with new appreciation. "You do have remarkable recall, René!"

The Frenchman shrugged. "It comes in handy. You suddenly needed a new source of income. A substantial source."

The Bermudian tapped his fingers together. "My lifestyle is extravagant, I must admit. But how fortuitous that we met, just as I was in — rather a quandary. Which you resolved. Although," he gave a slight shudder, "I still have trouble meeting the gaze of the Brigadier."

At his guest's frown, he nodded towards the library. "The portraits. My father, the only one in his class at Sandhurst to win the V.C. And *his* father, the Governor General."

"Of Bermuda?"

"Heavens no! Australia!" He sighed and shook his head. "I know they don't approve. Truth be told, neither do I. Detestable business, drugs! But surely they would not want to give up — all this?" With a sweeping gesture, he took in the pool terrace, the house behind them, and the rest of the top of the hill.

Dupré remained silent.

The other man smiled at his guest. "But your *élan,* your *savoir faire,* your — *je ne sais quoi* — made it," the perfect phrase eluded him, "somehow less detestable."

The Frenchman chuckled. "Plus, I did all the work. You provided the capital; I spent two years developing our network in the Caribbean, recruiting the agents we would need, preparing the way. I even arranged for my associate in New York to come down here and run our base of operations over in Somerset, so my face would not become familiar on the island."

"Brilliant," his host murmured.

"I did not return until a few days before the arrival of Vincennes, staying at Sandys House literally next door, posing as a captain of industry — *en retreat,* as it were."

His host sighed. "It was all going so smoothly, until — this. What made him do it?"

"Greed," Dupré replied simply. "He wanted — he *expected* — a third."

"A *third?*"

"Of projected net revenue."

"He wanted to be — *a partner*?"

"A *full* partner."

The owner slowly shook his head and tapped his long fingers together. "Is there no honor among thieves?"

His guest raised a hand. "I was shocked! As dismayed as you are! But I kept it light, as if it had not troubled me. I did not remind him of all we had accomplished while he languished in exile as a guest of his government. I let him believe that you would be as ready as I to accept him into our partnership."

The owner nodded but said nothing. Picking up a pair of high-powered binoculars, he trained them on the sailboats in the distance. "Gavin seems smoother today," he observed. "But Anson is still having his problems." He swung the glasses. "Ah, here come Lars and Søren. Now we'll see."

He lowered the glasses and turned to his guest. "The unseeded captains are already racing, but they won't face the seeded skippers until tomorrow." He sighed. "Match racing is such an elegant sport to watch! As polo once was. When I was a lad, my grandparents would take me. Their chauffeur would serve strawberries and clotted cream and Veuve Cliquot from the back of the Rolls. The players were all friends, of course. The Duke of Windsor was a friend of my grandfather's. I met him with Beryl Markham once. . . ."

With a sad shake of the head, he forced himself to return to the business at hand. "When did you decide—what needed to be done?"

"When he told me that he had stashed our property ashore and was not about to produce it until the three of us had met and sealed our new arrangement. I realized then that there could be only one outcome to the evening."

"You had convinced him you were not upset."

His guest smiled. "I let the *escargots* do that. He could smell them simmering, and he was hungry."

The sun was setting on the western horizon. Shading his eyes, the owner of the house watched it. "What did you use to—incapacitate him?"

"Something I picked up in Burma that leaves no trace. I kept it for years, on the remote possibility I might one day need it. I didn't think that day would be Saturday, but," he shrugged, "there you have it."

The western horizon was a fiery crimson, already darkening and shading towards purple as they watched.

"A shame the way things turned out," said the owner wistfully. "Monsieur Vincennes could have been of great service to us."

The guest nodded. "When I went over to Marseilles after his release, I told him: I hoped ours could be a long and profitable arrangement."

The owner sighed. "We might have even made him a partner eventually." He shuddered. "Getting him into the tub, even duct-taped, must have been—difficult. He must have weighed fifteen stone. And then?"

"He did have remarkable strength of will. He reminded me of my grandfather, during the war."

"Your grandfather was in the Resistance?"

The guest nodded. "When he was captured, he refused to eat or drink. The Gestapo finally broke him by forcing a tube down his throat and pumping liquid nourishment into him. His body betrayed him; it wanted to live."

"And that's where you got the idea."

"Yes."

"Well, all's well that ends well. By the way, thank you for sending my driver home before—"

The guest nodded. "I would have gone to collect Vincennes myself, except that would have entailed my being away too long from Sandys House." He looked at the owner. "You know I would go to any length to preserve your anonymity."

"I do know that, René, and I deeply appreciate it. Which is why I—never mind; there's no need to say what does not need to be said." He shivered. "Let's go in."

The interior of the house was cool white, with a blue

tiled floor and translucent, blue-tinted glass-block walls. They went through to the solarium which, cantilevered over the hillside, afforded another breathtaking view of the harbor. Taking chairs, they watched the continuing light show on the western horizon, muted now, in deepening shades of purple. Below, lights had come on like distant fireflies.

"Where is our property?" the owner asked.

"In St. Peter's Church, in a life vest, taped under the fourth pew from the back, on the left, as you face the altar."

"We'll leave it there for now. Tell me the rest."

"There's not much. I've sent my associate in New York a letter that I've written to the rental agency here. It's on my New York office's letterhead and is dated Monday, as if I'd sent it as soon as I was back in the office."

He smiled, pleased at his handiwork. "I informed them that although the lease runs to the end of next month, urgent business required me to return to New York immediately. The letter will have the key to the house and the car in it. I made copies of the keys and will continue to use house and car until the letter arrives, Thursday or Friday. Meanwhile, I have become Monsieur Laurent Devereux, who arrived Saturday and is staying at Sandys House for a week of rest prior to his business conference at the Princess."

The owner nodded. "Impressive, René."

"*Ce n'est rien.* I picked Sandys House because it was next door. I could slip out for the rendezvous with Vincennes and return as if nothing had happened."

"But something did happen."

"Yes. It was nearly one before I got back to Sandys

House. I made a call on the pay phone outside the lobby. As there are no phones in the rooms, it is not unusual for guests to use that phone. I even made a point of showing the night manager my cell phone, deploring its inability to hold a charge."

"Très impressif."

"I thought so," he said with a smile that soon faded. "By the way, how did you know I used duct tape?"

"From the police report."

"You saw the police report?"

"When it's necessary, I see — what I need to. It was necessary."

The guest stared at the owner with new appreciation. "What did it say, exactly?"

"That it was an execution, probably drug-related. That the perpetrator must have assumed the body would not be discovered for years — if ever. That the victim was presumed to have had his run-ins with the law, though the FBI and Scotland Yard have no record of him."

The Frenchman gave a low whistle. "Now it is I who am impressed."

The owner lifted a hand in a gesture of caution. "The inspector running the investigation is Harry Cochrane. I know his family; he comes from quality. It would be a mistake to underestimate him. "

"What else does he know?"

"This morning he wired Vincennes' prints to Interpol. So we can assume that by now he knows his identity. We must also assume he may have surmised why he was here."

The guest's expression grew grave.

"In a few days," the owner went on, "when *Laventura* makes ready to leave and her newest crew member fails to show up, they'll report him missing. That's when Cochrane will know how he got here. And when he sees the ports of call on *Laventura's* winter itinerary, he may deduce what Vincennes — *we* — had in mind."

The guest smiled. "It will be too late."

"Tell me," asked the owner.

"I will take the shipment myself."

"You?"

"Why not? In fact, it will actually be better if I go. Our people know me and trust me."

"How will you get there?"

"I'm working on that." He frowned. "How long do I have before they discover Vincennes came on the *Laventura*?"

The owner pursed his lips. "That will depend on what happens to Anson Phelps. Neil and Marcia Carrington, *Laventura's* owners, have come to watch him race. If he gets eliminated early, he could be gone by the day after tomorrow. If he makes it to the finals, he won't leave — and *Laventura* won't leave — until Monday."

The guest pondered that. "Either way, that doesn't give me much time."

"No."

The owner got to his feet, and so did the guest. It was completely dark outside. Both men looked down on the lights that wreathed the harbor like a diamond necklace. The owner looked at the guest. "You are absolutely certain there is no way that you can be tied to Vincennes?"

The guest thought a moment. "No."

"Why did you hesitate?"

"Well," he mused, "it is possible that there is a loose end that may need attending to."

"What do you mean?"

"There is a boy, a Somerset boy, who is one of my dealers for Ecstasy and now heroin. The weekly pick-up time for my East End couriers is Saturday night at eleven. If the post light is on, they may come to the door. If it isn't, they don't. That night it wasn't."

"Then what makes you—"

"Sunday afternoon I was in the bar at Sandys House, as were many of the guests. The boy came in. He saw me and ran."

The owner stroked his chin. "You think he might have seen something the night before?"

"I don't know how. The house was completely shuttered." He sighed. "But even if he did, he won't talk."

"How can you be sure?"

"Two weeks ago, he told me that he sensed his parents were beginning to suspect something, and he wanted to quit before they found out about his—extracurricular activity. I explained that our association was like the Irish Republican Army: 'Once in, never out.' He knew too much for us to ever allow him to retire. Besides, he was my access to Hamilton Academy. It would take too long to recruit another."

"How did he react?"

"Once he understood that he would have far more to fear from me than from his parents, there was no problem."

"What's the boy's name?"

"Eric Bennett."

"Ian Bennett's boy?"

"Yes," said the guest, mildly surprised. "You know that family, too?"

"I used to go fishing with his grandfather." The owner

frowned. "I would rather you not attend to that loose end, unless it is absolutely necessary."

His guest nodded, and the owner walked him to the door. Their meeting was ended.

"One more thing," he said, opening the door. "I will keep you apprised of the investigation's progress. But should things ever start to look bad for you, you must not expect me to do anything on your behalf. As far as the police are concerned, the possibility of there being a 'Mr. Big' behind the drug situation on this island is the product of some journalist's overheated imagination. A myth. Nothing—*nothing*—must disabuse them of that notion. Do I make myself clear?"

"Perfectly."

After dinner at the Frog & Onion that evening, Ron and Dan went over to the Bennetts' to see how Nan was doing. When she invited them in, Ron told her that he'd planned to call Ian first thing in the morning but had decided to do it right now.

"Oh, Ron, I'm so grateful! Something's terribly wrong — and I don't know what it is. Ian should be here."

Ron made the call and convinced his friend to come home on the next plane.

Nan was just bringing out some decaf when Eric blew in the front door. Before he could escape back out, or up to his room, Dan asked if he might have a word with him. A private word. They went into his father's study.

"I wanted to thank you for your help on the boat Sunday," Dan said. "I might have hooked that marlin without you, but I never would have kept it on, let alone gotten it in the boat."

"You did all the work," replied Eric, undeniably pleased.

"And you did all the coaching, telling me what to do next, and never losing patience or making me feel like a klutz, which I was." He looked the boy in the eye. "You're good with people, Eric. You make a person want to come back and fish with you again. And in your father's business that's the most important knack of all, even more than finding your client fish."

"Thanks, Mr. Burke." Eric murmured, looking at his shoes, at the Chelsea ship's clock on the wall, at the door. When Dan said nothing more, he asked, "Is that what you wanted to talk to me about? Because if it is, I've really got to—"

"No," said Dan quietly, "it's about something else— the thing you don't want to talk about."

If Eric had been anxious before, he was practically out of his skin now. But he could not very well leave.

"You know your mother's worried about you."

The boy nodded.

"Did you know your father is, too? He's cutting short his trip and coming home tomorrow."

"He is?" The boy looked both happy and apprehensive at the news.

"Yup. Mr. Wallace just called him and told him he thought he ought to come home."

"Because of me?" Mixed emotions crossed the boy's face like clouds scudding across the sky.

"I'm afraid so. And you know the first thing he's going to want to do, is talk to you."

The boy closed his eyes.

"Look," said Dan gently, "My son was your age once, and I know how hard it was for him to talk to his father. In fact, getting him to talk at all was like pulling a ten-penny nail out of an oak tree."

The boy smiled, and Dan suspected Ian Bennett had tried to pull a ten-penny nail or two in his day.

"I can remember the time my son 'borrowed' my four-wheel-drive patrol vehicle — the *town's* patrol vehicle — and tried to move a tree with it. The hardest thing he ever had to do was tell me. Sometimes," he mused, "it's almost too much."

Eric nodded vehemently.

"That's why I asked your mother if I could talk to you tonight, before your dad came home."

The boy waited.

"Son, I'm going to ask you one question. If you answer no, that'll be the end of this conversation. But if you answer yes, then we're going to have to talk some more." The latter braced himself. "Are you involved with drugs?"

For a long time the boy sat still as a statue. When he opened his mouth, no sound came out, but his lips formed the word — yes.

Late that evening, as Dan motored home, he did not turn his scooter into the drive at Sandys House. He had one more stop to make before he could call it a night.

At the Somerset police station, he asked the night duty sergeant if, by any chance, Inspector Cochrane was still there. The sergeant politely suggested that since it was well past working hours, perhaps he could return in the morning. "Any time after eight will be fine."

But noting he didn't say that the inspector had left for the day, Dan persevered. The inspector had interviewed him the day before, and he now had some information that might be helpful. Again the sergeant politely requested that he come back in the morning.

"I don't think this can wait till morning," Dan replied, whereupon the inspector, who must have caught at least some of this exchange, came out and wearily waved Dan to come back into the situation room.

Cochrane looked as if he hadn't slept in two days. "Yes, what is it?" Then he smiled and added, "I'm sorry, that sounded curt, even to me."

"It's all right," said Dan with a smile, "I've run a murder investigation or two myself. I know what it's like."

The inspector waited, too tired to reply.

"I think I can help. I've developed a—"

The Inspector exhaled. "Is *that* what this is about? You want to be involved in the investigation? I thought you were down here on holiday!" He made a supreme effort to be civil. "Look, Chief, thanks very much for your offer, but we're perfectly capable of handling this ourselves."

Dan smiled. "Which is exactly what I would have told you, if we were up on the Cape, and you'd just made the same offer."

Cochrane waited.

"I think I have a material witness for you."

"*What?*" In an instant, the inspector's fatigue vanished.

Dan told him of his talk with Eric. Of how the boy had gotten involved in the drug scene gradually but increasingly, until he had become a dealer and then a distributor. When he'd tried to quit, they'd put a real scare into him. But it was nothing like the scare he got Saturday night. He'd gone to make a pick-up when another young dealer, who'd just been up to the house and was scared out of his mind, told him that he'd witnessed a murder in progress — your murder."

"Who did it?" Cochrane demanded. "What was the name of the other boy? The one who saw it?"

"He wouldn't tell me." Dan shook his head. "I'm not exaggerating when I say that in twenty years of law enforcement, I've never seen anyone so terrified."

The inspector groaned. "Well, if he won't tell us, how can we put whomever they're afraid of behind bars?"

Dan smiled. "He slipped once and called the other boy 'Jonesy.' "

"Darryl Jones," the inspector said, nodding. "We've had an eye on him." He yawned. "Well, if Eric won't talk, maybe Jonesy —"

Dan interrupted. "Eric *will* talk. That's why I came over tonight. I've persuaded him that he has to come see you. And he's agreed. But only if I come with him."

Inspector Cochrane stood up, came around the desk, and smiling, stuck out his hand. "Chief Burke, welcome to the investigation."

Dan shook his hand and smiled. "Any service I can render, et cetera, et cetera."

"You can start by bringing him in here first thing in the morning. Actually, I'd like to see him right now, but it's late, and I don't want to spook him."

Dan frowned. "Tomorrow morning would be fine, except for one thing: He wants to tell his father first, and his father's in the States and not due back until the afternoon flight."

"I don't want to lose another day."

Dan nodded. "Normally I'd agree with you. But I've had a boy his age, and I think it's crucial they get started over again on the right foot. I know what it would mean to me if my son wanted to tell me before he went to the police."

"All right," the inspector agreed reluctantly, "I'll go along with you on this. Bring him in tomorrow afternoon, as soon as he's talked to his father."

All at once, he smiled. "Now that you're on board, Chief, I would be interested in your opinion."

"I don't know enough to offer one," said Dan. He thought for a moment. "There is one thing. . . ." And he told him about Eric's erratic behavior Sunday afternoon, when he entered the bar at Sandys House to pick him and Ron up. "I have the feeling that the person you're looking for was in that room. I'd have another talk with that Frenchman."

At 8:30 the following morning, René Dupré, a.k.a. Laurent Devereux, received a call on his cell phone. "We need to meet. Call me back on a land line where you cannot be overheard, at this number." And he gave him a number that only two other people knew.

Wednesday afternoon was O.K. Corral time for Anson Phelps and the boys from Marblehead (plus Colin Bennett). One of the seeded skippers had remained in New Zealand because after September 11, his syndicate, which had already invested $100 million in their effort, was loath to risk their ace flying anywhere near America. As a result, in the first round on Wednesday seven of the eight pairings would match a surviving unseeded skipper against a seeded one in a best-of-five duel. But the eighth match would pit two unseeds against each other: Anson Phelps and the very hot Danish captain, Søren Jansen, whom Anson had nicknamed Sørenski. The two were close friends who'd drained many a pint of Foster's together, but on the racecourse they were fierce competitors.

This afternoon they would meet on the two-buoy course, with two windward and two leeward legs. The first crew to win three races would go on to the Quarter Finals on Friday. The other crew would go home. They were welcome to stay to the end, but most did not care for the taste of ashes and departed as quickly as they could get their stuff together.

The two captains had eaten a late breakfast together. At the end of the long bar on the RBYC terrace was a huge stainless steel coffee urn and beside it, a smaller, hot water urn for the tea drinkers. The competitors were thin, short-haired, and deeply tanned, except around the eyes, where their Oakleys had shielded them. The uniform of the day was khaki shorts, boat shoes or sandals, and polo shirts, mostly white, with racing insignia from previous Gold Cups, the older the better. (No one but cruise-shippers wore short sleeved, button down shirts.) They were cheerful, nonchalant — but tension was already building under the smiles.

Søren, nursing a Bloody Mary, admitted to being a bit hung over — but not as badly off as two of his crew, Bjørn and Goran. They'd been billeted with Gladys Bancroft, one of the stalwarts of the RBYC, whose sons and now grandsons regularly rounded the cans on Saturday afternoons.

Bjørn and Goran, three sheets to the wind and surfing home on a breaking wave of Foster's, had gone to the wrong address. In the wee hours of the morning they had fumbled their way into the house — of the former prime minister. Shushing each other so as not to wake up their hostess, they had made their way upstairs in the dark and attempted to get into the large bed — which was already occupied by the former prime minister's wife.

She was, in a word, shocked! But impeccably polite. As was her husband who, clad in bathrobe and pajamas, bundled the tipsy Danes into his Mini and delivered them to their rightful abode.

"But," Søren had assured his rival, "they will be ready to sail this afternoon. And so will I."

A captain's mood invariably impressed itself on his crew. If the captain was calm and confident, so were they. Anson was tense. That morning, Charlie Thompson, the head of the Marblehead syndicate, had called him from 30,000 feet. He and his wife Katy were aboard his corporation's Lear, and with them was a potential new backer who could make it largely possible for them to put a second boat in the water. They would ETA Bermuda at noon, in time to get to the yacht club to cheer on the Marbleheaders. "And tonight, Anson," added Charlie softly, so his passenger pigeon could not hear him, "we're going to lighten his corporate wallet by twelve million dollars. So look good out there!"

"I'll give it my best shot, Charlie. I always do, man!"

All captains were tense before a race like this; the stakes were too high. And the tension mounted as they entered the pre-race tableau. At some of the tonier, blue-blazer yacht clubs of New England, the four-minute countdown to the starting gun was signaled by a ceremonial brass cannon aboard the Commodore's yacht. Things were a little less formal at the RBYC: The committee boat used an old shotgun. But the signal flags came up and down just as smartly, and the Race Director and his crew watched just as closely for the slightest infraction.

Half the races were won or lost right here, in the frantic pre-start maneuvering known as "the dance." The boat that managed to cross the line upwind had the initial advantage and was often able to maintain it. But cross one second too soon, and you had to circle back around and cross again.

Anson had allowed Søren to get the jump on him and

came across downwind, five seconds behind. At this point he should have shaken it off and concentrated on his tactics. Instead, he vented on his crew. And as their spirits sank, things started going terribly wrong.

Kerry yanked the jib line and managed to jam it—again. Then Anson really lost it, tearing a verbal strip off Kerry's back. Though they managed to get it unstuck, they were 32 seconds behind at the first buoy. In match racing, that was an almost insurmountable lead.

But the Marbleheaders were actually sharper rounding the buoys, managing to pick up six seconds at the first, eight at the second. On the second upwind leg, Anson tried every trick he could think of to get out of Søren's wind. He feinted and double-feinted. . . . To observers ashore the two boats were tacking and counter-tacking so fast they seemed to be almost shivering.

Once Anson even did the opposite of what his instincts were telling him, and Søren covered that, too, as if he was inside Anson's head. That really unnerved the captain of the red-spinnaker boat.

As they cleared the last buoy and set up for the final downwind run to the finish line, Søren had a ten-second lead. The Marbleheaders gained on them, but not enough; the red spinnaker crossed the line four seconds behind the blue.

As they readied themselves for the next race, the Marblehead boat seemed shrouded in a blue haze of invective. Anson was a towering inferno, and Colin caught the brunt of it.

"You were no help to me out there, man! No help at all! Where is the Beater? You said he'd be here, but he's not in the Marblehead boat, that's for sure!"

Colin made no reply. And to make matters worse, at

the beginning of the next race he blew the countdown, taking them over the start line two seconds ahead of the gun. They had to re-cross it, and it didn't matter that they were now sailing much better—calm, smooth, and in synch. It didn't matter that they actually picked up 43 seconds on the other boat on the last three legs. They still lost by six.

But at the end of the second race, Anson was no longer mad, no longer tense. What he was, was a great captain. "Now listen, guys, we've got them just where want them."

They looked at him, mystified.

"You know the best tank the army ever had? It's the Abrams."

Now they were truly mystified.

"It's named for General Creighton Abrams, and you know what he said during the Battle of the Bulge? 'They've got us surrounded again, the poor bastards!'"

Colin smiled as Anson went on. "Well, these poor Danes think they've got this match in the bag! But what's going to happen, as soon as we start pulling ahead? They're going to tense up! While we get even more relaxed. I mean, guys, we've booted it anyway, so we might as well have some fun. Relax and enjoy ourselves!"

The rest of the crew began to smile.

"We're sailing beautifully out there now, in case you haven't noticed. We may have only one bullet left, but, you know what? We're not going to miss. This boat is moving for us now. We're faster than they are, and they know it. Just keep cool, keep your focus, have fun! And when we get done this afternoon, get your laundry done. Because we're not going home. We're going to the Quarters!"

"All right!" cried Kerry, as the others grinned, believing.

"Kerry, you're smooth, man! And Alex? Just remember to breathe!"

They all laughed.

He turned to Colin. "You've got it now! The Beater's back! Don't ask me how I know, but I do. And pretty soon, you're going to know it, too!"

"I know it now," Colin declared. "Anson, Søren's been crowding the committee boat at the start. I know the Race Director. He doesn't appreciate that particular tactic. Watch what he does. If I'm right, he'll angle the start line. If we start at the other end, we should get a ten-foot lead."

"You sure?"

"Trust me."

"All right, Beater."

Colin was right. The boats crossed the line together, one second after the shotgun. But the red spinnaker was just a little ahead.

And Colin found he could read the wind again—the *next* wind. "When we round the buoy," he shouted to Anson, "hold off on the spinnaker. They'll raise theirs, but let them. Just use the jib. The wind's going to be coming from over there," and he pointed to the southwest.

As they came off the buoy, only the blue spinnaker ballooned out—and then, as the wind suddenly gusted across the course, the Danish boat started rolling from side to side uncontrollably, and there was nothing they could do to stop it.

Anson got ahead—and stayed ahead. "We're zoned, boys!" he cried, as they crossed the line nearly a minute ahead.

Just before the next race, as they circled tight to the start line, Anson shouted across to the other boat, "Hey, Søren-ski! Concede now, and we can start drinking early!"

"Big talk for someone who's got to win two in a row!" the Dane shouted back. "You want to put a grand on it?"

"Absolutely!"

They crossed the start line side by side, working a fickle, shifting headwind. But all Colin's old instincts were back. He knew what the wind was going to do, before the first telltale sign. As his confidence rose, Søren's waned, until he paid the Marblehead boat the supreme compliment: Whatever tack they took, he copied them.

That technique worked fine, up until the last buoy, when Anson wound up with the starboard tack, forcing Søren to give way.

Now they were even at two up, and Anson, was ecstatic. As they circled in the final countdown, he called out, "Sørenski! I've got a bungee cord, a long one — you need it?"

Colin winced, throwing a look at Anson, who just laughed. "I'm gaming him," he murmured. "Get him angry enough, he'll start doing stupid things."

He turned to the other boat and cupped his hands. "Yo, Sørenski! You're looking really good today, man! I hope someone's videotaping you! Highlights at eleven!"

"Anson, you —" and he called him a Danish expletive.

"Wait a minute," shouted Anson back, thumbing through an imaginary Danish-English dictionary. "Hey, man, that's not in here! But I think I got it from the context!"

That elicited a more vehement response. At the end of which Søren called to him: "You want to double?"

"Absolutely!"

This time, during the dance, Colin took them close to

the committee boat—a little too close. They actually brushed it, which earned them a penalty. It could have cost them the race—and the match—except that Søren was laughing so hard, he forgot to watch where he was going and sailed out of the box. Another penalty. The race was even again.

And it stayed even, with neither boat gaining an advantage. But at the final buoy, Colin sensed that the wind was about to lighten. "Anson, drop the jib—*now*—and when we're halfway round, start the spinnaker up."

"You *sure,* man?" It was a risky maneuver. If Colin was wrong, if the wind stayed up, the spinnaker would blow out.

"I'm sure. Do it!"

As they rounded the buoy, Alex hauled the red spinnaker up. In the other boat, Søren grinned, convinced they'd gotten greedy and blown it.

And then the wind dropped—just enough. Like a big red umbrella popping open, the spinnaker ballooned out—eight seconds before the blue one.

With that slenderest of leads, Anson gave Colin the con. The latter anticipated each of Søren's increasingly desperate maneuvers, so deftly it was as if he were inside the Dane's head.

The two boats sailed in tandem down the final leg, like skaters waltzing. The wind was steady now, and in the cerulean sky above them, two Bermuda longtails soared as one.

"This is why we do this, guys!" exulted Anson at the top of his lungs. "This is the way we always dreamed it would be!"

They were ahead by eight seconds, as they approached the finish line—and roared with laughter. On the committee boat, the Race Director and crew, in the event of another too close encounter with the Marblehead boat, had all donned their yellow life vests!

When they'd tied up and turned over the sails and the boat to the yacht club staff, they walked four abreast down the long dock to the club. In their red sailing shirts, with a certain swagger to their gait, they arrived, looking like resplendent matadors.

And were showered with praise. Charlie Thompson's friend was so excited, he was already talking about the second boat they would need. And one of Neil and Marcia Carrington's friends wondered if it was too late to join the Marblehead syndicate.

Towards the end of the evening, Anson, feeling no pain, took Colin aside. At the same table at which they'd sat at a few days before, he said, "Listen, Beater, it looks like the second boat's a lock. I want you at its wheel, man, and when we go for the Auld Mug, I want you right next to me, strategizing."

It was a perfect evening, thought Colin, as he drove the old Hillman home. Well, almost perfect. Perfect would have been to have Amy there to share it.

When he got back to the apartment, there was a FedEx waiting for him. Opening it, he started reading, and all his euphoria drained away. It was the decision from the divorce court hearing. The judge had awarded custody of their son to Amy, with once-a-year visitation rights. And there would be a lump-sum settlement for child support: $50,000. It was due in thirty days, or his property would be sold at auction.

He had no money, and the only piece of his property that was worth anything was *Care Away*.

29 | tying up loose ends

A weather front was moving in. Dark clouds roiled over Bermuda's low hills. Against them the white houses seemed stark and ghostly. It would rain soon.

The two men sitting on the blue tile terrace were not enjoying the view. They were not enjoying anything this morning — least of all, this hastily arranged meeting.

"We have a problem," said the owner in clipped, precise tones. "Let me rephrase: *You* have a problem."

Dupré waited.

"Remember that potential 'loose end' you told me about?"

"The boy Eric?"

The owner nodded. "Well, it seems there are two loose ends! And they are about to unravel."

"What do you mean?"

"Do you also have a young associate named Darryl Jones? Goes by the name of Jonesy?"

Dupré nodded. "He's in the Somerset Church's youth group."

"It would seem that, despite your precautions, your activities Saturday night *were* observed. Through a loose slat in the bathroom shutter. By Jonesy, who told Eric, who is scheduled to appear at the Somerset police station at four o'clock this afternoon."

"What?"

"To meet with Cochrane."

"Mercredi! You're certain?"

The owner did not bother to answer what they both knew was a foolish question.

The Frenchman reflected on the evening in question. "I did check the shutters from the outside of the house. Though I was not expecting to use the bathroom — in that fashion. The boy must have come up to the house, even though the post light was off. Must have nosed about, perhaps heard something. . . ." He looked at the owner. "Is there anything else you can tell me?"

"Yes!" declared the latter with biting sarcasm. "Concerning something *else* you should have told *me*." His colleague looked surprised; the owner had never taken this tone with him before. "Who's this policeman from Cape Cod? Staying at Sandys House, like yourself?"

"What, Burke? He's nothing!" He gave a dismissive flicking gesture. "I didn't tell you about him, because there's nothing to tell. He's a cipher."

The owner frowned at him over the tips of his tapping fingers. "Well, it seems that your cipher is going to accompany the boy to the police station. He has apparently gained the boy's trust and has persuaded him to talk to Cochrane."

Dupré stared at him, speechless.

Thoroughly disgusted with the whole turn of events, the owner looked up at the gathering storm. "We should go in now. In five minutes, we'll wish we had."

Dupré, deep in thought, followed him in to the solar-

ium. "Has the boy talked to Burke? Told him about—
me?"

"If he had, you'd be in custody. But I gather he's about
to tell Cochrane everything."

The Frenchman sighed. "Time to tie up loose ends."

"I should think so! Clearly it should have been done
before now."

"There's still time," said Dupré calmly. "I've provided
Jonesy with a pager. I'll use it to summon him to the
house after dark. He will be too frightened not to come.
And Eric I will see this noon."

"Won't he be in school?"

The Frenchman nodded. "They have a recess after
lunch. We have a system: Every Thursday, I drive past the
school at 12:40. He sees me, and we rendezvous at a corner four blocks away, as quickly as he can get there. I
supply him with what he needs, and he's back in school
by one o'clock." Dupré smiled. "Today is Thursday."

"He won't be—apprehensive?"

"Why should he be? He has no knowledge that we're
aware of his intent. And he's undoubtedly been advised to
act as if nothing is different. I'll wait at the corner for
him, as always. He'll get in the car, as always, and I'll
drive around the block, as always, while he tells me what
he needs."

It grew darker. Rain started to pelt the tall windows,
and Dupré stood and went to the nearest one. He studied
the pattern the drops made as they ran together, joining
into miniature rivers.

"One thing will not be as always," he concluded. "Instead of goods, I will have a syringe for him. When he
wakes up, he will find himself in a predicament similar to
Vincennes'."

The owner winced at the prospect of another liquidation, especially of someone he knew. "Is that really necessary?"

Dupré ignored him. "Except," he mused, "I may have to do Jonesy first. To ascertain if he's told anyone other than Eric."

He turned back to the rivulets. "Actually, I doubt I'll have to use the tub. The memory of it should be enough to loosen both boys' tongues. Then I will simply administer lethal doses of heroin, and," he smiled and raised his hands, *"voilà."*

Again the owner asked, "Is it — necessary?"

Dupré looked at him, not bothering to hide his fraying patience. "Since it is my neck in the guillotine, *comme il faut,* you will have to let me decide what is necessary."

He tracked one of the descending streams with his finger. "I must know if anyone else knows."

"I very much doubt it," said the owner, "or we would have heard."

Dupré nodded. "Even so, I must be sure."

The owner got up, signaling that their meeting was about to come to a close. "Perhaps, under the circumstances, it might be advisable to find somewhere else to dispose of — the evidence."

"Thank you," replied the Frenchman, bowing with exaggerated *politesse.* "Your advice is, as always, deeply appreciated." He thought for a moment. "I'll dispose of the bodies tonight. In a gully off the Railway Trail. The terrain is steep there, and dense. When they're found, OD'd on heroin — *if* they're found — the police will assume it was a drug party gone bad."

"Cochrane will know," the owner observed.

"No," Dupré clarified, "he will *suspect*. He won't know for certain."

The owner led his guest to the door. "Have you arranged your—departure?"

"I'm getting closer. I learned of an interesting possibility this morning, out at St. George's. In that regard, I'd appreciate you arranging an introduction for me with Neil and Marcia Carrington. Through them I would like to meet one of the Gold Cup captains, Anson Phelps, and through him—"

"Out of the question!" snapped the owner. "You know that your world and mine can never mingle!"

Dupré shrugged. "It would have saved me time, that's all." Then, annoyed at the owner's annoyance, he added, "Don't worry, I'll be out of your hair soon enough."

"It can't be too soon," replied the owner, not caring for the Frenchman's tone. "The police are confident that though they don't know the murderer's identity, they have him trapped. There are only two ways off the island—and the airport and cruise ship terminals are covered. They're saying it's only a matter of time."

"There's a third way," Dupré murmured.

"What?"

"Never mind." It was the first time he had not taken his partner into his confidence.

As they parted, neither man offered a hand in farewell.

Maud and Margaret were on the little balcony of their room, watching the sun setting over the Atlantic, enjoying the sound of the surf on the rocks below. The morning's rain had passed quickly, leaving everything fresh and bright.

On the table between them were two glasses with ice and two tiny bottles of J&B.

"The person I'm most concerned about is Jane," Maud announced, taking a drag on her slender cigar.

"Jane?"

"Our neighbor, remember?" She gestured in the general direction of the honeymoon suite. "Plain Jane MacLean. I like her!" she exclaimed, blowing a smoke ring. "And I *don't* like what's being done to her."

"We don't know anything is being done to her! I mean, you thought you saw something Monday morning, during that awful time on the beach. You just had a hunch, is all."

"We're *not* going through this again, are we, Mags? You know how right my hunches are."

"But we don't have anything else to go on."

Maud tapped the ash off her cigar. "What about his afternoon jogs?"

"I don't see what's wrong with that."

"Disappearing for two hours of prime time on his honeymoon?"

Margaret wasn't buying it. "She said at breakfast that she doesn't mind. Gives her a chance to take a nap."

Maud scowled. "She's putting up a brave front, poor thing." All at once she set her glass down and stood up. "We've got to help her!"

"Help her do what, for heaven's sake?"

"She's going to be badly hurt."

"But we can't help that."

"Maybe we can," her friend retorted, stubbing out her cigar.

Maud did not answer. She glared at the sun as if it were trying to stare her down.

"Maudie Brown! You swore to me, in the lobby of the Cairo Hilton, that you would never, never, never—"

Her friend waved a hand to stop the nevers. "This is different."

"It is *not* different! The *only* difference is that here we might not be in danger of starting World War III!" She glowered at her friend. "But knowing you, even *that* is not out of the question!"

Maud sighed. "Do you like Jane?"

"Of course I like her."

"You want to see her hurt?"

"Of course not."

"Then we've got to help her."

Margaret's voice was barely audible. "I don't want to ask what you've got in mind."

"Let's just see if his afternoon jogs are as innocent as they're meant to be."

"How are we going to do that? It's been years since I've done any running. And you—" she looked at her heavy friend and chuckled.

"I wasn't thinking of joining him," Maud snapped, not appreciating her cousin's levity. "I was thinking of spying on him."

"Oh, Lord!" moaned Margaret. "It's happening again!"

Maud shook her head in disgust. "I don't know why I drag you all over the world with me!"

"Because I'm the only one who'll put up with your nonsense!" Margaret shot back. "And I'm not putting up with it any longer!"

"All right, all right," said Maud, softening, "calm down."

They sat in silence for a moment. Then in a more placating tone, Maud pleaded, "Do this one thing with me, Mags, and if it turns out I'm wrong, we drop it."

Margaret's firm jaw remained set.

Her cousin upped the ante. "*And*—I promise to keep that promise I made in Cairo."

Margaret's eyes were cold. Her round steel-rimmed glasses seemed to underscore her steely resolve.

"*And*—we can go to Henley next spring for the Regatta."

The prospect of watching some of the best crews in the world competing together was almost more than one of Wellesley's great former oars could resist. The manicured lawns by the river's edge, the beautiful young men in their seersucker jackets and straw boaters. . . . There was an infinitesimal softening at the corners of her mouth.

Maud saw it, and softly, enticingly started the Eton Boating Song,

> "Jolly boating weather,
> And a hay harvest breeze,
> Blade on the feather,
> Shade off the trees. . . ."

Margaret, in spite of herself, began to smile. "That's not fair!" she muttered, but by the time her cousin reached the refrain, she had joined in,

> "Swing, swing together,
> With your bodies between your knees."

"All right," sighed Margaret with a shudder, "What exactly do you have in mind?"

"Well," said Maud, rubbing her hands together and leaning forward, "he's taken his scooter and gone over to the beach at the Southampton Princess, to do his jogging there."

"How on earth do you know that?"

"Because I eavesdropped. I overheard him telling Jane at lunch, in case she wanted to reach him by cell phone. He promised he'd be back by six, to take her to Il Palio for dinner." She looked at her watch. "It's almost five; if we catch a No. 8 bus, we can be there by 5:30."

"But he'll be almost ready to come back by then."

"Exactly! They'll be done jogging, and in the pleasant afterglow of all that exercise, they'll be enjoying a beer — no, too many carbos — a Pinot Grigio at the little bar by the beach."

"What if we get there, and he's not there?"

Maud shrugged. "Then we've wasted an hour and four bus tokens."

"What if he's there, but she isn't?"

"Then — we'll never, never, never do this again!"

Maud declared, mimicking her friend. "And either way, you get to feast your eyes on all those lovely boys at Henley. But if *I'm* right, and he *is* there, you and I are going to the Masai Mara in January! For two weeks! And this time we're going to do the hot-air balloon ride!"

They caught the No. 8 and arrived at Southampton Beach on schedule. It was a long walk down to the beach, and Maud was having a hard time. "Now I see why they have those nice blue trolleys for the hotel's guests," she gasped, as one passed them. "If I'm having this much trouble coming down, I'm never going to make it back up."

"It's all right, dear," said her cousin. "I've already decided we can splurge and take a cab home."

They reached the Cabana bar and restaurant facility, and Margaret was about to go in, when Maud grabbed her. "You can't just walk in there!" she hissed under her breath. "He'll see you!"

"*If* he's there," said Margaret, refusing to concede the point or lower her voice.

"Come on!" said her friend in her most urgent, conspiratorial whisper, and she went into the women's changing room. Margaret followed. "Now," continued Maud, "we're going to go out on the beach, and then come up to the bar from there, only we won't go in." She opened the door to the beach. See those bushes? We'll use them as cover, to check out the lay of the land, as it were." She paused. "If she's here, of course."

"Don't be crude, Maudie; it doesn't become you."

Once the two of them were behind the bushes, Maud peered out—and after a moment murmured, "Hah! Got you, you miserable, blow-dried creep!"

"Where?" whispered Margaret, tugging on her friend's arm. "Let me see!"

Reluctantly, Maud yielded the optimum vantage point.

"You're right!" Margaret whispered. "Again!" She watched Buff and the woman from the Red Lion pleasantly glowing, heads close together, sipping on straws in tall, reddish-brown drinks. "I think they're having Planter's Punch."

She turned to her cousin. "*Now* what do we do?"

"We don't *do* anything. We just watch."

They watched.

"This is so — *weird*," whispered Margaret, enthralled. "I've never done this before."

"What, spied on people? Why is it any different than what we do in restaurants? We eavesdrop like mad, even make up fantasy backgrounds for the people we're listening in on. Just think of this as eaves-*seeing*!"

After a while, Margaret whispered, "I'm beginning to see how this is such a turn-on for stalkers. It's kind of — *empowering*! We're seeing everything, and they don't even know they're being observed!"

"My turn," announced Maud, assuming the observation post. "Hmm, I think she just stopped glowing. . . . Uh-huh, if a person can *un*-glow, that's what just happened. . . . Oh, my stars and garters! Is she *ticked*! . . . She's standing up. . . . She's leaving . . . coming this way . . . we'll have to duck out of here in a moment."

Maud turned and was about to leave, but couldn't resist one more look. "Wait! He's coming after her . . . he's got her by the arm . . . she pulls free and. . . *Whoa!*" Maud winced and recoiled.

"What?" hissed Margaret. *"What is it?"*

"She slapped him! *Hard!*"

"Let me see!"

"Not yet." Maud held her away, without taking her eyes off the drama. "He's coming back for more! He's gotten around in front of her, to cut her off. . . . Oh, good for you, girl!"

"Tell me!"

"She just hauled off and belted him! And does she pack a wallop! Must work out on the heavy bag when she's not spinning! Now she's — that's telling him! Whoops, duck! Here she comes!"

The two cousins whirled away and bent over, apparently fascinated by a seashell — that looked exactly like all the others in its immediate vicinity.

The young woman passed by without noticing them. Rubbing the side of his face, Buff went away in the opposite direction.

In the cab on the way back to Sandys House, Margaret asked, "Just before we ducked, you said, 'That's telling him!' — What did she tell him?"

"Oh, just something crude that did not become her." Maud smiled at the memory. "But it was right on!"

That evening the two cousins were watching television in the TV room off the main lobby. There were no TV sets in the rooms, as St. John Cooper-Smith felt that if his guests came to Bermuda on holiday, they might appreciate a vacation from mindless, pre-digested entertainment. To first-timers complaining about no TV in their rooms, he would suggest "a little television of the mind" and would lead them to a library of well-thumbed mysteries.

Some discovered that they liked reading, even regarding it as a lost pleasure. It made for lively and enthusiastic breakfast conversation, over which St. John presided at the head of the long table, dispensing coffee from a huge silver samovar. Those already into reading, or back into it, would compare favorite writers and plot twists. Then the readers would encourage the nonreaders to give it a try. The occasional rainy afternoon produced an abundance of animated conversation, and people began congratulating St. John on inspiring a mini-renaissance for the literary-minded.

But he did realize that for some, giving up their daily tube fix, cold turkey, was asking a bit much. So he put in a TV room and let the addicts discover for themselves that, while they might have access to twenty or thirty channels at home, in Bermuda there were only three. Of which two often played the same program at the same time. While the third carried a cricket match so uneventful that even Bermudians sometimes thought of going out to the kitchen to watch the bananas ripen.

This night Maud and Margaret were watching Oprah. They were surprised to find her show on in evening prime time — until they realized how many islanders might prefer it to anything else they could get from the States.

Oprah was just plugging her latest book discovery, a Cape Cod mystery writer, when Jane and Buff came in from dinner. Glancing in the TV room, Jane saw them and smiled. When the cousins smiled back, she came in. Buff followed, not smiling.

"We had the best time!" Jane exclaimed. "That is the nicest restaurant! Great Italian food and an easy walk from here. You'll have to try it!"

"That's wonderful, dear!" said Maud. "We'll go tomorrow."

"And the maître d' —"

Buff yawned and interrupted her. "I'm going to bed; I'm afraid I overdid it this afternoon." He turned to Jane. "But you stay up and talk, if you want to."

He yawned again, and without waiting for a response, plastic-smiled and left.

"Honey," said Maud to her gently, clicking off the TV, "we need to talk."

ment. Then the monk frowned. "There's still no way this dealer could have known what Eric intended to do," he mused. "Unless — the boy happened to let something slip that made him suspicious. I mean, if I were Eric, and I knew this guy had killed someone, I would have freaked out, just being in the same car with him — even if I wasn't about to give him up."

The monk felt himself being drawn into the situation, but it seemed the right thing to do. "Have you told Cochrane?"

"Of course. He was the first one we told."

"What'd he say?"

Dan shook his head. "Same thing I would have: We're doing all we can. But until we have a name, or at least a description, we've hardly anything to go on." He paused, then added, "He did say he was going to pick up the boy Jones, as soon as he got home from school."

Bartholomew sighed and smiled. "In that case, they'll have their description soon enough. And their culprit. And Eric." He laughed. "Cheer up, Dan! This thing's going to have a happy ending!"

But Dan just shook his head. "I wish I could think so. My gut tells me otherwise." He managed a wan smile. "I'm glad you're here! I was going crazy out there on the bench, waiting! If you'd been much longer, I'd have freaked out, myself!"

Bartholomew nodded — and inwardly shuddered to think how close he'd come to being a couple of hours longer.

He took a deep breath. "First of all, you've got to stop blaming yourself. You did the right thing. I'm sure his parents don't hold you responsible."

"No, they've both told me how grateful they are."

Looking at his friend's haggard expression, Bartholomew realized that only time — and God — could ease his burden. "Look, Dan, get some sleep, or you'll be a wreck in the morning. And of no use to Eric or Cochrane or anyone else."

Dan nodded and got up. "Glad you're here," he murmured again, as he went out into the night.

The trouble was, having sent his friend back to Sandys House to get some badly needed sleep, Bartholomew couldn't get to sleep himself. He lay on the rack, staring at the darkened ceiling, his eyes wide as saucers.

That sometimes happened when he assumed the role of confessor. The penitent would be released from his burden, yet while Bartholomew instantly forgot the details, it sometimes seemed that the weight had been transferred from the shoulders of the absolved to the one pronouncing absolution.

Bartholomew had seen Eric only the two times: In church, then briefly as he exited the bar at Sandys House. But he kept seeing him in his mind tonight. Finally he decided he would deal with it as he had on other nights when sleep eluded him. He would go for a walk.

He got up, pulled on his navy blue sweats, his black walking shoes, and his new navy blue cap. As he was about to go out, he caught a glimpse of his reflection in the kitchen window and smiled. Dark clothing from head to toe—if he were a Navy Seal, he wouldn't be much more invisible.

It was a moonless night, which made it difficult to keep to the footpath to the Railway Trail, through the first field and around the freshly plowed one. It would have been impossible, had he not done it practically every day and on more than a few sleepless nights.

Once he reached the trail, he relaxed. While there were no streetlights (save one at the corner of the first cross-road, which was usually out), the trail was paved and smooth. So even though it was quite dark, particularly on moonless nights, he managed to stay in the middle by keeping track of the pitch-black foliage on either side. And certainly no one else would be out here.

Father Francis had warned him not to go out on the trail in the middle of the night. With the drug situation deteriorating, there had been a spate of robberies in this vicinity, and even a murder here last year. Yet for some reason, Bartholomew had always felt safe — though, he smiled ruefully, he may have put undue stress on his guardian angel.

He had walked perhaps a half mile west, into the cut through the limestone, when he became aware that he was not alone. He could not see anything. The cut, with its overhanging brush that shut out the faint starlight, was as black as the inside of a cave. Yet he was certain he had heard something, a sound he couldn't identify.

He stopped and listened. It was a sound that was not of nature. Man-made. Coming nearer.

He flattened himself against the rocky wall of the cut. The sound was coming from the direction of Sound View Road, the first road to cross the trail after it came out of the cut. He strained to see something, anything.

And then, just in from the road, the streetlight that was usually out sputtered briefly to life.

In that frozen moment, he saw a man pushing a shopping cart along the trail into the cut. Something large and bulky was in the cart. The light sputtered out. Bartholomew felt the brackish taste of fear rising in his throat. His breathing shallowed. He pressed his back against the rock as hard as he could and waited. And wished he could do something to still the pounding of his telltale heart.

The man and the cart came closer. He, too, was navigating, as Bartholomew had a few moments before, by keeping to the middle of the slightly less dense shadow. When he came abreast of Bartholomew, he stopped.

He's listening, Bartholomew thought. He's sensed something. He held his breath, wishing now that he'd forced himself to breathe more deeply.

The man remained perfectly still, no more than ten feet from Bartholomew, whose lungs were desperately scavenging what oxygen molecules remained in them. And then, a moment before Bartholomew gasped for air, the cart started to roll again.

Bartholomew waited for the man with the cart to emerge from the south end of the cut, before he followed. Filled with a profound sense of dread and foreboding, he nonetheless felt compelled to follow, to see this — whatever it was — through.

In the starlight now, Bartholomew could see the man's silhouette ahead, while he himself remained in the deeper shadow by the side of the trail. At a place where the trail ran by a steep gully thick with foliage, the man stopped. He looked back towards Bartholomew and waited a long time. Then from the cart he lifted the limp form of what looked to be a body, went over to the edge of the trail, and flung his burden down into the depths of the ravine.

Pushing the now empty cart, he reversed direction and came back towards the cut—and Bartholomew, who again flattened himself against the rock wall. This time the cart-man passed by without stopping. Letting him get a few paces ahead, Bartholomew followed.

Why? He demanded of himself. Why was he doing this? This was insane! He'd seen what he needed to see. He could bring the police back here. There was no point in doing any more!

Everything in him wanted to run, get as far away from here as possible! Yet, if that was a body—Eric's body (he forced himself to think it)—then he needed to see who this man was.

So—he followed as closely as he dared. Just before Sound View Road, the man stopped. Bartholomew stopped. The man pushed the cart into the brush by the east side of the trail, as if some shopper had "borrowed" the cart to get her groceries home, then abandoned it here.

Bartholomew was perhaps a dozen feet from him, when to his horror the streetlight chose that instant to sputter on. In that frozen moment, both men were transfixed.

Then Bartholomew ran back into the cut, as if the Hounds of Hell were after him. But there was only one set of footfalls echoing off the walls of the cut. The cart-man had chosen not to follow him.

Bartholomew had seen—and recognized—the face of the murderer.

And the murderer had seen the face of the witness.

33 | our turn

Still shaking when he reached the Quarry Cottage, Bartholomew was in turmoil. Thoughts, emotions, belief, perceptions — all crashed like roaring surf against the rocks of what he had just witnessed.

He should call the police. His cell phone was on the desk. Picking it up, he discovered that he'd forgotten to charge it. He could walk down to the main house, wake them up, and ask to use their telephone — and unnecessarily alarm the entire household.

He checked his watch: one o'clock in the morning. Plugging in the charger, which would have the phone usable soon enough, he sat down to pull himself together.

And realized that he was angry with God.

Snatching up his clipboard and pad he wrote:

Why did you let it happen? Why did Eric — if that was Eric — have to die?

It was not my will.

Is that what you say when people ask you about the Holocaust?

That was not my will, either.

But isn't that just a massive cop-out? I mean, you're God! You can do anything you want!

Not when it conflicts with man's will.

I don't get it! You are love, but you let hatred triumph. Where's the justice in that?

My son, why did I create man?

We've been through that: To be your companion, for time and eternity.

Correct. For man to be that, I had to give him free will. He had to want to be with me. He had to choose to set aside his will for mine.

You were taking quite a risk, weren't you? What if no one wanted to do it your way? Put down their will for yours?

Many didn't. You have no idea how much it hurt when some, for whom I had great love, turned away. But once I had set the machinery in motion, I could not change the rules just because I did not like the way it was working out.

Bartholomew smiled. You came close a few times. The Flood, the plagues, all those years of drought and famine. . . . But you do intervene, when we ask. Sometimes.

It is always my will for you to ask. It is not always in accordance with my will for me to answer in the manner you have requested.

Bartholomew was calmer now, but he still wanted answers.

What about Eric? He was so young. . . .

He was old enough to make choices. The day you saw him in the cathedral, he nearly chose me.

Oh, God! I almost prayed for him at that moment. If I had, would it have—made a difference?

Silence.

Bartholomew shuddered. Earlier, he'd sensed he'd somehow assumed Dan's burden for the boy. Now he knew it.

I wish there were some way of rewinding the tape.

The next time you have an impulse to pray for someone, do so.

What should I do now?

Call Dan.

He checked the cell phone; it had built up a sufficient charge. On the desk he found the piece of paper with the number of Sandys House on it and made the call.

The night manager sounded like he might have been catching a few winks himself. Bartholomew apologized for disturbing him, but said it was an emergency. A police emergency.

In a few moments Dan's groggy voice came on the line.

He told Dan what he'd seen.

"I'll call Cochrane."

Half an hour later, Sergeant Tuttle collected him and took him and Dan, who was in back, to the Somerset police station, where the duty sergeant showed them into the situation room. On the wall was an enlarged map of Bermuda, with a red grease pencil arrow to the reef in Sandys Cove where the body had been found. Next to it were posted several lists—the snorkelers, the guests at Sandys House and the Red Lion, and suspected drug dealers. There was a profile of Vincennes, provided by Interpol, and a timetable of events—the last being the scheduled interview with Eric.

Dan inspected Vincennes' curriculum vitae. "A pretty rough customer," he murmured.

"Who seems to have met his match," added Bartholomew.

The Chief turned to him. "You know, you took quite a chance out there. What if he'd come after you?"

"I had my feet in the running position," the latter said, with an apologetic smile. "I felt it was worth it, to find out who killed Eric — if that was him."

Sergeant Tuttle came in and offered them coffee, which they gratefully accepted. "Have to be black, I'm afraid. Milk's run out."

At that moment, Inspector Harry Cochrane arrived and went straight to the coffee maker, which was now empty. Opening the cupboard above it, he discovered that the coffee tin was also empty.

"Sergeant," he muttered, "do you suppose that in this entire establishment, there is one scrap of coffee left?"

Tuttle shook his head. "The day shift will be bringing some, no doubt. Along with fresh milk."

"Have mine," Bartholomew offered, extending the cup to him. "I haven't touched it. Just waiting for it to cool down."

Cochrane looked at him and smiled. "Decent of you. I should insist you have it, but my craving insists I take you up on it. Halves?"

"Put mine in the pot, too," Dan offered. "I haven't touched it, either."

Cochrane brightened. "Two-thirds of a cup is certainly better than none." He turned to Bartholomew. "So you're Chief Burke's monk friend. Tell me what you saw. Long version, please. Let me decide what's important and what isn't."

Bartholomew gave him the long version.

When he'd finished, Cochrane rubbed his eyes. "And

you think the body—if it *was* a body—might be one of
the boys we're looking for?" He turned to Dan. "We went
by to pick up Jonesy. He never came home from school."

Dan was stunned.

"I don't know for sure, Inspector," said Bartholomew.
"I've a feeling it might be."

"Well," said the latter, getting up, "we'd best go and
see. Sergeant Tuttle? Ask the duty sergeant if we might
borrow his clerk, and bring the portable floodlights."

In a few minutes there were two patrol cars parked on
the trail where Bartholomew had seen—whatever it
was—thrown down the gully. Tuttle and Officer Ellis set
up the floodlights on their tripod, but bright as they were,
they could not penetrate the dense foliage below.

"I'll go down there, sir," said Tuttle, before Cochrane
could ask.

Armed with high-powered flashlights, he and the clerk
ducked under the old wooden railing and prepared to descend. Before he did, he glanced at Bartholomew and
smiled. "This better not be someone's old mattress."

From the trail, Cochrane, Dan, and Bartholomew
watched the beams of the flashlights disappear in the underbrush, as the officers slowly made their way down.
Before long, they could see only occasional brief flashes.

Then the inspector's hand-held two-way talker crackled. "It's no mattress," said the sergeant. "We'll bring him
up."

Bartholomew fought the urge to ask which boy it was,
and looked over at Dan. His friend said nothing, but he
could tell from his eyes; he was hoping it wasn't Eric.

It took them more than a few minutes to bring the
body up to the trail. When they had, Bartholomew could

see it wasn't Eric. He looked at Dan. He had averted his gaze, a hand over his eyes.

The eastern sky was starting to lighten when they got back to the station. At the inspector's request, Sergeant Tuttle had taken the body to the hospital for an immediate autopsy. From the dilated pupils it looked like an overdose, probably heroin, but they had to be certain.

When Cochrane, Dan, and Bartholomew were back in the situation room, the inspector turned to the monk. "You said the streetlight came on, and you caught a glimpse of the man with the cart. Describe him."

Bartholomew did his best. When he'd finished, Cochrane smiled sadly and said, "You've just described a third of the adult male Caucasian population of Bermuda."

The Chief, lost in thought, now looked at Bartholomew. "Was his nose thin on the bridge and sharp-looking?"

His friend nodded.

"Narrow face, high cheekbones?"

Another nod.

"Dark hair, receding here and here?" He gestured to his forehead.

Nod.

"I know who it is," said Dan quietly but with great force. He turned to Cochrane. "And so do you. He's just described Laurent Devereux. At least, that's the name he goes by. He's a guest at Sandys House. I sat next to him at dinner Saturday night."

"Was a guest," corrected Cochrane. "He checked out yesterday morning. I know, because I wanted another word with Monsieur Devereux about the business conference he was supposed to be attending next week. The

Princess did have that event scheduled, but after September 11, too many registrants dropped out, and they canceled it. But they did have a list of presenters and seminar leaders. No Devereux; in fact, he wasn't even registered."

"So now what?" asked Dan.

"Yes, that's the question, isn't it," said Cochrane with a dour smile. "I'm curious, Chief; if this was your investigation, what would *you* do now?"

Dan thought for a moment. "Well, there are three of us who know what this guy looks like. I'd get a police artist in here, ASAP, to work up a sketch of him."

Cochrane nodded. "She's already on her way. Should be here about the same time as the coffee." He turned to a yawning Bartholomew. "That is, if you can stay awake that long. You're the only one who didn't get any sleep at all last night."

"I'll be all right," said Bartholomew, hoping he would.

"I have to say what I'm thinking," said Dan, obviously reluctant to, as if uttering the words might give them power. "Why hasn't he killed Eric?"

Cochrane nodded. "I've been wondering the same thing. The man kills easily, with no compunction. In fact, it would seem he derives a certain pleasure from it. So why spare the Bennett boy?"

"Bargaining chip," murmured Bartholomew, gazing at the wall map of the island. The other two turned to him. "He must be thinking the boy might be of more use to him alive than dead."

"How?" asked the inspector.

"I've no idea," said Bartholomew, shaking his head. Then he frowned. "You mentioned earlier there were only two ways off the island. What about a power boat?"

"Cape Hatteras is 631 miles from here. There are only

thirteen boats on the island's registry with that kind of range. And only three are still here. This time of year, the rest are all down in the islands, where the charters are. We've alerted the three captains to get in touch immediately if they're approached for any long-range charter."

Bartholomew was still frowning. "He's thinking that Eric might prove useful to him in getting off the island."

"How do you know that?" asked Cochrane.

Bartholomew shrugged. "A hunch."

Dan spoke up. "We've worked together on the Cape in the past. I've, um, found his hunches helpful."

"Right," said Cochrane, unimpressed. "Look, while we're waiting for the artist, would you mind going back with Officer Ellis and showing him where the perpetrator disposed of the shopping cart? A good print or two would be a great help. With that, and the artist's sketch, Interpol may be able to give us a hand."

He stood up and pointed at the open manila folder on the table. "I'm tired of being on the defensive with this Devereux, or whatever his name is. Tired of keeping personnel at the airport and the terminals with nothing more to go on than to watch for someone 'suspicious-looking.' Now it's our side's turn!" he declared. "And we're going to give him a taste of what our batsmen can do!"

"Amen!" exclaimed Bartholomew, who didn't even like cricket.

"Soon as the sketch is ready, it'll go on the front page of all the papers, and in all the TV news coverage. I wonder how Monsieur Devereux's going to like being Bermuda's Most Wanted! There won't be a hole big enough to hide him!"

On the highest hill on St. George's Island was a square steel building, painted white. Unimposing from the outside, its interior was another matter. For this was Harbour Radio, the eyes, ears, and nerve center of Bermuda. Equipped with the latest radar and state-of-the-art computers and monitors, it resembled the Combat Information Center of a nuclear aircraft carrier.

Every ship approaching or leaving Bermuda, no matter what size, was monitored here, and decisions were made as to which cruise ship would berth where. Their berths had been scheduled months in advance, but circumstances often changed, and it was Harbour Radio's responsibility to park them and keep track of them. There were five cruise ship berths on the island — two in Hamilton, two at St. George's, and one at the Dockyard. If a sixth ship came calling, as sometimes happened, Harbour Radio would assign her an anchorage in Great Sound, where she would be serviced by a special ferry, that would bring her passengers ashore.

This afternoon the first watch was quiet and uneventful, the way every watch officer preferred it. It remained that way until 1325, when it got unquiet in a hurry.

"Mr. Shackelton, you'd better see this." The first petty officer called from the fax machine.

"What is it, Moberley?"

"Weather advisory. Bermuda Weather Service. Basically what they're saying is, their millibars have just fallen off a cliff!"

"What are you talking about?"

"Have a look, sir! There's a severe tropical depression building."

"How far from us?"

"That's just it! It's *here!* We've got convection stacking vertically, a warm core developing, and get this: It's starting to spin!"

The watch officer stared at the fax. "We're talking hurricane," he murmured.

"I know!" exclaimed Moberley. "And the whole thing is building up right on top of us!"

Shackleton muttered an unprofessional oath and soon had the weather monitor showing them the same thing Bermuda Weather was seeing. It was eerie. It looked like an ancient Chinese wash of a tsunami. The afternoon had just turned into every watch officer's worst nightmare.

He got on the phone to his counterpart over at Bermuda Weather. "Where'd this thing come from, Terry?"

"Beats the hell out of me! Looks like we're just lucky enough to be on the trailing edge of one front, about to be overrun by another, with a third coming down fast from the northwest. I've been in this business a long time, Shack; I've never seen anything like this!"

Shackleton glanced over at the chart to see where the

cruise ships were. There were only two still at the island — the *Scandinavian Sovereign* over at Ordnance Island, and the *Royal Dane* over in Hamilton. "So what are we looking at?"

"Worst case or best case?"

"Give me the worst, and we'll hope for the best."

"The worst is that in a couple of hours we're going to have thirty to forty knots from the north, but that's just for openers. By nightfall it could be double that. Or more."

Shackleton's eyes widened. "*Or more?* You're talking hurricane, Terry!"

"Tell me about it! This thing's going to *be* a hurricane by the time it gets the hell out of here! We're telling everybody, and asking them to tell everybody else. You, too, will you?"

"Count on it. We'll close the airport, call the radio stations. What does Miami say about it?"

"The hurricane center? Oh, they're watching it. They're a little embarrassed, judging from the careful but rapid upgrading of their cautions." He gave a wry chuckle. "But they're only embarrassed. You know who's going to get it in the neck, don't you. I can already see the letter to the editor: 'Once again our vaunted meteorologists at the Bermuda Weather Service have let us down,' et cetera, et cetera."

Shackleton smiled. "Head them off at the pass, Terry. Get up a press release, explaining the most extraordinary weather event Bermuda has experienced in the past thirty-three years."

"You know, I like that. Thanks, Shack."

"Catch you later, man. I've got a couple of big ones to get out of here."

He turned to the first petty officer. "Moberley, get ahold of the *Dane* and see how fast she can clear Hamilton. Then call the *Sovereign*. The wind's stiffening in the channel. She may not be able to get out. It'll be her captain's call. Tell him, if he decides to ride it out where he is, we'll put a couple of tugs on her, to hold her." He looked at the chart. "And then get on to the *Pacific Princess* and tell her she'd better stay down in Barbados and not even think about coming in here tomorrow."

He picked up the phone and called the Yacht Club. "Hilary? It's Shack, over at Harbour Radio. I've got some bad news, I'm afraid. . . ."

When he finished, he just shook his head. This was going to be a long afternoon. And a longer night.

The ironic thing about a tropical depression was that if you didn't happen to notice how fast the barometer was falling, you'd have no reason to suspect big trouble was coming. The wind might be picking up, but the sun was still out. Of course, if you looked up, you might notice the high stratus clouds moving a whole lot faster than usual, almost as if someone was projecting them in time-lapse photography.

Colin had no reason to look up that afternoon. He had, in fact, never felt less like looking up. Today was a lay-day for the Marblehead crew, while they waited to see whom they would face in the Quarterfinals tomorrow. But he was at the club anyway; he had to see Anson.

He found him eating some late scrambled eggs and chatting with Kerry. "Anson, can I talk to you?"

"Sit down, man, you want some breakfast?"

"I'm not very hungry."

Anson, chewing, looked up at him.

"It's, um, private," Colin said.

"Hey, man, no prob," said Kerry jauntily, "I'm done anyway," and he left the two of them alone.

Colin told him about the FedEx from Georgia.

"Bummer!" murmured Anson through a mouthful. "Your soon to be ex-father-in-law sounds like a real piece of work!"

"He's that all right," Colin muttered, and sighed. "I've got to come up with the settlement money or lose my boat." He paused. "I was wondering if you might be able to spare some cash."

"Sure," said Anson, swallowing, "how much you need?" He took another bite.

"Fifty thousand."

Eggs nearly spewed. "Man, I don't have it! Everything I've got is tied up in the syndicate. House is mortgaged — the works."

"It's okay," said Colin. "Just thought I'd ask. As you can imagine, I'm a little desperate."

"Yeah, man! Your boat! That's terrible!" He thought for a moment. "Look, I can give you two. Hey, man, you won that for me yesterday — as soon as Sørenski comes up with it. And look, I'll add the thousand I bet him yesterday, but that taps me out. It's a good thing we won!"

"Thanks, Anson," Colin said, getting to his feet. "You're a stand-up guy."

"Hey, man, me and the Beater are going to be doing a lot of sailing together."

That reminded Colin of the other Rolex, still in its presentation case. It should fetch around $3000. Great, only $44,000 to go!

At the bank he was informed that they did not consider a Venus 34 suitable collateral for a loan. "Sorry, Mr. Bennett, but we're just not set up to be a used-boat brokerage."

After that, he went to Sandy Harrison's boatyard, to see if he was still interested in having him as a partner. Sandy definitely was. Enough to advance him say, $20,000? Sandy considered that, and then agreed — under terms that would make Colin more of an indentured servant than a partner. He told Sandy he'd have to think about it.

He had one last hope. Ian.

As he turned the old Hillman in the direction of Somerset, the car seemed to run a little easier, as if it knew it was heading home. The one-car-per-household rule for the island might have persuaded him to get something newer, but the Hillman had been his father's. For that reason he held on to it, coaxing season after season out of it.

Entering Middle Road, he realized he hated asking his brother for money. He hated asking Ian for anything. Ian had always been the responsible one, the one his parents had been proud of. And Ian had lived up to their expectations. He had worked hard, put enough money aside for Eric to go to Harvard, Oxford, anywhere.

But Eric had insisted that all he wanted was to be a captain like his father. So Ian had planned eventually to use the tuition money as a down payment on a second boat, *Mercy* — bigger and faster, with a spotting tower. He would give *Goodness* to Eric as a graduation present, once he finished Hamilton Academy.

Colin, on the other hand — no, let's not go into Colin, he thought, that subject was a little too painful.

He was surprised to see a police car in the driveway of

the modest family domicile. He was stunned to see the expression on his brother's face, as he came out to greet him.

"Colin, thank God you're here! I've been trying to get you! Oh, God, Colin! Eric's been—kidnapped!"

Colin was shocked speechless.

"He was into drugs," his brother stammered. "We didn't know. And now some dealer has got him!" Ian broke down, and Colin, staggered, reached out and held him.

"Oh, my God! I can't believe this!" his brother said over and over.

Colin took him inside. A woman officer was trying to comfort Nan in the living room. They went into Ian's study. And for a long time, neither of them spoke.

Then Colin asked when it happened, and his brother told him all they knew, which wasn't much. "And each hour we don't hear something, like a demand for ransom, it's less likely he's—alive." His brother just shook his head, unable to say more.

For a long time they sat in silence. Then Colin said, "I wish there were something I could say. I keep thinking: What if it were Jamie?"

"You don't have to say anything," his older brother replied. "You're here. That's all that matters."

He lowered his head and shut his eyes. "Oh, God, I had such plans for him, such hopes."

"Ian, don't do that," his brother said, trying to muster courage he didn't feel. "You don't know that he's not all right."

Colin stayed with him, until Inspector Cochrane arrived—with no new news. Then he want back to the club. He had nowhere else to go.

He'd not mentioned his own predicament; it had never occurred to him.

35 | thieves' honor

Outside, the wind began to lash the palm trees. In the blue-tiled solarium, the owner paced, hands clasped behind him. His guest merely watched.

"I want you off this island in twenty-four hours!" exclaimed the owner.

"You don't want that any more than I do," replied his guest with a quiet smile.

Put off by his calm demeanor, the owner wheeled on him. "You don't seem to get it! *They know who you are!* A witness saw you dispose of the Jones boy's body. An artist has done a sketch. It's going to be on the news tonight, and on the front page of every paper tomorrow! A remarkably good rendering, by the way; you really should have it framed!"

Dupré stood up and shot him a glance. He'd had enough. "No, Monsieur le Grand!" he retorted, a hard edge to his voice. "It's *you* who don't seem to 'get it'! If I go down because you have refused to help me, guess who's going down with me!"

The owner glared at him and said nothing. Then he slowly smiled. "I was wondering if it would come to this.

I can promise you that before you could open your mouth to implicate me, you'd be shot 'attempting to escape.'"

Instead of replying, the guest held up a large manila envelope, stamped and addressed. "This is a letter which I'm about to mail to my associate in New York. In it are three other sealed envelopes addressed to Bermuda's Prime Minister, to the Leader of the Opposition, and to the Governor General. My cover letter instructs my associate that in the event of my untimely demise while in custody, they are to be mailed immediately. Each contains the identical document — a detailed description of our operation from its inception. Dates, times, names, Bermuda bank accounts, Swiss bank accounts, plus the names of our agent on each island. Your role, my role, Vincennes' role — *le tout ensemble!*"

The owner blanched.

Dupré let him chew on that. Then in a more moderate tone, he added, "But if I die under circumstances that are not suspicious, they will not be sent. Or if I am caught through my own stupidity, I will keep my mouth shut. I will preserve your precious anonymity — and the possibility of eventually resurrecting our joint venture."

His partner relaxed somewhat, but the Frenchman wasn't finished. "Stupidity is one thing, however; the callous refusal of aid to a comrade in peril is quite another. That is tantamount to betrayal."

Both men knew that, as it once was in the Resistance, in their high-risk field of endeavor, betrayal was the darkest of crimes.

The owner smiled. "I think we can reach an accommodation. What exactly is it that you would like from me?"

"As I said before, I want to meet the Carringtons. At

the club. This afternoon. They know Anson Phelps. And he knows someone who can help me."

"Sorry, but I told you that was impossible. Nothing's changed, I'm afraid—"

The Frenchman simply waved the envelope.

The owner stared at it, perhaps imagining the reaction of—his friends—when they read its contents. "All right, I'll make a call," he said with a sigh. "But I want that envelope before you leave."

"Oh," replied the Frenchman with a wry smile, "there is one more thing. I need $50,000, U.S."

"There's more than that in either of the accounts."

"And whose name are those accounts in? Monsieur Devereux, I'm afraid, has been declared *persona non grata*. I'd be picked up immediately."

The owner tapped his fingers together, his brow furrowed as he considered his options. There were none. "Wait here. I'll get it for you."

"I'll come," countered his guest.

"Suit yourself."

They went into the library, a long paneled room whose temperature and humidity were carefully controlled to protect the five thousand volumes on shelves from floor to ceiling. To reach titles on the upper shelves, there was an elegant wheeled step-ladder of Bermuda cedar.

At the far end was a huge oil portrait of the owner in a colonel's field uniform, with a burning jungle in the background. On the wall to the left of the portrait was a dress sword, and beneath it on the polished teak floor a regimental drum. To the right of the portrait was an illuminated display case with all the owner's decorations.

As the Frenchmen examined them, the owner seemed

pleased. "I still wear them," he murmured, "to the Governor General's reception on the Queen's Birthday."

His guest made no reply.

The owner pushed a hidden button on the frame of the display case, and it swung away from the wall, revealing a small safe. He stepped in front of it, to block his guest's view of exactly where the dial stopped, as he spun it deftly, left, right, and left. Opening it, he brought out five packets of U.S. hundred dollar bills.

The Frenchman, looking over his shoulder and seeing more packets in the safe, said, "Better make it eight."

"You said $50,000."

"I'll need walking around money."

"That's ridiculous! You'll be carrying cashier's checks for $20 million!"

"All sealed, with receipts for each agent, in waterproof wrapping. What would you have me do? Borrow from our employees?"

The owner turned back to the safe and withdrew three more packets, which he handed to his guest. Then he closed the safe firmly, as if to emphasize that there would be no further demands.

"I shall keep an account of your expenses!"

"Suit yourself," replied the Frenchman with a shrug.

But he did relinquish the envelope. Honor was restored.

"Darling, are you almost ready?"

"I'm in the shower, darling."

"I know that. Are you almost ready?"

"How can I be ready if I'm in the shower?"

"Darling, I told Dieter our ETD was 1800 hours."

"And darling, I told *you:* Never talk nautical to me."

"Sorry."

"But you keep *doing* it! If you were sorry, you'd stop!"

"All right. I told Dieter we wanted to leave at six."

"What time is it now?

"Three-twenty."

"See? You can do it, if you want to."

"Do what?"

"Talk normal time."

"Darling, are you almost ready? I want to say good-bye to Anson."

"You think *I* don't? *I'm* the reason we're here, remember?"

"Yes."

"And *I* invited Tim and Lydia, and Stuart and Stacey."

"You'll be glad to know, they were able to get on the last plane."

"That's a relief! I wouldn't want that on my conscience."

"Listen, put a shake on it, will you?"

"Darling, I'm packed! Have you checked us out?"

"Yes."

"Then cool your jets! I'm almost done!"

"I got a call from the Vice Commodore. Apparently there's a French entrepreneur over at the club, who might be interested in joining the Marblehead syndicate. He asked me to introduce him to Anson."

"Well, why didn't you say so? All that mumbo-jumbo about 1800 hours! Darling, be a darling and bring me that towel?"

36 | force nine

On the flagpole in front of Harbour Radio, the red flag of Bermuda with the Union Jack in the hoist quadrant was starched by the rising wind. High above, the clouds were racing as before, but the sky was no longer blue. It was a milky, gray-white.

Inside the command center, every scope was manned, and voice communication was kept to a minimum. Only Senior Watch Officer Shackleton could ask questions, and he asked a lot of them. The answers were instantly forthcoming.

"Moberly, any idea how long this — *thing* is going to sit on us?"

"Bermuda Weather does not expect movement until early tomorrow morning. Then it will track out of here to the north."

"Current wind velocity?"

"At 1500 hours, it was steady at thirty to thirty-five knots, gusting to fifty."

Shackleton moved down the row. "Marshall, what have we still got to worry about in Hamilton?"

"The *Royal Dane* has cleared the channel and is now

in open water. The yachts *Fairborn* and *Allesandra* are due to weigh anchor within the hour."

Shackleton moved to the next scope. "Lightbourne? St. George's."

"The *Scandinavian Sovereign* couldn't make it. She's going to tough it out at Ordnance Island."

"Get the tugs on her that I promised. And tell her to double her lines."

"The captain's already done that, and the tugs are underway."

"Good. What about yachts?"

"All away, except *Laventura*. She's due out at 1800."

"Some people always wait to the last minute," muttered Shackleton.

The alert bell rang. "Mr. Shackleton?" It was Moberly. "Hurricane Center in Miami's just upgraded our little event again. It's now a force nine gale."

Chaos reigned as Colin pulled up to the club. The Gold Cup had been canceled. Boat owners were taking what measures they could to ensure the safety of their craft.

In the midst of all this activity, the inside paneled bar was an oasis of calm. People were having drinks there, as if nothing unusual was going on about them. It gave Colin the eerie feeling of what it must have been like in the First Class Lounge on the *Titanic* — after the iceberg but before the summons to the boat deck.

One of the group at the bar was Anson, who detached himself and waved him over. "Where've you been, man? Your cell phone's not working."

Colin pulled it out and looked at it. "I turned it off over

at my brother's and forgot to turn it on again." He remedied that. "My nephew's missing. The police think it may have something to do with the murder."

"Oh, man, that's heavy! Are the police—optimistic?"

"Not really. They've never dealt with anything like this." Colin looked at his friend. "How come you're still here? I heard nothing but storm warnings on the way over."

"I'm on the last flight to Boston, if it still goes." Anson glanced at his watch, a black-faced Submariner like Colin's—awarded them on the same long-ago afternoon. "I'll be heading for the airport in about ten minutes. I was just hanging, to see if you'd show before I had to go."

Anson lowered his voice. "Listen, Beater! I've got a hot one for you. You know your—problem?" He beamed. "I may have the solution."

Anson nodded toward the bar, to the group he'd just left. "See the guy with Neil and Marcia? He's French, name of René Dupré. The Vice Commodore put him in touch with them. He's a venture capitalist, heading up a consortium of high rollers in Paris. Since France doesn't have a boat in the next America's Cup, he wants to join our syndicate. I gave him Charlie's card and told him to call him."

"Charlie's gone?"

Anson nodded. "Bugged out a couple of hours ago, at the first sign of bad weather."

Colin glanced at the bar. Each evening the Carringtons had insisted on buying them supper, which was fine with him. And now Marcia, seeing him looking their way, waved. He waved back. The Frenchman looked vaguely familiar. Had he been at the White Horse a couple of nights ago, when Colin had stopped for a nightcap?

He frowned. "Nice for you, Anson, but what's that got to do with me?"

"After I gave him Charlie's card, he asked me if I knew anyone with a sailboat for charter. Said he'd been working wicked hard all year long — as point man for his group — and wanted to go on holiday. A *long* holiday — all winter long. Soon as possible. He wanted to hire a boat and its captain to take him down to the islands, and just beat around the Caribbean." Anson grinned. "I immediately thought of you, man."

Colin stared at his friend, hope beginning to build for the first time since the FedEx had arrived. "Is he — for real?"

"I think so. I said I knew someone who might be available, and of course, Marcia, piped up, 'Oh, you mean, Colin?'" He shook his head. "That woman —"

"Hurry up, man," Colin urged his friend. "You've got to go, remember?"

"Oh, yeah." He glanced at his watch, and his eyebrows rose. "I really do! Anyway, he asked me how much this Colin would charge, and I asked him how much was he prepared to pay."

Colin shook his head and grinned. "I can't believe this! Go on."

"When he mentioned two thousand a week, I said no way! The gig's worth at least three. He said, *three*? I said, we're talking about the best skipper in Bermuda! And what's more, he's going to need a signed contract for twenty weeks. A letter of agreement will do, but he's got to see half the money up front!"

Colin's mouth fell open. "Did he — swallow that?"

Anson laughed, "Well, he looked as if he was going to choke, but — he accepted it." He clapped Colin on the shoulder. "Man, that's thirty long! And with this," he produced an envelope with Colin's name on it, "you're two-thirds there! Just take the boat and this client and — disappear. By the time you come back here, you'll have your nut."

Colin was dumbstruck.

"Come on, man, you got to meet this guy, 'cause I've got to go!"

"Wait a sec," Colin said, his voice thick, "I got to tell you, Anson; you're the—" He couldn't finish it.

"Forget it, man," Anson replied gruffly, taking his friend by the arm over to the group. "Like I said, me and the Beater's going to be doing a lot of sailing together."

To the Frenchman he announced, "Here's the man I told you about. And now I've got to take off!" And he did, like a shot.

"Colin," said Marcia, ever the hostess, "this is René Dupré. He knows friends of ours at the Cap, and he wants to charter you for the whole winter! Isn't that absolutely fabulous?"

Colin looked at the Frenchmen, who met his gaze. Neither man spoke.

Marcia, puzzled, was about to speak, when Neil turned to her and quietly said, "Just shut up, darling."

"But shouldn't they be negotiating, or something?"

"They are."

"Oh. A guy thing."

"Yes, darling. Be still now."

Colin didn't care for the feeling he was getting from this man. He seemed charming enough, but there was cold steel behind those eyes. In fact, under any other circumstances he'd decline this proposition — graciously, of course. This was not a man he wanted to spend a week with, let alone a winter. But beggars could not be choosers, he reminded himself, and he could put up with a lot to keep *Care Away*. For three grand a week, he could even put up with this one's *faux* charm.

Colin turned to Marcia and gave her the full Lands End smile. He hadn't used it in years, but it still had the desired effect. "Marcia," he said sweetly, "we need to be alone now, for just a few moments." He beamed at her. "We're going to sit down over there, do our deal, and come back, soon as we're done, I promise."

"Actually, take your time," Neil said. "We've got to leave ourselves. Right now," he said, glancing at Marcia, so she would know he meant it. "We're sailing at — 1800 hours." (Marcia would just have to learn that this was the way men of the sea talked.)

"Well, I hope it all works out!" gushed Marcia at Colin. "From what René tells me, you're going to be in a lot of the same ports we are, at around the same time. Think of the fun we'll have!"

"Come along, darling. It's nearly 1630."

Colin and the Frenchman sat down. "I gather Anson gave you my terms."

The Frenchman nodded.

"They're acceptable?"

"Quite."

Colin smiled. "Good. I also understand you'd like to leave ASAP. Is Saturday soon enough? The storm will be well out of here by then, and far enough to the north that we should have smooth sailing all the way down."

"I want to leave now. This afternoon."

"Oh, man! Have you got *any* idea how rough it's going to be, if we head south?"

"The Carringtons are leaving now."

"Yeah, under power. They'll be seventy miles south of here by the time this storm reaches its full intensity! I talked to their captain last night. Their real captain. Their engine's bigger than my whole boat! And they've got enough fuel to motor halfway to England, if need be."

Colin laughed sardonically. "I've enough fuel to make it back into the harbor, if anything happens — as long as I'm not more than twenty miles out."

The Frenchman looked at him with his ball-bearing gaze. "I don't care how rough it gets. I want to leave this afternoon."

Colin took a long time before replying. "Well, I'm sorry, but I just don't think it's a good idea. *Laventura* can get away from this storm. We can't."

"Are you scared?"

"You bet! Only a fool wouldn't be. I've been through two gales at sea. I don't ever want to go through another."

"I was told you're the best sailor on the island."

"Anson tell you that? You should take what he says with a grain of salt."

"Anson — and others."

So he *had* been at the White Horse! Checking him out! "I'm sorry, Monsieur Du—"

"René," the Frenchman interrupted. "If we're going to be spending the winter together, we might as well be informal."

"Well — René, the answer's still the same. Unless you agree to wait until Saturday, you and I are not going to be spending the winter together — and incidentally, I do *cherchez les femmes; les hommes* are not my cuppa."

The Frenchman inspected his nails. "Regarding our departure, how much would it take to overcome your — reluctance?"

"What do you mean?"

"Well," Dupré pursed his lips, "suppose I were to increase the advance—give you, say $45,000, up front—would that do it?"

Colin looked at him, his eyes narrowing. Someone at the White Horse must have talked. He tried to remember whom he told about the judgment. It was probably Mike. The bartender was a friend—but hardly a Sphinx.

He took a deep breath. If he said yes, that would make a total of $48,000, plus what he could get for the Rolex. He could keep *Care Away.* And he wouldn't even have to ask his brother for a loan. But it would mean putting his beloved boat—and himself—at extreme risk.

When he didn't respond, the Frenchman said quietly, "I will pay in cash."

Colin exhaled. $45,000! What kind of venture capitalist carried that kind of cash around?

As if he could read that thought, the Frenchman explained, "In my business, checks often bounce. Even checks that one would assume were good as gold. Also, cash clears immediately—whereas, for a check of that size, one might have to wait a week for it to clear." He smiled. "By that time, we'll be halfway to Antigua."

He had a point—several points, in fact. Yet there was a distinctly unsavory aroma about this deal. The only people on the island with that kind of cash were druggies. But he was a friend of Neil and Marcia's, and was going to join the Marblehead syndicate. He *had* to be all right!

Colin took it to the bottom line: Life without Amy and their son was misery. Life without *Care Away,* too, would be—unbearable. Not worth living. Might as well put his life on the line.

Looking at his watch, he said, "I'll pick you up at the

37 | one by land, two by sea

The silence in Ian Bennett's study was broken by the brass ship's clock ringing three bells — half past five. Then the silence returned, undisturbed by the three men present.

Dan Burke had finished telling Ian of gaining his son's confidence, to the point where the boy had told him of his involvement with drugs and of young Jonesy telling him he'd just witnessed a murder. Knowing how bad his friend felt about how things had played out, Brother Bartholomew had come with him to support him on this errand of conscience.

At length Ian said, "Well, I'm glad you told me all this, Chief. It fills in the blanks." He looked out the window. "I'm glad he told someone. He was never able to talk to me — about anything that was important to him." He put a hand over his eyes.

"He wanted to," murmured Dan, looking up. "That's why he didn't go to the station that night, or first thing in the morning. He wanted to wait till you got home, so he could tell you himself." He paused. "And since I've a boy his age, who has a hard time talking to me—I let him."

Bartholomew spoke. "I realize how bad it looks, but I've got to remind you: We don't know for sure that Eric's dead. If the Frenchman was going to kill him, he would have done so at the same time he killed the Jones boy."

Ian looked at him, not daring to hope. "What do you mean?"

"He might see Eric as being of use to him, getting away."

"I don't see how," countered Dan. "As the inspector said, there are only two ways off the island, by plane or cruise ship. The police have copies of the artist's sketch, and tomorrow it'll be everywhere." He turned to Ian. "They'll get him."

"There may be a third way off," said Bartholomew quietly. Both men looked to him. "In a small boat."

"No!" declared Ian. "There aren't half a dozen charter boats still here with that kind of range—"

Dan finished it for him, "—and the police have already contacted them."

Bartholomew didn't answer. He was looking at the wind whipping the surface of Ely's Harbour. "He could go by sailboat."

They stared at him. Slowly, reluctantly, Ian nodded. "It's possible. But if that's what he's planning, he's stuck here until after the storm. No sailboat's crazy enough to leave in the teeth of a force nine gale!"

The Chief nodded. "By the time the weather clears, every man and his dog will know what the murderer looks like."

The phone rang. Ian started to reach for it, but the policewoman in the kitchen with Nan reminded him, "Mr. Bennett! Let your wife answer! We have the recorder hooked up in here, and a relay to Bermuda Telephone."

Nan took it. She kept the person on the other end talking the requisite 45 seconds. Unfortunately, it was not a request for ransom money.

Nan, wrung-out and cried-out, came into the den. "It was just a friend of your brother's," she told Ian. "Someone named Mike at the White Horse. He said Colin's about to leave for Maine, and he'd left off a package for you."

Ian stared at her. "Colin never said anything about going to Maine!" He snatched up the phone book, looked up the White Horse and dialed it.

"You say Colin's leaving for Maine?" he asked when someone answered. "I don't believe it! Not in this storm! He's smarter than that!" Pause. "But that's insane!" Pause. "Did he say what was in the package?" Pause. "My God!" Pause. "No, he never told me!" Pause. "Has he left yet?" Pause. "Okay, I'm coming out there!"

He hung up the phone. "Colin is sailing for Maine!" he told the others. "This Mike person's the bartender at the White Horse. He thinks the package might be some or all of a divorce settlement — $50,000!"

He shook his head. "I knew Amy had gone back to Georgia, but I didn't know it had gone this far." He frowned. "Where would he get that kind of money?"

They all knew at the same moment.

"I'm calling Cochrane!" exclaimed Dan, grabbing the phone. Getting through quickly, he relayed the situation and told him what they suspected.

"Inspector," he concluded, "if you're going after him," he glanced at the other two, "we want to come." Pause.

"We're aware of the danger, and we accept the responsibility." Long pause. "But—"

Dan returned the receiver to its cradle. "Cochrane thinks he may have already left, so he's taking the fast police boat out to St. George's. The territorial limit's twelve miles. He's confident they can catch them before they reach it. But he doesn't want any civilians involved. *Civilians*," he spat the word out in disgust.

"If we were up on Cape Cod, you'd have said the same thing," Bartholomew reminded him.

Ian was doing some figuring on a piece of paper. "They should be able to do it," he announced. "Colin's Venus can't make more than five knots on his engine, and he won't be able to put any canvas up till he gets in open water." He did some more figuring. "The police boat, Rescue 2, is a rigid inflatable, powered by twin Yamaha 150s." He shook his head. "I've seen that sucker flat out. It was planing! Had to be making forty knots!"

"Yes, but for how long?" asked Bartholomew.

"Its range? I don't know." He thought for a moment. "It has to be forty or fifty miles—enough to get from downtown Hamilton out to the territorial limit in any direction—and of course, back again."

Dan stood up. "You heard me ask if we could go. He thanked us very much for all our help and input, but said they'd take it from here. He reminded me the Frenchman's extremely dangerous and wouldn't hesitate to kill again."

"Is he armed?" asked Bartholomew.

"Guns are illegal on Bermuda," replied the Chief, "but hey, so are drugs. If he's got one, he's got the other. That's why Cochrane doesn't want us anywhere near him. He's taking Tuttle with a scoped rifle. Plans to drop him, soon as he gets a clear shot."

The sea in St. George's Harbour was as ugly as Colin had ever seen it. The more time a sailor spent on it, the healthier became his respect for it. Colin had logged enough time to know that this was the last place he wanted to be. And the sea was giving every indication that in a short while it would be a lot worse. Maybe bad enough to make this not worthwhile, even if it cost him his boat.

At the tiller of *Care Away,* he kept her heading with the waves, as long as they were carrying him towards the narrows into Smith Sound. Her little engine was doing its best, but he was not sure how she'd do with the sea on her port beam as they headed for Bremen Cut, instead of following, as now. He was at the point of bagging the whole thing.

Up ahead, through the rain that was starting to fall, he could make out the East End Wharf, and there was his passenger waiting, wearing a yellow life vest, his bags beside him, his car parked behind him. Odd that Dupré should be wearing a life vest. He did not strike Colin as a fearful man. *Care Away* had six vests stored under the aft seats. Not wearing one, even in weather like this, was preferable for the freedom of movement. And if he needed one, he could get to it in a few seconds.

The approach was going to be tricky; he threw the fenders over the side. Just then a rogue wave, bigger than the rest, lifted his stern, exposing the propeller, which revved wildly, till he could back off the throttle. That settled it. They weren't going. He would lose *Care Away,* but he was not ready to lose his life.

He swung expertly around to the leeward side of the wharf, and Dupré gathered up his gear and started towards him.

Colin shook his head and shouted to make himself heard over the wind. "We're not going!"

The Frenchman ignored him, tossing his duffles and hang bag into the aft end.

"Did you hear me?" cried Colin. "I said *we're not going!*"

Dupré leaned close to him. "We have a deal, Monsieur Bennett. No one backs out of a deal with me."

"Well, I do. Look, we can go Saturday, like I said. And I'll give you back the extra — inducement. But we'd lose her out there!"

"I thought you were the best!"

"I am! That's why we're not going! I want to still be the best tomorrow!"

Dupré glared at him. "We are going *now!*"

"Then you're going to have to swim, because this boat's not going anywhere!"

"Wait here. I have something that will change your mind!" Before Colin could answer, Dupré turned and went back to his car.

"Look," Colin called after him, "if it's more money, forget it! There's not enough money in the world to—"

He stopped. The Frenchman was getting something out of the trunk of his car, something large. A person!

Colin squinted in the rain and the failing light. It was a man, arms duct-taped behind him, more duct tape over his mouth. There was a wire noose around his neck, attached to a two-foot pole that Dupré was leading him along by. Before they reached him, Colin knew in his heart. It was Eric.

In his other hand, Dupré had a 9mm Glöck automatic. "Now, we're going, I think you'll agree. I didn't want to do it this way, but you've forced my hand."

He prodded Eric towards the boat, and Colin, for the safety of the boy, helped him aboard.

"Now, cast off!" ordered Dupré, jumping aboard himself. "And remember, try anything, anything at all, and I will shoot the boy first."

He shook his head. "*Quel dommage!* We would have had such a nice winter."

⛵

Guiding *Care Away* through the cut in the dwindling light and rising sea, Colin forced himself to do risk assessment. His life and Eric's depended on it.

What were their chances of survival? Minimal. As long as he had enough light to see by, he could keep her from swamping. But after dark? He'd have to risk putting up some canvas, in spite of the wind. Sail due south. It was the only way to get out of the maw of this storm.

What were their chances of rescue? Minimal. No one knew they were gone. No one had even seen them leave.

If only he'd told Dupré to meet him at St. George's, instead of St. David's. Never mind that now. Focus on the now and the soon.

How long was their situation tenable? If they didn't founder, four hours, maybe six. Then fatigue would become the overriding factor. Normally, as owner/captain of the boat, he would be in command. But with Admiral Glöck on board, all rules were waived.

Should he resist? Or cooperate? Or seem to cooperate? They were in a hostage situation. Eric was the most at risk. Dupré could get him to do anything he wanted, merely by threatening to do harm to his nephew.

Until he started to fall asleep. Then what?

He looked over at the Frenchman, who was watching him. He still held Eric by the noose attached to the pole. The wire had already cut his neck. His blood stained the front of his school uniform. One yank on that pole, and the wire would reopen the wound. A hard enough yank could kill him. And Colin had no doubt the Frenchman would do it without hesitation. He would have left him in the trunk of the car, had Colin gone willingly.

His and Dupré's eyes met, and he sensed the Frenchman was doing his own evaluation. The one unknown was just how much he knew about ocean sailing. Probably enough to keep on a southerly heading. And if he knew how to use a GPS, it would not be too difficult to get where he wanted to go. The only thing he didn't know was how to set the automatic pilot. And Colin determined not to teach him. That knowledge might be all that would keep Dupré from putting him and Eric over the side.

Which was going to happen eventually anyway, Colin realized. There could be no returning to civility now. The only question was, how soon?

They had reached open water. And eight-foot swells. The boat was riding them, but her engine was laboring. "We're going to have to switch to canvas," he called to the Frenchman over the sound of the storm. "She doesn't have enough petrol to go another hour this way."

Dupré nodded. "Do it."

"I could use the boy's help."

"Do it yourself. I'll man the tiller and keep the boy company." Tucking the Glöck in his belt, he took over the helm.

Colin unreefed the mainsail and raised it four feet. It was all he dared. Even with that little canvas showing, *Care Away* heeled over and drove forward. But she was under sail now, and Colin could cut the engine. As he did so, he was dismayed to see how well Dupré managed the tiller. He knew what he was doing.

Just then, the cell phone in his pocket went off. Colin pulled it out and answered it. "Ian?" He put his hand up to his other ear, to hear his brother better. "Say again?"

The Frenchman reached over Colin's shoulder, took the phone out of his hand, and tossed it over the side.

Colin glared at him. And tried to keep his expression from revealing what he had just heard. They were coming!

Below, the ship's radio crackled to life. "Harbour Radio calling southbound vessel, three miles from Bremer Cut." The call was repeated three times.

"I ought to answer that," said Colin. "They can see us on their radar."

The Frenchman pondered this, as the radio crackled again. "Southbound vessel, be advised: We have received your distress signal. Rescue 2 is on its way to you. Stay within the limit."

Dupré made up his mind. "Take this," he commanded, turning the tiller over to Colin. He peered into the hatch, keeping his hand on the pole attached to Eric's neck. With his other hand, he took the Glöck from his waist and shot the radio.

Colin looked at him in disgust. "You'd better pray we don't need that to save our skins!"

Dupré ignored him. "What distress signal?"

"I don't know what he's talking about!"

The Frenchman leaned towards Colin and suddenly smashed him in the side of the face with the pistol. "I said, what distress signal?"

Wincing in pain, Colin angrily replied, "And *I* said, I don't know what he's talking about!"

"Shall I shoot the boy?"

"I told you, I don't—"

Taking careful aim, the Frenchman shot Eric in the upper left thigh. The boy screamed. Colin screamed. "Are you *crazy*? I said I don't know what he's talking about!"

Dupré smiled. "Now I believe you. Which means they were lying. Why?" He thought about it. "They want you to know help is on its way. Rescue 2 is a police boat, isn't it?"

When Colin didn't answer, Dupré took aim at Eric's other thigh.

"All right! It is a police boat!"

Dupré scanned the horizon behind them. Visibility was deteriorating, but there was nothing to be seen. "What did he mean by the limit?" he demanded of Colin.

Silence. Dupré raised the Glöck.

"The twelve-mile limit," Colin shouted, to keep him from firing. "It's international waters beyond that."

"So they must get here before we get there, *n'est-ce pas*?"

Colin nodded sullenly.

"How many miles have we gone?"

Colin shrugged.

"Guess!" Dupré ordered, waving the Glöck toward Eric.

"Six, maybe seven."

"And how long will it take?"

"At this rate? About an hour."

"In the end," said Dupré pensively, "it always comes down to a matter of time."

Heading east on South Road after the Trimingham roundabout, there was a long downhill straightaway. Dan cranked the right-grip throttle wide open and held it there, as the scooter's speed climbed past 40, 50, all the way to 60 mph. Good thing it wasn't raining—and as if the thought had summoned them, the first drops began to hit the pavement.

With a bend coming up and the road now slick, he backed off a little, but only a little. Until he felt the rear wheel begin to slide out from under him. He was barely able to correct it before losing control entirely. Badly shaken, he thought: A man could get killed doing this! He backed off a little more.

The wind had picked up—just how much, he discovered as he roared down the hill past the Swizzle Inn and caught his first glimpse of the long causeway that connected St. George's Parish with the main island. On either side of the causeway, the wind had whipped the sound into an evil, milky-green soup, with whitecaps everywhere and spindrift flying off the tops. The wind was at least 30 knots.

And blowing directly across the causeway. Waves

were crashing against the low concrete wall on the windward side, the tops of them coming straight over the wall and flooding the road. There was no traffic out there, for good reason: The causeway was impassable.

He started across.

A wave broke, drenching him and throwing him and the bike sideways. He barely managed to avoid the opposite wall. After that, he hunkered down as low as he could get, his eyes barely above the handlebars. The next wave hit him, but did not move him sideways as much, and he began to believe that he was not going to die out here, after all.

Once he got off the causeway, it was better. The straightaway past the airport was the longest on the island, and he again cranked the throttle wide, passing a startled taxi in the process. He knew that the police seldom stopped rental scooters (the ones with the red license plates), not wanting vacationers to leave with a bad taste in their mouths. He hoped they'd make an exception for one going two and a half times the national speed limit; he could use a police escort just now. Of course, when you *wanted* to be arrested, there was never a patrol car in sight.

The rest of the way into the town of St. George was twisty and tricky, but after the causeway, nothing fazed him. When he reached the dock, there were two patrol cars, and no *Care Away*. Ducking behind a building to get some shelter from the rain, he called Ian.

"Missed them by about twenty minutes, I'd guess," said Dan. "They're probably in the narrows by now."

"Well, we've had a bit of help from the wind, and should make it to St. Catherine's in about ten minutes. Can you get there?"

"Roger that."

"Take your time. It'll be all over by the time we get there, anyway. Rescue 2 passed us a few minutes ago, going like the proverbial bat. They were on top of the waves and flying!"

In the cabin of *Goodness,* Ian was at the wheel, negotiating each ten-foot wave as it came. He glanced over at Brother Bartholomew, and from the latter's expression assumed he was battling seasickness. "Keep your eye on the horizon," he shouted, to be heard over the sound of the storm. "Don't look away from it. It'll help your ear adjust your inner balance."

Bartholomew nodded and managed a weak smile, but it was not primarily a queasy stomach that concerned him just now (though he was doing a fair amount of swallowing, to remind peristalsis it would be inappropriate to reverse itself).

What was disturbing Bartholomew's inner balance was a sickening sense of *déjà vu.*

For this was the nightmare! The one he'd had after seeing "The Perfect Storm" — in which he'd relived how his father had died.

Only he wasn't asleep now, in his bed at home. He was wide awake. Living it. He swallowed hard. It was not the heaving sea that had put this brackish taste in his mouth; it was the raw terror.

Taking his eyes from the horizon (just for a moment), he risked a glance at Ian. The man was resolute, even grim. But not afraid. Maybe this fear that gripped him was exaggerated. Maybe what they were doing was dangerous—but not suicidal.

And then *Goodness* buried her nose in the next wave, and she took green water over her foredeck.

"Hate it when that happens!" cried Ian. "Puts too much strain on the engine."

Bartholomew nodded and swallowed harder.

Abruptly Ian pulled back the throttle, and veered the boat to starboard. "St. Catherine's. Can you see the Chief?"

"Can't see anything through this rain."

"I've got to concentrate on the approach. You keep an eye out for him."

"Wait! There he is!" shouted Bartholomew. "He just got there!"

In five minutes, Dan was on board, and they were back out on the roaring sea.

"Pull on a slicker," Ian called to Dan, nodding towards the hatch to the hold. They're in the port gear locker. It's a little late to keep you dry," he said wryly, "but it'll keep you warm."

To Bartholomew, he said, "See if you can raise Harbour Radio on 2182 kHz. I'd like to find out what's going on out here."

Bartholomew turned to the frequency. It crackled, and he said, "Hello?"

"No, no, let me have it."

Bartholomew passed the mike on its coiled cord to Ian.

"*Goodness* calling Harbour Radio."

"Go ahead, *Goodness*."

"That you, Shack?"

"Ian, what are *you* doing out there? Nobody's supposed to be out on a night like this."

"Just trying to help my little brother."

"Yeah, well, we've got him in sight, seven miles south of Bremer Cut. But listen, Ian, Inspector Cochrane in Rescue 2 said that if we heard from you, we were to send you home. And that it was *not,* repeat *not,* optional."

"Roger, optional, Harbour Radio — you're breaking up a little there — we opt to carry on. How about a SitRep?"

There was silence as the Senior Watch Officer contemplated giving him a situation report. "Well," he said at length, "if it was my brother, I'd be out there, too. All right, here's what we've got: *Care Away* is three miles from the limit, making about eight knots, tracking one-eight-five. She's about four miles from you on a bearing of one-two-zero. You should have a visual pretty soon."

"We can't see jack out here! Where's Rescue 2?

"Between you and them. We've been vectoring them for an intercept. They should be to *Care Away* in four minutes." There was another voice in the background. "Hold a minute; I've got to take this."

In the gathering darkness, Bartholomew thought he saw something ahead. He pointed to it, and Ian, squinting, said, "That's a red light on a pole — we've got Rescue 2!"

The radio came back on. "Ian? Shack here. That was Cochrane. They've just lost their starboard motor. Can't plane. He wants you to come by and pick him and one of his men up."

"Oh, he does, does he? Well, you tell him — never mind, I'll tell him myself!"

With his back braced against the aft wall of *Care Away's* cabin, the Frenchman trained the boat's binoculars on the scene behind them. It was almost dark, nearly impossible to see anything. But not quite. He gave Colin and Eric a running account.

"The police boat, which until a moment ago was in, as you say, hot pursuit, now appears to be disabled."

He moved the glasses slightly to the right. "There is, however, another craft farther back—a small, conventional powerboat." He turned briefly to Colin. "Could this be your brother?" He turned to Eric. "And your father? Coming to your rescue? We shall see."

He turned back to the scene in the distance behind them. "The powerboat is stopping alongside the police boat. Someone's just gotten out of the police boat and into the other boat."

He frowned and let the glasses hang down by the strap around his neck. "And now another man. With a rifle. That's not good."

He looked up at the nearly dark sky. "*N'importe*, in ten more minutes, they won't be able to see us. *Mal-*

heureusement, someone ashore is obviously guiding them to us."

He turned to Colin. "How far are we now from 'the limit,' as you say?"

"How should I know? Not more than a couple of miles, I should think. I could call Harbour Radio and ask them, but then, we don't have a radio or a cell phone, do we."

The Frenchman shook his head. "You disappoint me, Colin. You take me for a fool. I was informed you have the best navigational equipment of any boat in Bermuda. Suppose you go below and bring your handheld GPS up here." Colin didn't move. Dupré jabbed his pistol into Eric's leg wound. The boy shrieked in pain. Colin swung down the hatch and in a minute was back with the GPS and a folded map. From the coordinates it gave them, they were barely a quarter of the distance from the limit that Colin had estimated. The invisible line in the water was half a mile ahead. Six minutes—at most.

The Frenchman raised the binoculars and resumed his narrative. "They are, perhaps, two miles behind. And they are definitely gaining on us. It is going to be a close thing. Very close." He lowered the binoculars and looked at Colin. "Can you make this boat go any faster?"

"Listen to her bow wave, man! Feel the vibration in her keel? She's got to be making close to eight knots. She's never gone this fast!"

"It's not fast enough! They won't catch us before we cross the line, but we'll soon be within range of that rifle." He raised the glasses again. "In fact, the man with the rifle appears to be getting ready to take a shot."

He said to Colin, "Move over here, so that you are between me and them."

"Suck eggs!"

Dupré aimed carefully and shot Colin in the upper thigh, exactly as he had his nephew. Colin cried out and doubled over, grabbing his leg.

In the next instant there was a sharp crack next to the Frenchman's head, and the running block flew to pieces. It controlled the mainsail which, suddenly freed, swung wide, bringing *Care Away* to an abrupt halt and leaving her wallowing broadside to the waves.

The Frenchman was shocked. "That was meant for me!" Realization of his partner's subtle betrayal sank in. "Get that sail under control!"

"I don't know if I can," said Colin, still holding his leg. He pushed the tiller away from him, and the boat swung into the wind.

"What are you doing?" demanded Dupré.

"How else am I going to bring the main within reach?" Colin retrieved it and looked at the shattered block. "I can't fix this."

"Liar!" cried the Frenchman. "I was told you could fix anything!"

Blasted Town Crier, thought Colin. He was going to have a word with Mike, if he ever got out of this.

"Fix it — now!" ordered the Frenchman, waving the pistol in Eric's direction.

Wincing and groaning, Colin turned the tiller over to Dupré and worked his way forward, taking the topsail halyard and making it fast to a cleat at the base of the mast. Then, he ran it aft on the starboard side, through the outermost scupper hole to the starboard toe rail. "It'll work for a while," he gasped, when he'd finished.

"Good! Now, as I said a moment ago—"

The top trim of the hatch, four inches from his face, exploded into splinters.

"I want you *here!*" cried the Frenchman, indicating that Colin should position himself between him and their pursuers.

When the latter did not move, he jerked on the pole, hard, so that the wire re-opened the wound on Eric's neck. This proved too much for the boy, who until then had bravely held himself together. As blood oozed from his neck, he began crying hysterically.

Enraged, Colin gathered his good leg under him and prepared to lunge at the Frenchman, when he found himself staring into the muzzle of the Glöck. "Go ahead!" shouted Dupré. "You're of little use to me now, anyway!"

Colin forced himself to relax and, as instructed, put himself between Dupré and the other boat.

He would bide his time, wait for his chance. For the first time in his life, he realized he was prepared to take another man's life. In fact, he was looking forward to it.

With the delay to jury-rig a workable mainsheet arrangement, the other boat was almost on top of them. Colin guessed they were beyond the twelve-mile limit now, but at this point no one was thinking about that.

It had grown too dark for the rifleman to risk another shot, even had Colin not been in his direct line of fire. But in a few more minutes, it wouldn't matter. *Goodness* was so close, he could almost make out his brother's face.

His brother could certainly make out theirs. Ian had a searchlight atop his cabin for feeling his way back into Ely's Harbour on a foggy night. He suddenly switched it n, momentarily blinding everyone in the sailboat. He must have been overjoyed, Colin thought, to see Eric — *live*!

But now the Frenchman demonstrated his own marksmanship. Disdaining the fashionable two-handed grip, he stood sideways to his adversaries, and, feet apart, gracefully extended his arm like a master of the épée (which he had once been, as captain of cadets at St-Cyr). He fired three rounds in rapid succession. The first went through *Goodness's* front windshield, in the vicinity of the driver. The second went through the scope and into the eye of Sergeant Tuttle who died instantly. The third extinguished their searchlight.

"That should give them cause to reconsider," gloated the Frenchman, as darkness returned.

But *Goodness* continued to bear down on them.

"Why aren't they stopping?" cried Dupré, grabbing Colin and jerking him back in front of him. "We're in international waters!"

"Maybe Bermuda's 'rules of engagement' make an exception for hot pursuit," Colin replied, and then smiled wryly. "Make that lukewarm pursuit."

There was another light on them now, from a handheld flashlight. The Frenchman, skilled as he was, could have shot whoever was holding it, but he had something else in mind. Something for which that light would be necessary.

"Time to play my last card," he informed Colin. "Fortunately, it's an ace."

A small, round hole appeared in the mainsail, less than a foot from the Frenchman. Someone else was using the rifle, sans scope. But he remained unperturbed. "You have life vests aboard," he asked Colin. "Where?"

"You're sitting on them."

Dupré glanced at his seat, saw that it was a bench, opened it, and took out two yellow vests, which he chucked into the dark waters. Then, using the pole, he drew Eric to his feet and — pushed him over the side.

"You —" cried Colin, diving after his nephew. He had to keep Eric afloat, since his arms were taped behind him, and his mouth was taped. If he could somehow locate one of those vests. . . .

As Dupré had anticipated, with two people they cared about now in the water, his pursuers gave up the chase and started searching for the men overboard. But just to make it a little harder for them. . . . He took careful aim at the figure holding the flashlight.

Another hit. The flashlight dropped — presumably over the side, since it did not reappear. Dupré took the tiller and sailed off into the darkness, leaving the power-boat frantically circling in the distance.

There was no question of his being in international waters now. The pursuit had been broken off. He had won.

41 | frog-gone conclusion

Aboard *Goodness* there was darkness and consternation. At the wheel, Ian was able to use only his left arm, his right hanging useless at his side. Beside him Cochrane searched the waters ahead for any sign of life, but he was looking at black on black. The same was true of Dan and Bartholomew in the back.

Then Dan remembered his "piece"—the ancient flare pistol that had belonged to Ian's father. He fired it straight up, and in the burst of light, they saw movement in the water off their port bow.

"There they are!" Ian cried, overjoyed. "Both of them!" And sure enough, in the water on the side of the huge wave opposite them, were two tiny figures, clutching a yellow life vest between them. He swung *Goodness* over and gunned her down the wave, heading for them.

Only one person was less than overjoyed. As they roller-coastered down the wave towards its trough, Bartholomew realized that this—right here, right now—was the worst part of the worst nightmare of his life. The wave opposite was looming higher and higher. The front windshield already had a hole in it. If they took dark water over the bow now. . . .

He gripped the side of the boat in frozen panic. Down and down and down the boat plunged. And then the illumination from the flare died away, leaving them in darkness. Again, just as he had in the nightmare, he felt the icy fingers of terror reach up into his entrails and slowly close into a fist.

But there was a difference between that dream and this reality, he reminded himself. In the nightmare, he had not prayed. Now, he did. Eternal Father, strong to save. . . .

I will never leave, nor forsake you, came the thought, and the fist of fear in his gut began to release its grip.

Dan fired another flare. As light returned, they pulled alongside the struggling figures, and Dan and Cochrane hauled them aboard, unassisted by Bartholomew, who could not let go of the rail.

Cochrane started to assess Eric and Colin's physical condition, as they lay on the deck alongside the lifeless form of Sergeant Tuttle. Dan tapped him on the shoulder. "Let Brother Bartholomew do that. He used to be a corpsman." Then glancing over at his friend, he caught the look on his face.

"Bart, you're needed over here!" It was a command, not a request, and it had the effect of snapping Bartholomew out of his trance. The ex-Marine came over and knelt between the wounded men. With his hands he gently but swiftly surveyed the nature and severity of their wounds. "No broken bones," he announced. "But we've got to staunch the blood flow." He called to Ian. "You got a first-aid kit?"

"In the cabin. On the wall to the left." Dan went and got it. Fortunately, it was a large one, complete with gauze rolls, tape, scissors, and antiseptic. He soon had his patients' wounds dressed. He pointed to Colin's leg. "As this one has no exit wound, we'll have to get you to hospital, so a doctor can dig the bullet out."

He looked down at Eric. To Ian he said, "Your son's lost a fair amount of blood, but other than that, he should be okay."

"Thank God!" exclaimed Ian, as it grew dark again.

"Hey," called Colin, from where he lay on the deck, "aren't we forgetting something?" They looked at him. "He's getting away! With my boat!"

Cochrane frowned. "If we call Harbour Radio for a fix on him, they'll tell us to give it up. Which I'm not inclined to do."

"None of us are," agreed Dan.

"Well, use your own radar!" shouted Colin, still supine. "C'mon, Ian, didn't they teach you anything in those fancy schools?"

His brother laughed and turned to his radar, forgotten in the chase. "There he is! A thousand yards off our starboard bow!"

Swerving to the right, he jammed the throttle full forward. Her engine groaning, *Goodness* lunged through the sea.

The darkness was so complete and the seas so high, that even with the radar, *Care Away* was invisible until they were almost on top of her.

Cochrane braced himself against the side of the cabin, the rifle ready, determined to avenge the death of his fallen comrade. "Don't worry," he said, seeing Dan's expression. "I'm not going to kill him. He knows too much that I want to know."

"Well, keep in mind he's awfully good with that side arm."

"There he is!" cried Colin, who had pulled himself upright. And there he was — less than fifty yards ahead of them.

"Look out!" cried Dan, as the Frenchman raised his pistol and took aim.

They ducked, and Dupré's shot went wild.

All at once, Colin's jury-rig on the mainsail gave way, as he had planned it to. *Care Away* rocked to port, her main boom swinging wide. Had Dupré done exactly what Colin had under similar circumstances, *Care Away's* nose would have come into the wind, and he could have retrieved her sail.

But he did the opposite. He jibed. And suddenly, gale-force wind got behind the sail and violently flung it in the opposite direction. The massive boom whipped across the boat, catching Dupré in the midsection, lifting him out of the boat, and depositing him in the black sea.

Flailing wildly, the Frenchman struggled to keep his head above water. But his life vest contained, not foam pads, but 20 water-sealed sets of cashier checks, laboratory plans, formulae and methamphetamine starter doses, one for each port of call. Instead of buoying him up, 40 pounds of dead weight was dragging him down. His life vest was his death vest.

Dan fired off his last flare just as they reached him. He had gone under. Bartholomew was about to go after him, when Dan grabbed his arm and held him back. "No! We've lost enough people out here tonight!"

In the bright illumination overhead, they could just make out the Frenchman's face, looking up at them as he

nk. A string of tiny bubbles came up from the corner of
s mouth.

Then he was gone.

&

For a moment, no one spoke. Then Colin murmured,
.es grenouilles sont finies."

Ian looked at him, surprised.

"Frog-gone," his brother loosely translated, then
ded, "What? You think I didn't learn anything at all
ose academies?"

He pointed at *Care Away*, whose mainsail was flop-
ng loose. "If you guys don't mind, I'd like to get my
at back!"

"Can you sail her?" asked Bartholomew, concerned.

"With one arm — make that leg — tied behind me!"

Then he thought better of it. "Actually, why don't you
me along? In case I faint, or something. I'll let you do
l the work; I'll just tell you what to do."

Bartholomew nodded, but Dan looked carefully at his
end. "You okay with that? It's going to be a pretty hairy
le."

"Piece of cake," said Bartholomew, grinning.

The No-Name tropical storm reached its peak at midnight and started to track away from Bermuda to the north-northwest, at ten miles per hour. In its wake there was wind damage everywhere — trees down, power out, boats sunk at their moorings. The front page of the *Mid Ocean News* featured a big photo of the *Scandinavian Sovereign* with a massive dock ballard hanging down from her nose. And sure enough, the *Royal Gazette* carried a letter by an indignant citizen shaming the Bermuda Weather Service for failing to issue proper warning.

By the following afternoon, the airport was open, power was mostly restored, and things were getting back to normal.

Colin's bullet had been removed, and he was recovering nicely in a semi-private, drifting in and out of sleep, when he had a visitor.

"Colin," she said softly, "how — are you?"

His eyes opened — and he thought he must still be dreaming. It was the one person he wanted to see most — and whom he'd given up on ever seeing again.

He couldn't speak.

"Anson came and got me," she said at last. "He flew to Boston, but then got right on a plane to Atlanta. My father wasn't going to let him see me, but he couldn't very well stop him." She smiled. "You know Anson, when he makes his mind up."

He grinned and nodded.

"When I left here, I was sick as a dog, and sick of you, and—"

"I remember."

"So, by the time I got to *Live Oaks,* I was totally bummed. Daddy got Doc Tatum to load me up with antibiotics and antidepressants, to the point where, according to Anson, I was practically drooling." She laughed. "It wasn't *that* bad!"

He smiled. "Anson's been known to exaggerate."

"Anyway," she concluded, "I didn't really want to push the divorce thing, but I was kind of out of it. And you know Daddy."

She shook her head. "I was not at the hearing. And until Anson told me, I had no idea there was a lump-sum settlement." She looked down at him then, and her voice broke, as she said, "I would *never* have let him take *Care away*!"

"It's okay, hon," said Colin, patting her hand and smiling weakly.

"No, it's not okay!" she insisted, squeezing his hand. "Anyway, when Anson asked me if I was happy, all I could say, he told me later, was that I wanted to be with you."

There were tears in Colin's eyes.

"That was enough for him. He bundled me and Jamie into his rental car. My father was furious, but Anson,

well, he can get awfully angry, too!" she recalled with
smile.

"Tell me about it!" Colin chuckled.

"Anyway, he drove us to Atlanta, and stayed with u
and got us on the first plane here."

Colin shook his head. "If this *is* a dream, I don't war
to wake up. It's the best I've ever had."

She frowned. "While we were in Atlanta, I called Ia
He said he'd meet me. On the way here, he told me abou
all that happened." She shook her head. "Wow."

"Yeah, that about sums it up."

"Thank God, you're okay!" She looked down at th
heavily bandaged leg. "You *are* going to be okay, aren'
you?"

"I am now," he said, beaming.

Then he grew serious. "You know how they say you
life passes before your eyes, just before you drown? Well
it did. I was in the water at night in a raging gale, my le;
shot, trying to keep Eric afloat, and—I sort of had a lif
review."

He looked at her. "You know what the best thing in i
was? You. And the next best thing? Jamie. And I vowe
that if I lived, I would find you and tell you that."

She lifted his hand and kissed it.

When she could speak, she said, "I saw a few thing
myself, waiting in the airport."

She looked at him. "I'd been on the verge of coming
back, and I suspect Daddy sensed it, which was why h
was pushing so hard on the divorce thing. But it wasn'
until Anson talked to me while we waited at the airport
that I saw some things. I saw you through his eyes. I sav
the Beater, one of the best sailors on the planet. I sav hov

sailing was your life and your passion, and how wrong it would be for you to give it up."

Colin didn't know what to say.

Amy did. Her eyes were shining now. "Thanks to Anson, we were in the Crown Room at the airport. There was an old *Time* magazine that had an article about home schooling. About how Harvard and other colleges are dying to get home-schooled kids because they have good study habits, are emotionally more mature, and less likely to trash the campus."

"Don't tell me!" he said, laughing. "We're going to home school Jamie!"

She nodded. "We're enrolling him right now in *Care Away* Academy! Do you love it?"

"I do love it. I love *you*!"

"And we're going to do this together," she rushed on. "Don't get the idea I'm going to do all the teaching. You're going to teach him math, which he'll need for navigation, and mechanics, so he'll know how to keep his boat shipshape, and French, for when we go to the Med—"

"Hmm, I might let *you* teach him French," Colin said with a rueful smile. He looked up at her, pleading. "Amy, tell me this dream will never end."

"It never will, darling. I promise."

In the airport restaurant that afternoon, waiting to board the plane to New York, Maud and Margaret, and Jane and Buff were having a late lunch.

Maud was her usual blunt self. Fixing Buff with her gaze, she said, "You think you have your priorities straight now?"

"I do," he replied, meeting her gaze so that she could see that he meant it.

"And you," she turned to Jane, "the one who married him for better or for worse? The next time it gets worse, you're not going to mouse around. You're going to tell him what he's got to jolly well do to make it better? Do you read me?"

"I do!" she exclaimed, laughing.

"Then I now pronounce you new man and new wife! And to celebrate, I think we should have a bottle of their best champagne — which *you*," she informed Buff, "are cheerfully going to pay for!"

"I'll drink to that," he said cheerfully.

"And so shall we all!" agreed Maud heartily.

"Shh, Maudie," said her cousin, "Not so loud! You don't have to make a perpetual spectacle!"

"Of course I do! I'm unsinkable, remember?"

Atop his hill, on the blue-tiled terrace surrounded by bougainvillea, the owner did his best to appreciate the clear and sparkling sunset.

To be sure, the Swiss account had been drained. And he had permanently lost his eyes and ears in the police department. And he would be forced to sell the coffee plantation in Jamaica to cover his losses. That was the most unpleasant part, no longer being able to escape the island's cold, damp winters.

But he chose to look at the bright side. Though their operation was compromised, he was not. His accomplice had drowned without revealing anything — or he would not be sitting here now. That meant the network was still intact. All it needed was a little patience, until fate brought him another accomplice with a fresh infusion of capital.

In the meantime, he would still wear his medals to the Queen's Birthday Party on the Governor General's lawn, the third Monday in June.

Yes, there *was* brightness after rain.

Ian Bennett took Dan Burke to the airport. "I'll ship your marlin, soon as it's ready," he said, smiling. "The taxidermist I use is a real craftsman. You'll be pleased."

"I hope Peg will," replied Dan, who was having second thoughts about introducing such a sizable artifact into their rather modest living room.

Ian laughed. "Oh, there'll be a period of adjustment; there always is. But eventually she'll be as proud of it as you are."

At the airport, they shook hands. "Chief, come back soon for a real fishing vacation. And next fall, when Nan and I come up—"

"We'll invite you over, so you can admire that thing collecting dust over the sofa!"

Father Francis and Brendan Goodell brought Brother Bartholomew to the airport. Their passenger did not talk much on the ride, but they didn't notice. They were nattering away, as usual. "Tourism's really hurting after nine-eleven," the old priest was saying. "I hear all the hotels are laying people off."

As usual, Brendan took the opposite tack. "But the reinsurance industry took the hit and survived. The island's got new respect in that quarter."

"I hear the Minister of Tourism is meeting daily in emergency sessions with his counterparts from the other islands."

"Maybe so," replied Brendan, "but Ezra, the bartender at the Coral Beach Club, tells me that a number of their regulars changed their vacation plans and came back because they didn't want to fly so far. Guess if you're a terrorist looking for a plane to kill a building with, you pick one with ten or twelve hours of fuel on board, instead of four or five."

"Besides," the priest agreed, "you'd have to look pretty hard to find someone here who didn't like Americans."

In the back seat, Bartholomew caught the scent of cedar and hyacinth through the open window. And on South Road, he gazed at the bright blue Bermuda waters and allotted them a double-page spread in his album of forever memories.

Father Francis had been right. He was leaving with a heavy heart. But he hadn't thought it would be this heavy. He had almost lost it this morning, at his last Mass. The window was open at the back of the tiny three-pew chapel, and in the middle of the service, a small, black form had entered.

No one noticed at first, except Rheba, the old black lab by Father Francis's side. Bartholomew turned and saw that it was Noire, come to say goodbye. He reached over, and she let him brush her ears one time. Then she leapt up on the windowsill and was gone.

The sister beside him leaned close and whispered, "Don't worry, Bart; we'll take care of her."

He choked up. So—what was it about this place that had so gotten to him?

Getting close to God.

Finally.

He recalled what had come to him on the ferry, a week ago—it seemed like a year ago.

You can take what you've learned home with you, and you can remain as close to me as you choose.

They had arrived. It was time to say goodbye. He hugged Father Francis and thanked him. "You know what you said about leaving?" Bartholomew said. "You were right."

"I know."

"I'll be back."

"I know."

A planeload of new arrivals was just coming through customs. They were greeted by a Calypso band, courtesy of Bacardi's. "Welcome to our island Paradise," they sang. "Welcome to Bermuda."

43 | compline

As soon as he reached the Friary that evening, Bartholomew went to find Anselm. He didn't have far to look; the Senior Brother was in his favorite chair in the library. Bartholomew was glad he was alone.

Anselm got up and gave him a hug, then waved him to the chair beside him. "Well?"

"What can I say?" answered Bartholomew. "It was all you knew it would be—and so much more than I thought."

"I didn't know how it would turn out," said his old friend. "I prayed for you every day." He smiled. "And I hear from Father Francis that you and Chief Burke managed to get involved in another—situation."

Bartholomew chuckled and nodded.

"Did it interfere with your retreat?"

The younger monk shook his head. "My retreat ended, just as the other began." He thought a moment. "In a way, it prepared me."

Anselm looked out the window at the night. "Tell me what you learned down there."

Bartholomew took a long time before replying. "That

ust in God is the bedrock of our life here. That my will
far stronger than I supposed. And far less inclined to
ubmit to God's will. But—I can be as close to Him as I
oose, in my heart."

Anselm stood up. "Then it was an excellent retreat,
artholomew. It's time for Compline."

Compline was the last service of the day, the "putting
e Church to bed," as it were. Joining the other brothers
the new basilica's robing vestibule, they observed since as they donned their robes. Except for the Grego-
an chant, they would continue Grand Silence, as it was
lled, until after Matins in the morning.

Slipping into his robe, it occurred to Bartholomew that
was the first time he'd worn it in nearly a month. Funny
ing, it seemed to fit better now.

As they formed up in a column of twos, waiting to
ter, by chance Novice Nicholas wound up beside him.
artholomew looked at him and smiled. Then, without
eaking, he put an arm around his shoulders and gave
m a hug.

There was one more friend he wanted to greet that
ght, back in the friary. But Pangur Ban merely looked
 at him and stalked away, as if to say, you can't just
alk out of people's lives that way.

Later that night, however, long after lights out, the
oor to their room pushed open a little, and a heavy lump
nded on the end of his bed. He was careful not to dis-
rb it.